THE OXYGEN MURDER

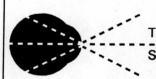

A PERIODIC TABLE MYSTERY

THE OXYGEN MURDER

61472

CAMILLE MINICHINO

THORNDIKE PRESS
An imprint of Thomson Gale, a part of The Thomson Corporation

Detroit • New York • San Francisco • New Haven, Conn. • Waterville, Maine • London

THOMSON

★ ™

GALE

LIBRARY OF CONGRESS CATALOGING-IN-PUBLICATION DATA

Minichino, Camille.
  The oxygen murder : a periodic table mystery / by Camille Minichino.
    p. cm. — (Thorndike Press large print Americana)
  ISBN 0-7862-9138-9 (alk. paper)
    1. Lamerino, Gloria (Fictitious character) — Fiction. 2. Women physicists — Fiction. 3. New York (N.Y.) — Fiction. 4. Large type books. I. Title.
  PS3563.I4663O99 2006b
  813'.54—dc22   2006028933

U.S. Hardcover:
ISBN 13: 978-0-7862-9138-0
ISBN 10: 0-7862-9138-9

Published in 2006 by arrangement with St. Martin's Press, LLC.

Printed in the United States of America on permanent paper
10 9 8 7 6 5 4 3 2 1

For my dear sister, Arlene Minichino Polvinen, who delivered life-saving oxygen throughout her long career in anesthesia

ACKNOWLEDGMENTS

I'm very grateful to the many writers, family members, and friends who reviewed this manuscript or offered generous research assistance, in particular: Robyn Anzel, Nina Balassone, Judith Barnett, Sara Bly, Don and Liz Campbell, Margaret Hamilton, Dr. Eileen Hotte, Jonnie Jacobs, Rita Lakin, Anna Lipjhart, Margaret Lucke, Dr. Marilyn Noz, James Oppenheimer, Ruth Oppenheimer, Ann Parker, Arlene Polvinen, Loretta Ramos, Sue Stephenson, Jean Stokowski, Karen Streich, and Barbara Zulick.

As usual, I drew enormous amounts of information and inspiration from Robert Durkin, my cousin and expert in all things mortuary, and from Inspector Christopher Lux of the Alameda County, California, District Attorney's Office.

Any misinterpretation of such excellent resources is purely my fault.

Special thanks to Marcia Markland, my wonderful editor, who has been with me in one way or another from my first book; and to my patient, extraordinary agent, Elaine Koster.

I'm most grateful to my husband and web-master, Dick Rufer, the best there is. I can't imagine working without his love and support.

CHAPTER ONE

You'd think it would be impossible to find yourself alone in New York City. Especially on a bright Sunday morning in December, only a couple of blocks from the dazzling supersigns of Times Square.

A short distance away, elbows and shoulders overlapped at crowded intersections. Couples and families had to hold hands to stay together. Holiday shoppers, packed as close as particles in a nucleus, strained their necks toward the glittery, animated ads for cameras and underwear, baby clothes and whiskey, surround-sound systems and Dianetics.

But here I was, the only person in the tiny, dark lobby of a narrow brick building, about to enter the smallest, oldest elevator I'd ever seen. Picture a dusty reddish-brown box with metal construction on three sides and a rickety accordion gate on the fourth. I hoped the indentations peppering its walls were only coincidentally shaped like bullet holes.

The blast of heat, comforting at first after the near-freezing temperature and gusty wind outside, now added to the swirls of dust around my nostrils.

I stepped inside the cage and pulled the squeaky gate across the opening. In the back corner, a janitor's bucket and mop took up a quarter of the floor space. The smell of chlorine tickled my nose.

I could hardly breathe.

I looked up at the dented metal ceiling. Too bad there were no oxygen masks, like those demonstrated by our flight attendant on the plane from Boston's Logan Airport.

I was no stranger to creepy environments — hadn't I lived above my friends' funeral parlor for more than a year? Done my laundry a few meters from their inventory of preservative chemicals and embalming fluid? Still, an uneasy feeling crept over me in the unnatural quiet of this space. I hunched my shoulders and pushed a scratched button with a worn-down label. Number *4*, I hoped. I worked my jaw to loosen it.

The elevator jerked into motion.

I longed for a sign of life, some sound other than the creaking machinery of the old cage. Where were the alleged eight million citizens of the nation's largest city? Not to mention the hundred thousand or so tourists supposedly passing through JFK every day. Where were the blaring car horns, the noisy taxis, the thundering buses? Where were the sirens of the famous NYFD? The old building seemed soundproof, leaving no noise inside except that of the whirring, rasping gears taking me upward toward . . . *what?*

It had seemed like a good idea at the time. Four of us had flown into La Guardia two days ago, but everyone else was too busy for this errand. My best friends, Rose and Frank Galigani, were having breakfast with relatives, the parents of their daughter-in-law, Karla, who was originally from New York. My husband of four months, homicide detective Matt Gennaro, was tied up, so to speak, at a police conference, which is what had brought us all to New York City in the first place.

So it had fallen to me to go to the home-cum-workplace of thirty-something Lori Pizzano, Matt's niece. His late wife Teresa's niece, more accurately. We'd had dinner with Lori last night, and she'd left her prescription sunglasses at the restaurant. As the only one of us truly on vacation this morning, I'd offered to return them.

I'd pictured something more exotic when Lori gave me directions to her "film studio in Times Square."

The old elevator took forever, fitting and starting its way up, past two other red metal doors, each with its own blend of scuff marks. I saw graffiti-lettered FAGETTA-BOUDIT twice and wondered what daredevil wrote it, swinging around, hovering over the open shaft. Here and there bleached-out streaks hinted at unmentionable stains.

At the fourth floor, the cage jerked to a stop, landing me across a narrow hallway from the threshold to Lori's apartment, the large metal door of which stood wide open.

Strange.

I checked my watch. Quarter to nine. I was cutting it close. Lori had said she usually went ice-skating around nine on Sunday mornings. Surely she couldn't have gone already, leaving her door open for me? My stereotypical New Yorker used two dead bolts and a chain to secure her door even when she was home.

From my place in the elevator I scanned the area, noting an eclectic blend of work and living furnishings, with an occasional partition in the form of a standing screen, a drape, or a curtain. Easy chairs in muted colors mixed with high-tech-looking work-tables and computer stations.

"No more cutting room floor," Lori had told us last night, expertly twirling spaghetti in a half-indoor, half-outdoor Little Italy restaurant. She'd worn a purple scarf, a lacy knit that seemed to offer no warmth against the cold air coming under the door from Mulberry Street but had much to recommend it as a fashion statement. "It's all videocam to computer or TV screen, direct. The editing is all done electronically, and the product is a videotape or a DVD."

"Imagine," said Rose, my lowest-tech friend.

"I have to admit, though, I have a soft spot in my heart for film," Lori said. "As far as prints go, you can't beat the resolution of fine-grain film. I still have a little darkroom in my studio."

I'd enjoyed hearing Lori talk about her latest success, winning an award for a short film on September 11 families. "Not that it translates to a lot of money," she'd said. "But I love my work, and there's always that huge grant out there waiting for a documentary filmmaker."

Her Uncle Matt seemed proud, and I guessed that at times like these he thought of his first wife, Teresa, Lori's aunt. Judging from photos in Matt's albums, there was a striking resemblance between Lori and the young Teresa, both petite in stature but with soft, round features, both with an intense and confident air.

I realized I'd been standing in the stopped elevator, going nowhere. I grasped the metal slats of the accordion door, unwilling to leave what had come to feel safe. The cage. The yellow mop and me.

"Lori?" I squeaked.

No answer. Except for a slight scratching sound. Mice? I felt a deep shiver and looked around me, as if someone might have managed to slip in beside me during what had seemed a long ride.

I shifted my body and stuck my head as far through one of the diamond-shaped openings as I could. My feet seemed glued to the tacky floor.

One more time, a little louder. "Lori?"

No answer, until — a siren, finally, from the street. The blast of noise shook me out of my inertia. I took a breath. All I had to do was enter the loft, deposit the glasses on a table, and make my exit. Nothing to it. Nothing to be afraid of. Maybe I'd take the extra minute to leave a note, that's how unafraid I was.

I pulled Lori's glasses, encased in hard

plastic, from my purse and tapped twice on a metal slat.

I sang out a warning. "Hi, Lori. It's me, Gloria. I have your glasses." I'd been going for *light and cheery* but instead heard *strained.*

Finally, I pulled at the elevator's rusty door: *I'm coming in. Mice beware.*

Only four steps into the apartment, long before I reached the small wooden table, I saw her. The glasses fell from my hand and crashed to the floor.

A woman was sprawled on the bare wooden floor, in front of a rack of electronics. A soft upholstered couch had been overturned, its flowery pillows scattered near her body.

Lori?

My heart jumped and my pulse raced. The light was dim, blocked by a neighboring brick building not five feet away from the window, but I could see the woman's hair: an unusual color, almost gold, closer to amber.

A wave of relief went through me.

Not Lori's tight dark curls. A large frame, not Lori's petite shoulders and short legs.

Not Lori, but still a woman in trauma.

I felt, rather than saw, a figure at the far end of the loft, leaving by the window.

15

I hurried toward the woman, skirting around one of the loft's many posts, at the same time pushing 911 on my cell phone.

Rumble. Crash. Crash.

Loud noises from outside sent an adrenaline rush through me. The noise was close — too close. And too many decibels for mice. I stepped back, hovering between wanting to help the woman and longing to rush back to the elevator and flee the building.

I heard a moan from the woman. I leaned down to say something soothing. More likely, something foolish, like *Are you okay?* I touched her rich golden hair and shrank away from the stickiness. I smelled her blood. There was a large pool of it under her head, or maybe a small pool, I couldn't tell, but it was enough to make me woozy.

Help her, I told myself. But I was unable to move.

I clung to the cell phone as if that in itself were productive.

Finally, the dispatcher's voice came over the line. "What's your address, please?"

I took a breath and rattled off the West Forty-eighth Street address.

"Yes, they're already on their way," the dispatcher said. "Please don't hang up this time. Now, is anyone else there with you?"

"I didn't hang up." I said. "This is my first call to you."

Had I given the wrong address?

I could already hear the ambulance stopping at the entrance four floors down.

So this was what they meant by a New York minute.

CHAPTER TWO

The next hours were a whirlwind of cell phone calls between Matt and me, between Lori and Matt, and between Matt and his NYPD buddy, Buzz Arnold. By the time I got back to our hotel room in the late afternoon, I was ready for a nap.

Rose, on the other hand, was ready for a briefing.

New York was full of extremes, on both ends of the spectrum. The tallest buildings, but the smallest elevators. The largest pretzels, but the tiniest restrooms in restaurants. The most famous city park — twenty-five million people visited Central Park each year, I'd read, and more than twelve hundred of its benches had been "adopted" — but the most meager hotel rooms. The one Matt and I shared had a closet that would be better described as a niche, so shallow that the clothes had to be hung parallel to the opening, one hanger in front of the other, facing out. Metal brackets provided for two such rows of hangers. I smiled at the sight of Matt's blue tweed sports coat next to my pantsuit, each facing out into the room, shoulders touching.

I wished I were closer to his real shoulder. I looked down on Eighth Avenue from nine floors up, only three short blocks and one long one from Lori's loft. The day had turned dark and rainy, to match my mood. My new digital camera was plugged into its charging dock on the small bedside table. I doubted I'd use it very soon.

Rose sat on the only chair in Matt's and my room; I sat on the bed, my legs dangling uncomfortably. I shifted around until my knees reached the edge of the mattress.

"You must have been scared to death, Gloria," Rose said. Then she put her fingers to her lips — coral, to match her jacket. "Oh, what a thing to say. I'm so sorry about the young woman."

I nodded, distracted. Yes, I'd been scared to death, and yes, so sorry about the woman identified as Amber Keenan, Lori's camera-woman. I felt a strange connection, as if I'd named her upon seeing her hair. I couldn't help feeling guilty, too. I'd taken a CPR class a couple of years ago, but it would never do me any good if I was afraid to use it when it counted.

Three decades as a physicist hadn't prepared me for emergency situations. The biggest crises I'd faced in the lab were times when my laser failed to operate a few days before I needed data for a conference. Or when a professor I'd refused to date was appointed to my doctoral thesis committee.

"Come back, Gloria." Rose waved a beige room-service napkin in front of my face.

Rose's name suited her, too. Rosy complexion (though the yellow walls, reflected in the mirror, flattered neither of us), rosy highlights in her hair (mine was dull and graying), rosy disposition (mine matched my hair), and a spectacular rose garden in front of her Revere, Massachusetts, home.

I wondered if Amber had amber jewelry, if everyone gave her amber presents, as so many friends gave rose things to Rose.

As if it mattered.

"She was alive when I got there, Rose. I can't help thinking I could have saved her life."

Rose wagged her coral-tipped finger at me. "No, no, we're not going there. Didn't they say she never would have made it?" She patted my chubby knee, encased in wrinkle-free knit pants. "Anyway, you hardly had a minute before the experts arrived.

Who knows? You might have made her worse in her last hour."

I failed to see what would have been worse than letting Amber die, but I didn't challenge Rose's logic-gone-awry, which in normal circumstances brought a smile to my lips.

"Thanks," I said. No sense in having two of us depressed.

We were waiting for Matt to bring us news from his NYPD friend. He and Buzz had spent Saturday at a conference session called "We Own the Night," learning about helicopters equipped with cameras that could "see" into buildings. Matt explained how this night-vision technology, long used by the military, had been adopted by law enforcement; its results were now admissible in the legal system.

Usually I was the one giving the science lesson, but this time I'd done my best to avoid curbing his enthusiasm by expanding on the basics of infrared thermal imaging.

Too bad one of those high-tech birds hadn't been flying over Lori's West Forty-eighth Street apartment building this morning.

I hadn't been able to tell the police very much. I'd closed my eyes tight and tried to envision the crime scene. The interior dark brick walls were the color of blood; the black and silver electronics components piled one on top of the other in chrome racks cast eerie shadows against the brick. I remembered the flowery pillows strewn around Amber's body and the light denim-colored couch that looked as though it would be so comfortable if it had been right side up. I recalled seeing a purse on the floor near Amber's hand, its contents scattered. A see-through cosmetics bag. A package of tissues. Videotapes and DVDs everywhere.

Describing the rumbling and crashing noises I'd heard was harder than I expected. What exactly did it sound like, the police wanted to know.

"A person? Or could it have been an animal?" Detective Glazer leaned into me, giving me the idea that I might be a suspect. My stomach clutched until I looked more carefully at his face. A gentle countenance, enough like Matt's to relax me.

"I'm not sure," I said. I felt helpless and dumb.

"Or could it have been a breeze, knocking something over?"

"I think it was a person, leaving by the fire escape," I told him, "but I didn't actually see anything or anyone."

I struggled to retrieve more information from my brain. This time I tried looking up and to the left, for an image of the scene. It didn't help. No glimpsed patch of clothing, no hint of a body part, long or short, dark or light, flitting down to the street level. Trying to re-create the moment left me with the feeling that there might not have been a sound at all. Maybe my scared psyche made it up, as an excuse for not trying to help Amber.

"Did it look like Amber had just walked in?" Glazer asked. "Did you see her coat, for example? Or keys? Maybe she'd done a little shopping?"

I squeezed my eyes shut. No shopping bags. Keys? I couldn't remember.

"Excuse me, but wouldn't the police have seen these things when they got there?" I ventured.

"If they were still there, yes."

I gave Glazer a questioning look. Then I realized he was asking me in a roundabout way if I'd removed anything from the scene. Clearly he didn't know my stunning record of consulting service to my detective husband and the Revere Police Department. Or maybe he did.

Nice as he was, Glazer had shared little

23

with me. I learned simply that the call before mine from Lori's loft to 911 had also come from a cell phone, and it would take a while to identify the owner. Or it would take a while to release that information, I guessed. Then I was sent to my room, so to speak, and advised not to leave town.

"Did you tell them you're married to a homicide cop?" Rose asked me, after I'd given her the briefing. "Not that I was witness to the union, of course."

Her last remark was accompanied by a deep frown. Rose had barely forgiven Matt and me for depriving her of the pleasure of a wedding. We'd gone off for the weekend to a B and B in Vermont and come back married. Rose claimed it was nothing short of eloping.

"It's what kids do," she'd said. "When they have to."

We knew what she meant.

Matt and I called our decision mature and efficient, a favor to our family and friends. We'd been part of an elaborate wedding in California over the summer, and neither of us could bear another round of fuss over flowers, caterers, and endless errands having to do with white lace.

"We're not in Revere anymore, Rose," I

said, skipping over the no-wedding issue. "Matt has no standing in Manhattan."

"Well, did you tell them you do police work yourself?"

"You know I get called in only on science-related cases."

She sat back, smiled, and uttered a loud *hmph.* "You'll find a way."

I didn't contradict her.

"Apparently, science is involved," Matt said. "Lori and Amber were working on an environmental sciences documentary." If he was surprised by the reaction — a burst of laughter from me, and an "I told you so" from a grinning Rose — he didn't show it.

Matt had arrived soaking wet from a late afternoon downpour. When he sneezed, I felt a rush of concern. I checked my husband's face for signs of fatigue — in truth, for signs of a cancer that he seemed to have beaten but that never left my mind. He gave me a smile that told me not to worry. *Only a sneeze,* it said.

He was wearing his blue suit, his Monday suit, on a Sunday. A weekend conference had thrown us off his wardrobe routine.

Rose relinquished the chair to Matt and brought him a mug of hotel coffee. I hung his jacket on the shower rod and toweled his salt-and-pepper hair, a match to mine in color, if not in thickness.

"This is nice," he said, smiling.

"It doesn't come free," Rose said. "You have to talk to us. Is there anything we can do to help Lori? What's going on with the investigation?"

"First, not right now, but Lori will be by later," he said, grimacing after a sip of coffee that had been brewed in the bathroom. "Second, there's not much to tell. Amber was Lori's primary camerawoman. She was DOA, sadly. Cause of death, suffocation."

Lack of oxygen to the brain. Was one of those lovely pillows a murder weapon? Why the blood, then? Had Amber been hit first? I shook away the awful image and focused on Matt, who'd continued talking.

"Lori's not doing too well," I heard him say, wondering what I'd missed. "I told her she should come here as soon as she finishes up at the precinct."

Rose and I sat on the swirly-patterned yellow bedspread, hands folded. *And?* we asked, with our posture, if not words. After one more swallow of questionable coffee, Matt took out a notebook and flipped a couple of pages. Just like home.

"Buzz did tell me about a few leads they'll be working. He's not primary on the case, but he's in the loop and he promised to brief me. First, Amber had just broken up with her boyfriend. Also, workwise, this documentary was not exactly welcomed by a couple of companies that are out of compliance with some environmental regs, and" — Matt closed his notebook and slapped it on his knee — "Amber had been moonlighting for a PI firm. She worked on the side for a Tina Miller Agency, staking out and photographing suspected adulterers, frauds, and other creeps." He looked up. "Buzz's term."

"We knew you wouldn't use that term," Rose said, with a wave of her hand. "So there were lots of people with a motive to kill her." She folded her hands in her lap and took on a pensive look, as if she'd been entrusted to solve this crime but didn't know where to begin.

Were we really doing this in a Big Apple hotel room, on what was supposed to be a vacation? Why weren't we at the Statue of Liberty or a Rockettes matinee, like normal people? Instead we were dealing with a crime scene, leads, and motives for murder. I'd already started a mental list of suspects: A. PERSONAL; B. WORK RELATED.

Oh-oh. I gasped with a sudden realization. "If Amber was killed because of something in the documentary, that means —" I stopped when I realized I'd been expressing my thoughts out loud.

Matt took a deep breath. "That Lori could be at risk. I know."

Rap. Rap. Rap.

A soft knock on our door. We opened to Lori Pizzano, her curls and her jacket dripping. It was hard to tell tears from raindrops on her face. She'd brought her own coffee, in a paper cup with a Timothy's logo. Smart woman.

Our fussing over her prompted a weak smile. "Thanks. I'm okay, considering my place is a crime scene."

"Are you finished with downtown?" her Uncle Matt asked. I found it interesting that we all knew what he meant.

"Yeah, your friend, Detective Arnold, was very nice to me. He stayed with me until the others came to interview me. He said he knew you from rookie days?"

"Yep, Buzz lived in Revere back in the day, then moved to New York about fifteen years ago. Good guy. I'm glad he treated you well. Did he give you a Yogi Berra quote?"

Lori shook her head and shivered at the same time.

"He will next time." Matt scratched his head. "Funny I can't think of one right now.

Buzz has a million of them."

Rose took Lori's shiver as a cue and trotted to the floor-mounted heating/cooling unit. "It's chilly in here," she said, bending to adjust the knobs. The gracious hostess, even in a hotel room, and one that wasn't her own. The fan kicked on, and dusty air blew through the room.

"They wanted to know where I was this morning. I told them ice-skating, like every Sunday morning in the winter, and of course Amber has a key, so she could get into the loft anytime." Lori patted her index finger absentmindedly on her lips, as if she were keeping time with a tune only she could hear. "I didn't know whether to tell him everything, though," Lori said, her voice softer, nearly drowned out by the fan.

Matt's eyebrows went up. He pulled one of his dry jackets from a hanger and placed it around Lori's shoulders. "If there's something that might help the investigation . . . ," he said, in a gentle, casual, voice. Impressive, considering what he must have been thinking. *How could you, my niece yet, not tell cops investigating a murder everything? Immediately.*

"I just can't believe this, that Amber is actually dead. I mean, we weren't that close, just work colleagues, you know, but . . . she's dead." Lori's eyes filled up. Rose went to the bathroom, a few steps away, and came back with a wad of tissues. "I feel so guilty. I should have tried harder to talk some sense into her. I told her she was getting herself in too deep."

"Too deep in what, honey?"

Honey? That was a new one. Matt wasn't strong on terms of endearment. He had one other niece and a nephew, both teenagers, his sister Jean's children. I'd never heard Matt call Peter and Allyse anything but their names. Of course, I'd never heard Matt interview them in a murder case, either. Maybe this was from his bag of interrogation tricks.

Lori blew her nose, then reached for her coffee, which I coveted. The paper cup had been perched on top of my hard-sided suitcase, which was squeezed in between the bed and the chair.

"Amber's the best . . . *was* the best photographer Tina — she's the PI — had, so she gave her all these big cases. Like, one time there was a guy with a huge claim against a brokerage on Seventh. Scaffolding fell on him or something, and Amber was supposed to follow him around and show that his limp was phony. Well, she was on the curb trying to sneak a picture of him getting into his SUV with his skis, and she ended up nearly getting run over by the guy. She broke her ankle rolling out of the way."

"So you were trying to talk her out of doing stuff that was too dangerous?" Matt walked around behind Lori. He adjusted his jacket, the Thursday gray, on her shoulders and rubbed her back.

To me, it was better than watching the ballet Rose wanted me to attend. I loved seeing Matt at work.

"Yeah, but not just physically dangerous like that. She'd been —" Lori jumped up, leaving Matt's jacket behind. "Oh, God, I don't want to talk about this. Amber's dead, and it doesn't matter anymore." Lori's voice was shrill. She leaned against the door to the corridor, one hand near the handle. I thought she was going to bolt out of the room.

Matt pulled her back, put his jacket over her shoulders again, and hugged her.

The interview was over. The rain slid down our window. Christmas lights on a nearby rooftop blinked on and off. For a moment everyone was in freeze-frame.

Followed by bustling activity.

Rose washed the coffee cups. I brushed off Matt's wet suit coat. Matt got out one of our maps and had Lori point out the locations of her favorite restaurants.

Lori didn't feel up to joining us for dinner, she told us. She'd take the subway out to Queens and stay with a girlfriend until she could get into her loft again.

"We'll put you in a cab," Matt said. "It's too cold out there to be walking around. We can pick up some sandwiches downstairs first, for you and your friend."

"Whatever. Anything for a distraction," she said.

I moved in on an opportunity to provide a diversion.

"Lori, I know this is not a great time, but if you have a few minutes more, I'd love to hear about the environmental project you're working on."

Lori's eyes widened slightly. "Yeah, well, it's very exciting. At least it was until now." She took a breath and swallowed, as if to prepare for a change of topic. "Okay, well, there's nothing like a global issue to put things in perspective. I've been working with two companies in town, Blake Manufacturing and Curry Industries. Here's my tag line. 'Oxygen — like any good thing, too much or too little can ruin your health.' "

"I like it," I said.

"Hmmm," Rose said. "Mae West said, 'Too much of a good thing is wonderful.'

Or maybe that was Groucho Marx."

I cleared my throat and Rose fell silent.

Lori went on, becoming more animated, gesturing with her hands, Italian-American style. "See, ozone, which is a form of oxygen, can be bad for you. If you breathe in too much of it, like if you work in a refrigerator factory, it inflames your lungs and you can be asphyxiated."

I wondered if Lori realized Amber had died of suffocation, a close cousin to asphyxiation. I hoped she didn't think of it at this moment.

"*But,* the earth as a whole is starting to have too *little* ozone. The ozone layer around the earth" — here Lori swung her arms in a large circle — "is there to protect us from the harmful ultraviolet rays of the sun."

Rose and Matt shot me a look. Rose rolled her eyes, as she usually did during science lessons. I shrugged: *It worked.* Lori was temporarily distracted from the tragedy of Amber's death.

"So the first segment of the documentary would be on what's called ozone depletion. Do you know there are people who actually smuggle CFCs into the country? Like, twenty thousand *tons* of CFCs — that's short for chlorofluorocarbons, like Freon — they're used in a lot of household materials, and eventually they end up where the ozone layer is and —" Lori stopped short and looked at me. "Oh my God, listen to me. A real scientist here and I'm going on and on."

I waved away her remark. "You're doing very well, Lori. I'm sure by now you're more well versed than I am in environmental issues."

"Well, I *have* done a lot of studying, but I'd love to have your input. I know the problems, but I don't know how it happens, like, what are those CFCs doing to the ozone layer exactly? If we're going to nail someone for violation — I know I'm sounding like *60 Minutes* here — we have to know what we're talking about."

"Is that what you're going for? Nailing someone?" Matt asked.

"Okay, bad choice of words. I'd like the video to explain what the issues are and point out that we're not all as aware as we should be."

"Gloria, maybe you could help. You could be an informal consultant on Lori's documentary," Rose said.

I frowned and shook my head. "No, no, I —"

Rose tilted her head and raised her eyebrows. A subtle, wordless interruption, but a connection born of years of friendship told me she was way ahead of me. It was a simple equation: *Consulting with Lori* equals *chance to investigate Amber Keenan's murder,* and a chance to make up in some way for my failure to respond when she lay dying at my feet.

"Would you?" Lori asked, her tone hopeful.

"Would you?" Matt asked, his tone just this side of threatening.

I swallowed and weighed the advantages of keeping my distance from anything connected with the Amber Keenan case. Then I heard the loud wail of an emergency vehicle from outside our window.

"I would," I said.

CHAPTER THREE

When Frank Galigani arrived, our little hotel room was at capacity. As much as we wanted to hear about his day — he'd spent the afternoon with a mortician who was part of an emergency response team — we decided to postpone the report until later, when we were comfortably seated at dinner.

Rose and Frank left for their own room, three floors down. I knew they'd appear in the lobby at eight o'clock, even more sharply dressed and put-together than they were now. For us, on the other hand: Matt would straighten his tie and put on a dry jacket, and I would give some consideration to brushing my hair before rendezvousing at the concierge's desk.

Matt insisted on accompanying Lori to the street and seeing that she and a bag of food got into a taxi headed for Queens. He wrote down her friend's phone number before they left the room. I was sure Matt's solicitude stemmed from a number of things — ranging from the concern of a loving uncle to the precautionary outlook of a homicide detective who worried about her being a target.

Matt had given me family background on the plane ride to New York: Lori's mother died when she was barely nine years old, and her father moved a new wife into their home within three months.

"Rita, the new stepmother, wasn't the maternal kind," Matt said. "So I sort of adopted Lori until she left Revere and came here to go to college at Columbia. She's lived in New York ever since."

My heart went out to the young woman who'd done so well after such a tough start in life, effectively orphaned at nine. I also wondered what Lori had held back from the NYPD, and whether Matt had been able to coax it out of her.

To think, until this morning, I had only a vacation to worry about.

Now I had a murder.

I also had an errand to do.

It had stopped raining, but I shoved a fold-up umbrella into my tote, between a notebook and a copy of *New Scientist,* always handy in case I became bored with Gotham.

I went out the side door of our hotel and headed up Eighth, knowing Matt would be with Lori, in front of the hotel on West Forty-fifth Street, either in the deli or on the street waiting for a taxi.

The first block offered everything a person might need. Flowers, prizewinning produce, a falafel wagon, a check-cashing office, T-shirts, used books (on a sidewalk table, in spite of the low temperatures), Rolex watches displayed in an attaché case. I tried to pick out the natives on the crowded street. It was easier years ago, when most New Yorkers wore black, no matter what the season. Then, you could pick out the visitors simply by clothing color: White jeans and a pink sweatshirt in December signaled a tourist from Stockton, California, or Phoenix, Arizona. Now, pink was the new black, and I couldn't tell the natives from the tourists.

I felt at home myself. Rose and I had arranged annual extended weekend reunions in New York during the years I lived in California, many times coinciding with an American Physical Society conference I'd attend at the Sixth Avenue Hilton. She'd take a train from Boston to Penn Station,

I'd fly into JFK, and we'd meet in a downtown hotel. Rose would choose one cultural event, like a drama on Broadway, to force me to, and I'd drag her to the Hayden Planetarium or to some abstruse exhibit of the notebooks of Sir Isaac Newton to peruse four-hundred-year-old prose, some of it in Latin.

The rest of the time we walked and talked, about her three children, the state of the world, or my latest lab mishap.

The air today was cold and fresh, perfect for mental acuity.

I started a mental list.

Number one: check noise — my reason for this trip to Lori's building. I felt compelled to survey the outside area around her West Forty-eighth Street address, to see if there even was a fire escape, or a trash can that could have been knocked over in the alleged escape attempt I thought I'd heard.

No one, I rationalized, could call that *investigating.*

Number two: check TOMS. I needed to review the data on ozone depletion from TOMS, NASA's Total Ozone Mapping Spectrometer. I knew about the Montreal Protocol, implemented in the late 1980s. Member countries approved a plan to control the production and consumption of substances that can cause ozone depletion. The agreement had been amended to ultimately ban CFCs altogether, with consideration given to developing nations that might need time to improve quality-of-life technologies.

What I hadn't kept up on was the quantitative data. The last I'd heard, early in the new century, was that the earth had lost 3 percent of its ozone layer.

Number three: brush up on ozone monitoring in the workplace. At the other end of the ozone spectrum was the problem of too much of it. In some industries, employees were at risk of serious overexposure to ozone inadvertently generated through their occupations.

I wished I'd brought my laptop, but at the last minute, I'd given the space to a pile of science magazines (the only kind I read). I'd look up the locations of Internet cafés so I could do some research and have a coffee at the same time. I figured New York would have one on every corner.

Number four: check violators. While I was there, roaming around in the ether, I might as well research some of the companies that had already been found in violation of the guidelines. I hoped that would lead me to other possible noncompliance spots: If Lori and Amber were about to expose anyone for violation of CFC regulations or ozone monitoring, it would be a powerful motive for murder. The penalties for smuggling CFCs or evading the special excise taxes on them were severe, sometimes including a prison term — an unwelcome prospect for a high-living CEO. The same was true for ozone monitoring violations.

I didn't linger long on the idea that it was Lori's apartment that was the crime scene — and Lori who would be the more likely target in this scenario, not Amber. I swallowed hard. Surely no one would mistake the honey-haired Amber for the short, dark Lori Pizzano.

My alibi was ready, in case I got caught doing more than what might be required to help Lori with the documentary. I'd tell my husband and my friends that I was preparing for my next Revere High School science class talk. In fact, I probably would use the material for that purpose, thus adding truthfulness to my résumé.

I breathed easier.

I used the long block between Eighth Avenue and Broadway to focus my attention on Lori's building, looming ahead.

From the outside, at a casual glance, the

building showed no signs of a recent struggle, except for the presence of a uniformed officer on the front stoop. I walked past the building, then turned to pass it in the other direction. As far as I could tell, no one noticed this peculiar maneuver, not even the cop. Like the other pedestrians — the pretheater dinner crowd, I guessed — I kept my eyes guarded, not making eye contact with anyone, except for the occasional *'scuse me* after a bump.

On my second walk-by, I stopped in front of the narrow passageway between Lori's building and the next one. I peered down the alley and took a few steps into it. A row of trash cans as long as my first helium-neon laser tube lined one wall. Fire escape steps and platforms stood out from the buildings on both sides of the alley, nearly meeting in the middle. The set of steps on Lori's building stopped about three feet above one of the cans, next to a large Dumpster. I counted windows and saw broken flowerpots on the old metal landing at the fourth floor.

Never did a dark, trash-filled alley look so good to me.

Rumble. Crash. Crash.

I heard the sounds again in my mind. I knew that if I still lived in California I'd have run for the doorjamb, thinking an earthquake was rumbling through.

I shuddered at the idea that I might have shared Lori's airy loft, even if only for a few seconds, with Amber Keenan's killer. I wished I'd had the time to ask Amber what she'd gotten herself into lately, what might have caused Lori to worry about her.

I looked up again at the fourth-story windows. I wished I'd been able to commandeer tanks full of oxygen, grasp Amber's last breaths, and stretch them into enough for a lifetime.

Matt was waiting for me in our room. He wanted to know how and why I'd snuck by him as he ushered Lori into a cab.

"I thought you'd be visiting with her for a while," I said.

A brief *huh,* not a question, was his only utterance.

"I left you a note," I said, doing what I supposed many of Matt's interviewees did during his silences — digging in deeper. In any case, I never was convinced that my simple OUT FOR A WHILE on a scrap of paper would suffice.

"That's *what,* not how, or why, or where."

I gauged the response seventy-thirty,

teasing-serious. Making this calculation was an important skill I'd developed over our time together.

"I needed some air?" I hadn't meant it to be a question, but Matt's frown, with its yellowish glow from the walls, intimidated me.

"You're aware this is not even *my* jurisdiction, let alone yours?"

I could tell that *What could you possibly mean by that?* wouldn't work. "I know, and I swear I did nothing even vaguely illegal." I crossed my heart and saw the hint of a smile.

Another *huh* from Matt.

"Not even an obstruction of justice."

He held up his palm. "Okay."

It seemed too easy, but I didn't question his willingness to drop the subject. I had a new topic ready.

"Is it time for an ozone lesson?" I asked.

A smile. "I guess it wouldn't hurt."

Whew.

"We'll start with oxygen, which you already know is number eight on the periodic table. So it has?"

"Eight protons in the nucleus."

Another inaudible *whew.* We'd had occasion to discuss the periodic table before this, and it was gratifying to know he'd retained some facts. On the other hand, I didn't want to resort to kindergarten tactics and make a big deal out of a small success. Teaching one's husband, I'd learned, is a tricky business.

"Ozone is a simple molecule, made of three oxygen atoms. It's just O_3." I showed him three fingers to reinforce the image. "You probably already knew that."

"I didn't."

I reached for the pen and pad of paper by the phone and started a sketch, severely handicapped by the unavailability of Power-Point. A wiggly circle for the earth. Four more or less concentric rings around it for the layers above the surface: our atmosphere. I shaded an area. "The ozone layer is in the second layer, the stratosphere."

Matt scrunched his face. Thinking. Remembering. "Let's see, ninth-grade science — Mr. Russo, who was really hired to be our field hockey coach. We went to the finals that year. Beat Winthrop, as I recall."

I poked my index finger into Matt's chest. "Well, therein lies the problem. Mr. field-hockey-coach Russo. We ought to be hiring teachers who know science and let them wing their way through sports coaching, instead of the other way around."

Matt grinned. I knew he agreed.

Matt was perched on the heating/cooling unit, while I sat on the chair in front of him. I had the superior view. Outside our window was a dense group of New York buildings, their floors and windows lit in a random fashion. Some windows were dark; others offered a bright look into an office or hotel room. I loved the geometry of the view: thousands of rectangular windows, with fire escape ladders slashing diagonally across them at intervals; at street level, an array of conic-section awnings decorated with a street number or the name of a restaurant. In this holiday season, more than the usual number of lights flickered at the tops of skyscrapers.

I stared at small office Christmas trees and festive lighted garlands strung around rooftop gardens.

A mesmerizing scene.

But I had a student in front of me. I picked up where I left off. "The ozone layer acts like a blanket, absorbing the harmful ultraviolet rays from the sun." I drew the sun at the edge of the paper. The completed drawing looked like one that could adorn the refrigerator of a family with a six-year-old. "Without this ozone cover, when the ozone layer is depleted, in other words, we're exposed to serious sunburn and potential risk of skin cancer."

I saw Matt's attention drift. I needed to remember to limit the length of science sentences.

"That was nice today, by the way, getting Lori to talk about oxygen," he said.

I waved my hand in the air. "Science cures."

"So you say." He leaned forward and kissed me. "I'm trying to compliment you. You put Lori at ease, and that was important."

I nodded and whispered a thank-you. The best I could do — I hadn't had a lot of training in accepting praise.

"Were you able to find out what Lori did *not* tell the police? Whatever it was that Amber was too deep into?" I asked, putting quote marks in the air around the last phrase.

" 'Fraid not. But we'll see her again tomorrow."

Matt stood, came behind me, and put his arms around me. I leaned back, my ear at his heart.

We looked at our watches. Almost ten to eight.

In our immediate future, for the Galiganis, Matt, and me, was dinner again in Little Italy. Sure, New York City was known for a wide variety of ethnic restaurants, and you might think we'd try a different neighborhood on our third night. But not two Galiganis (one née Zarelli), a Gennaro, and a Lamerino (me, joining the 17 percent of New England brides who did not adopt their spouse's name). We were drawn like iron filings to the magnetic Italian neighborhood just east of SoHo.

Frank Galigani had the idea that trying a new Italian establishment each night was diversity enough. He'd ticked them off on his fingers. "You've got your Sicilian, your Neapolitan, your Abruzzese . . ."

I guessed that Lori, who'd told us that on Saturday she'd feasted on a Bavarian breadbasket for breakfast at the Neue Galerie off Fifth, and sushi for lunch in Chelsea, would have laughed if she'd been there to hear it.

"Too bad we have to leave," I said.

Matt squeezed my shoulders. "Later."

I gave him my best smile. "Later."

CHAPTER FOUR

Zio Giovanni's must have been the narrowest restaurant in this city of extremes. There was room for one short row of tables for four along one wall, and one row of tables for two along the other.

So, when the marching band came through, we barely had room to lift our forks without pulling elbows in, close to our bodies.

Seven old men, all looking like my father, Marco Lamerino, in Santa outfits with floppy hats, marched in with big brass instruments. The Mulberry Street Marching Band (a name we created for them, on the spot) lined up in the skinny aisle and played holiday music for about ten minutes.

The four of us joined the other diners in singing the words now and then, when we knew them, and humming when we didn't.

The medley was eclectic. "Silent Night" morphed quickly into "I Saw Mommy Kissing Santa Claus" and then back to "O Come, All Ye Faithful." The group was gone before anyone could think of tipping them.

"I didn't think they did things like that anymore," Frank said after they'd left.

"They do everything in New York," said our young waiter.

I believed him.

The four of us had dinner together in Revere so often, it seemed quite natural for Matt and me to be sitting across a red-checked tablecloth from Rose and Frank Galigani in New York City. We'd selected Zio Giovanni's mostly because it was a non-gentrified restaurant, with scuffed, uneven floors — increasingly hard to find, with blond wood paneling and ferns creeping into the neighborhood's dining facilities. Another plus: Zio Giovanni's had no hawker on the sidewalk recruiting customers.

We resorted to our firmly established rhythm as each of us took a turn at leading the conversation. Like a four-way *How was your day?*

Frank, who'd worked in one or another aspect of mortuary service since he was in college, always had stories of questionable appropriateness for mealtime. His particularly tough challenge of reshaping the mouth of a young woman who died in a head-on collision. A new glass trocar, providing visible flow of the fluids drawn from his "clients." A state-of-the-art technique for sculpting an ear out of wax and pieces of tape and plastic to replace one lost in a shooting accident.

Tonight he described a missing nose on the last client he'd prepped before our trip. That he simultaneously hacked off a piece of salami from the antipasto tray only added to the realism of the story.

Rose announced that she would enlighten us on the mortician's role in disaster preparedness. After she and Frank had breakfasted (while I was alone in a creaky elevator) with their daughter-in-law Karla's parents, Grace and Roland Sasso, they'd met with a woman who was a member of a DMORT — Disaster Mortuary Operational Response Team.

Rose started, however, with a report on the Sassos, their oldest son Robert's in-laws. For Rose, family always came first. I was glad to be part of hers.

"Grace and Roland are such wonderful people. They've lived in that same apartment building all their lives. They wouldn't give it up for anything. Last year —"

"DMORT, Rose?" Frank said. I figured he didn't want to waste a perfectly good turn at conversation with family gossip.

"DMORT. It was so interesting. It's not something that gets publicized," Rose said, neatly buttering a warm slice of Italian bread that I knew she would never finish eating. My plate of eggplant, on the other hand, would soon be so clean as to look unused by the time the kitchen crew got to it.

"You don't necessarily want people knowing that a bunch of embalmers are standing around an accident scene, or whatever," Frank said. "We're thinking of joining the regional group in Massachusetts. They need funeral directors, MEs, X-ray technicians, fingerprint specialists, you name it."

Frank paused for a sip of wine and Rose stepped in again. "When there are mass fatalities — like in an airplane crash or an earthquake or a flood or —" Rose paused, her face taking on a sad expression, and we all automatically looked south.

"Or an attack," Frank said softly, patting Rose's hand. "We're talking about large numbers of people who need to be identified and stored."

"Stored?" I asked. I'd been a tenant in the Galiganis' mortuary — a live one, that is — until I moved in with Matt, so I might have known better than to ask about storage. I figured it out in time to hold off an explanation. "Never mind," I said.

"Not exactly what you find listed in the *I Love New York* tour book," Frank joked.

Matt had nothing to report. He confessed he'd napped through one of his conference sessions and slipped out for coffee with a buddy during another. He deferred to me, to report on what he called "the oxygen front."

"What I don't get," Rose said, "is how come we survived the old, unregulated days. I mean, we sat on Revere Beach for hours without sunscreen number such-and-such, and we ate raw cookie dough, right? Suddenly all the things we thought were okay when we were kids aren't safe anymore? Like these CDCs, or whatever was making our refrigerators run. Were we that stupid? Or are we being paranoid now?"

Rose always got to the heart of things, in spite of mixing up acronyms. Understandable that CFC would be replaced by CDC, the Centers for Disease Control, in her memory, given her profession.

"Very good questions," I said sincerely. "A little of both, I suppose. CFCs were a boon when they first came on the market — around the time we were kids."

Rose patted her nicely highlighted hair.

"Maybe when *you* all were kids," she said, with a wide grin. She wore a short jacket with fringe on the collar and cuffs and all the way down the front — the new frayed look that I didn't understand. Especially when you added a large faux flower, constructed from more of the frayed fabric and pinned to her lapel. My black washable knit outfit came from an outlet store that specialized in travel clothes.

"About CFCs," I said. I knew my minutes were numbered, so I kept on track. "We used to think CFCs — like Freon — were ideal for both industrial and home refrigerators, among other things. They were so much better than the stuff they replaced. Originally, sulfur dioxide and ammonia were the refrigerants of choice. So everyone was thrilled to substitute something nontoxic, nonflammable, noncorrosive, and very stable, like CFCs. Then we realized that the chlorine part of the CFC molecule was a hidden hazard."

I surveyed my audience, all paying rapt attention to their food and drink. Frank caught the last segment of spaghetti on his fork. Matt picked at the crumbs on his bread plate, looking at the basket as if deciding whether to have another piece. Rose sipped water after unobtrusively swallowing a calcium supplement.

"I think I'll leave it at that," I said, returning to my eggplant. "Keep you all in chlorinated suspense."

A laugh all around.

Rose was ready to tell us of their visit with the Sassos, whose residence was in the West Seventies, not far from the American Museum of Natural History (I could live with that).

"Last year the building went co-op, and Karla was able to help them buy their place," Rose said. "They're so proud of her success as a lawyer, as we are, too, of course."

"She makes a very good living," Frank said. "I guess divorce is lucrative for attorneys, if not for the clients involved." He paused. "I guess you could say that for me and Robert, too, about the mortuary business."

Matt and I laughed. Rose gave him a strange look.

"Karla's due in New York herself later in the week," Rose said.

"To spend the holiday?" Matt asked.

"As close to Christmas as she can get," Frank said. "William is at that age where he doesn't want to leave all his friends while they're on school vacation. So Karla will do an early celebration with her parents, then be home in Revere for the big dinners."

"Can't miss the big dinners," I said.

"Too bad we're not going to overlap here," Rose said. "We'll be long gone from New York."

"Maybe not," I said, all too aware that we had return tickets to Boston for Tuesday morning. Matt's conference ended tomorrow, Monday afternoon, and we'd allowed ourselves one extra night for enjoying the city together.

Heads turned; forks and knives were silenced.

"Huh," Matt said, in his *Really?* tone, perhaps the least stunned by my remark.

"Well, there's Lori to take care of. And the police did ask me to stay around."

"Indefinitely?" Rose asked, her eyes wide.

"To investigate?" Matt asked.

Frank laughed. Then we all did.

"Well, what do you say?" I asked, swinging my head to encompass everyone at the table.

"I think I'll head back Tuesday as planned," Frank said. "I talked to Robert this afternoon, and we've got every parlor filled."

I pictured them all: the main Parlors A and B off the foyer of the Galigani Mortuary. Parlor C at the back, a smaller, make-shift area for busy times. For so many months, my home had been the small apartment on the uppermost floor of the building, topping off the stack that comprised the embalming room in the basement, the parlors and Frank's office at street level, and Rose's office above that.

"Hmmm," Rose said.

I knew the look and the hesitation. Rose needed to hear from me that I wanted her to stay on with me.

I didn't.

I needed unencumbered sleuthing time, not the special museum exhibits and Broadway shows that were the highlight of Rose's New York vacations. I couldn't let her know that, though.

"I hope you can stay, Rose," I said, with as convincing a smile as I could manage.

"Okay," she said.

I doubted that I fooled her with my forced enthusiasm, but the special communication of a long friendship was at work. I knew she was pleased.

The three of us looked at Matt, who'd been drumming his fingers on the table next to his bright blue bottle of sparkling water. "Honey?" I asked, in falsetto.

Rose and Frank laughed, a sign that the

word hadn't quite run its course for this trip.

Matt stopped drumming and made a half-and-half motion with his hand. "Can't deny my bride," he said. "And I've always wanted to see Rikers Island."

It was all funny enough to cause Rose to drop her multivitamin into her water.

I thought about asking our waiter what the specials were for the rest of the week.

CHAPTER FIVE

Lori clutched her purse in front of her and stepped onto the N train. Monday morning commute time. No seats. She wrapped her arm around a pole and adopted the familiar position for reading a newspaper standing up while traveling fifty miles an hour. Although she hadn't taken the subway much since moving into the midtown loft, she'd had enough experience reading and doing homework underground during her college years at Columbia.

She folded the *Times* arts section lengthwise and tried to focus on a review of a play she'd been wanting to see, but all she could think of was her last fight with Amber yesterday morning. She didn't know either of them was capable of such angry words.

"You have to stop this, or I'll turn you in," she'd told Amber. What did that mean? *In* to what? To Amber's PI boss? Or was Lori going to storm into the nearest police precinct and tell them that her colleague was a blackmailer?

If she did that, she'd have to tell them she was a blackmailer herself.

It had seemed so innocent at first, collecting a few extra bucks for a good cause — and Pizzano Productions was certainly a worthy recipient of a little money from people who would hardly miss it. All Lori's videos had important social consequences. Not that she was in the *Fog of War* category yet, but someday maybe. Her piece on charter schools had aired on public television, and she'd done films on the lake cleanup, the right of gay couples to adopt, the sad state of nursing homes, the dwindling resources for at-risk children. All of them meaningful.

She'd have to except that one short piece during her internship, on the homes and gardens of New Hyde Park, Long Island, undertaken only because Professor Simms, who lived there, had insisted.

It was Amber who'd nearly destroyed Lori's dreams. "Think of this little scheme as collecting grant money or donations," Amber had said in her speech about why blackmailing was nothing to feel guilty about. "You know, like on PBS, when they say 'viewers like you.' " Her laugh was cynical, unbecoming a lovely twenty-nine-year-old Columbia journalism grad.

Lori thought back to when Amber first took the job with the private investigator, Tina Miller. The gig was to be temporary, just a few cases, to pay off her student loans and get a little ahead. Amber's assignments were usually low-key, like doing background checks for employers, following up on insurance claims, or taking a telltale photo here and there. Lori had agreed to let Amber use the equipment in her studio for a small fee.

Then Amber made Lori another offer. Instead of paying for studio time, Amber would cut her in on some special deals. Lori still wasn't exactly sure why Amber didn't continue to work solo. Maybe she needed to let someone else know about her exciting life, the risks she was taking. Amber had never been one to keep things to herself. More than once she'd called Lori immediately after a date to report on every detail, steamy or otherwise.

Amber had made her blackmailing scam seem almost part of her job. Whenever she learned that one of Tina's clients was a high roller with a lot to lose, Amber would move in: She'd withhold incriminating evidence from Tina and the client and sell it directly to the mark. Lori had let Amber talk her into taking a piece of the action, though everything in her said it was wrong and could never end well. All Lori had to do was look the other way while the occasional roll of film was being developed or a video-tape processed or a digital camera memory card slipped into one of Lori's computers. No big deal. Besides, it would be just until Amber could afford a place and equipment of her own.

"Eventually I'll have nothing but the best, like my new direct-to-DVD camera, and you'll be welcome to use it," Amber had told Lori with a grin that struck her as sinister.

Amber loved to show Lori photos from her little sideline. A prominent councilman parked on a known hooker corner, his window rolled down, apparently setting up a fun night. A well-known married business-man slipping into a gay bar. Another mar-ried man with a cute young thing on his arm in a Lower East Side bistro. Harmless amusement. Until Amber arrived with her thumbnail contact sheet.

Then Saturday night — the last straw. Amber showed Lori a set of pictures she'd snapped while she was following a married woman who took her six- or seven-year-old son with her to a motel to meet her lover.

"I shot through the window of the room," Amber had said. "Nearly fell into some thorny bushes." She paused, as if waiting for applause for her heroism in the line of duty or sympathy for the scratches she exhibited on her arm. "Look at this photo. You can see the little boy working at his PlayStation while his mother —"

"Don't show me any more of these," Lori had said.

"Okay, if you just want the money, fine with me."

Talk about calling a spade a spade.

Lori wanted out, and she had meant simply to reason with Amber on Sunday morning, not fight with her. Now Amber was dead, and Lori couldn't even get into her own apartment. She wondered how thoroughly the police would search the place. Would they check each and every file? She thought of sneaking back in, but it might already be too late.

They might already have found the evidence.

Uncle Matt would do anything for her, but not even a homicide detective could get her out of this.

Lori felt deep pain in her hand and realized she was clutching the N train pole so tightly her fingers hurt.

On the street, Lori kept her head down against the wind — and against making eye contact with happy-looking tourists. She resented every smiling, skipping kid, every wreath, and every red and green shopping bag. She couldn't even think of Christmas. Cameras hanging around people's necks reminded her of Amber the photographer; the window mannequins brought back thoughts of Amber the cool dresser; women walking happily together took her back to the days when Amber and Lori were good friends. The church with the tiny cemetery in back was a place to bury Amber.

Lori had checked her messages on both her loft phones from Cindy's apartment in Queens. Her private line was noticeably free of anyone looking for her, in large part because she'd been too embarrassed lately to keep up with most of her friends. On her work answering machine, on the other side of the loft, there were several messages. Besides her own business calls, there were two from Amber's ex-boyfriend, Kevin, and one or two older-sounding guys looking for Amber, probably marks. Another thing Lori hated — that Amber gave out the studio phone number to her sideline victims.

The message Lori cared about most was from Craig Daly, her editor and sometime soundman, with a question about footage he and Amber had taken at a welding plant. How much emphasis should he put on the welders as opposed to the product, and so on? It was nice to hear his voice. Craig's behind-the-scenes-guy personality appealed to her. A lot. She had no idea if he thought of her as anyone more than his producer, however. As good as Lori was at flirting, she couldn't do it with Craig. One of these days, she'd just come out with it and invite him on a date.

The N train pulled into Forty-ninth Street, her stop. She needed to put thoughts of Craig on hold and mentally prepare for her breakfast with Uncle Matt's new wife.

Lori's plan was to let Gloria go on and on about oxygen and ozone. Hopefully, the late Amber Keenan wouldn't even come up.

CHAPTER SIX

My plan was to get Lori talking about Amber.

Where was she from? Who was the boyfriend she'd just broken up with? Was it a nasty split? Had anyone been bothering her lately? Maybe one of the creeps Matt's friend Buzz talked about, someone she'd caught in a compromising situation. I had full confidence in the NYPD's ability to investigate Amber's death (wouldn't they be relieved to hear that?), but guilt over my cowardly ineffectiveness during Amber's last moments drove me to at least *wish* I could help find her killer.

It would be easy enough to get information about which companies were in violation of CFC regulations and which employers were heedless of ozone exposure limits. I needed Lori to tell me about Amber.

My morning catch-22 was, How do you find the location of an Internet café without using the Internet? It had been years since I thought of something so low-tech as yellow pages, and in fact there weren't any in the room. Unless they were stashed under the bed. There was no other spot for them in the tiny space.

I resorted to another old-fashioned method of information gathering: calling the front desk. From a very young woman with a heavy accent I learned there were at least four such establishments within walking distance of the hotel. I settled on Coffee And, not the closest place, but I loved the name. I remembered my father's daily *coffee and,* the *coffee* being espresso, the *and* being not a doughnut or a Danish but a shot of whiskey.

Between that tradition and the wine Marco Lamerino and my uncles made in our cellar, it was a wonder I ended up a teetotaler, and even more of a statistical wonder that I met another nondrinker in Matt.

"I don't have any brain cells to spare," he'd said.

I knew another reason was that his job brought him up close to the effects of excessive drinking. He'd often moralized about the large percentage of crimes that could be linked to alcohol — domestic violence, child abuse, vehicular homicide. Meanwhile, Rose and Frank were perfect examples of responsible wine imbibers. For years Rose had tried to tell me what I was missing in the taste of a good wine.

"I don't need one more thing that will add calories to my diet," I'd told her.

Her confused look could only come from one who had trouble keeping her weight above a hundred pounds so she could donate blood.

Lori and I had agreed that I'd call her when I had an address for our meeting. She picked up after three rings.

"Looking forward to talking about oxygen, CFCs, and all that cool stuff," she said.

"And I'm looking forward to getting to know you better," I said.

Losing Rose was easier than I thought it would be. She wanted to go to church with her husband.

Frank never missed a chance to stop in at St. Patrick's Cathedral on Fifth Avenue, to visit the shrine of St. Francis of Assisi, his patron saint.

"You might say he was the world's first environmentalist," Frank had said at dinner, as if to entice me into devotion to St.

Francis, based on his proclivity toward science. "The protector of animals and the environment, he's called. All of God's creatures were drawn to him. He fed the birds, wrote hymns to the sun and the moon, that kind of thing. He even had a prayer for pets. 'May my pet continue to remind me of your power.' Good stuff."

"You don't have any pets," I said.

Frank shrugged. "Even so."

"MC may get a puppy," Rose said, bringing her only daughter and my godchild into the conversation. She smiled and folded her arms across her chest, as if she'd just cleared everything up.

"I'll bet St. Francis would have been on the enlightened side of CFC issues," Matt said. Always the one to bring us to the present, peacefully.

"Right you are," Frank said.

"You don't mind if I go with Frank, do you, Gloria?" Rose asked. "It's not that he goes to church that often." She poked her husband on the arm. "Only if it's the biggest one in the country."

Frank reached into the pocket of his Italian silk jacket and pulled out a brochure from our hotel's pamphlet rack. He put on his glasses and read to us, in a sermon-like tone. "The *Pietà* in St. Patrick's is three times larger than the one in St. Peter's in Rome. One of the altars was designed by Tiffany."

"And we know God cares about these things," Rose said with a grin.

We all knew that Rose, the only one of us still a practicing Catholic, prayed regularly for our souls, most often at St. Anthony's Church in Revere.

"You go along with Frank," I said to Rose, magnanimous friend that I was. "I'll just be doing some boring Internet searches."

She gave me a look: *Right.*

I kissed Matt good-bye as he left for his conference, secretly hoping he wouldn't get out early, and walked toward Coffee And, between Fifth and Sixth on West Fiftieth. Today's "and" for me would be a chocolate croissant, I decided, always thinking ahead to the next sweet. The sidewalks were teeming with tourists on their way to and from the enormous Rockefeller Center Christmas tree, the lighting of which Rose watched on television, religiously, every year.

I remembered her critique of this year's show, aired just before we left for New York. "I don't know many of the performers anymore," she'd said.

"Except for Tony Bennett," Frank added.

We were all glad for the familiar voice, now representing a whole past generation of Italian-American crooners.

The brisk air, the animated pedestrians, and the noisy traffic energized me, and I reached the café fifteen minutes before Lori was due. Enough time to order breakfast, log on, and check into ozone crime in New York State. I had no problem finding a seat with a computer terminal, and near a window so I could watch for Lori.

Not the sexiest of offenses, crimes against the environment would probably never draw television audiences of millions of people. Nevertheless, unlawful disposing of hazardous waste, the transport and illegal use of CFCs, and the transport of endangered species were crimes with widespread impact. Looking at the mass of numbers that made up NASA's charts of data, though, I couldn't blame the average citizen for his glazed-over look when the topic came up. We needed more simplified information and more big-picture discussion, I decided.

Finally, I located a site with descriptions of recent violations. I was pleased to scroll through cases that resulted in criminal action.

A White Plains businessman who made millions by selling ozone-depleting gases on the black market was sentenced to six years in prison and ordered to pay three million dollars in restitution. The latter penalty meant simply that he had to forfeit his eight-thousand-square-foot mansion in Connecticut.

The man's accountant was also found guilty, on charges of complicity in tax evasion, and sentenced to four years and a fine of two hundred thousand dollars, which he probably covered by selling a couple of his cars.

I thought of Lori's "neither too much nor too little" theme: In the upper atmosphere, CFCs create a hole, and the result is too little ozone, exposing us to damaging UV radiation. At the earth's surface, too much ozone is a respiratory irritant and harmful to health, especially the health of children and the elderly.

I did a search for employers found in violation of ozone exposure limits in their industrial environments.

In the past year, water-treatment plant personnel and employees of a welding company had been victims of overexposure to ozone. Another company had failed to provide protective gear when the PEL — permissible exposure limits — couldn't be met.

I started to list the names of the guilty parties until I realized that the people Amber and Lori were threatening to expose probably hadn't been caught yet. What I really needed were the oxygen files. Ha, what a good title for a best-selling spy thriller, I thought.

I drummed my fingers next to the keyboard for a minute, gazing back and forth at the interior café surroundings and the street outside for inspiration. The light shades and the counter in the café had a modern, burnished-metal look. The cappuccino rivaled the best I'd had; the croissant was fresh and flaky. The people passing in front of my window — here a head of neon green spikes, there a long, silky fur coat — seemed much more heterogeneous than any slice of the population of Revere.

All that stimulation gave me an idea. Maybe the oxygen files were out of reach for the moment, but Tina Miller, Amber's employer, would have PI client files — and her place wasn't a crime scene.

Click, click, click.

Within a minute I had an address and a phone number for the agency. Lori entered the café just as I wrote down the information.

I made a quick plan to walk to the agency

— not that far away, on West Fifty-seventh Street — after Lori left and before Rose and Matt were available again.

My vacation had become busier than my regular life.

Lori took a seat and looked around the café with approval.

"How'd you find this? I thought I knew all the hot spots."

"An eighteen-year-old concierge advised me," I said.

"Cool."

Lori grinned, improving her drawn appearance only slightly. She had on a black jacket with quilt stitching and a different lacy scarf from the one she'd worn the first evening. This wrap was red and orange, with bits of fluff throughout. I'd seen the same style on many young women in New York, and I was positive Rose would buy a couple before she left. Maybe she'd be the one to move the new look northeast to Boston and Revere. In our short time in New York, she'd already picked up two Coach-like bags and a pair of chenille mittens, both from sidewalk vendors.

In the overheated café, I pulled off my cardigan and added it to the jacket over the back of my chair. The outside air had grown colder over the weekend, but no more rain was in sight.

"I've been thinking about Amber, wondering if she has any family around here," I said.

Lori took a long breath and shook her head. "They're all still on this wheat farm in Nashville, Kansas." She paused. "Not Tennessee. Kansas. It was such a stereotype, I couldn't believe it the first time I went there. Even her name. You know, *amber* waves of grain, that's what her parents named her for." Lori stared off at a distant spot in the café, as if she were trying to see all the way across to Kansas. A small smile took over her face. "Her brother, Billy, literally had straw in his hair. He and Amber argued all the time about big city versus small town. He was very hot, though. I could have had a thing for him if he were a tiny bit older and willing to leave the farm."

Lori stopped abruptly. I gathered she hadn't meant to say as much as she did.

"Do you know what Amber did, specifically, for the PI agency?" I asked.

"Gloria!" The very buff young counterman in a long-sleeved black tee sang out my name.

My second cappuccino was ready.

Foiled.

I'd hoped that catching Lori off guard about Amber's moonlighting might loosen her up and evoke an unfiltered response.

"I'll get it," Lori said, rushing toward the counter. She seemed relieved to be leaving me, even for a few moments.

Lori came back with my drink plus a plain coffee and a croissant for herself. She had her answer ready.

"Amber did just routine work, you know, like background checks and taking pictures of the scene of an accident, like for an insurance company or some lawyer."

"Did she follow any unsavory types?" I asked. *Wink, wink.* Just an old retired lady looking for a vicarious thrill.

Lori stirred a packet of sweetener into her coffee. "Only if you think it's unsavory to cheat on your wife." She winked at me, as if to tell me, gently, that she saw through my attempt at casualness. "You know, what I'd really like to know is the exact way that too much ozone hurts you, and the way that CFCs destroy the ozone layer. What happens, atom to atom, if that's the right way to ask?"

When had I not wanted to talk about science to anyone who would listen? Here was a person seriously interested in hearing me expound on the mechanism of ozone depletion. Instead of reveling in the idea, I was intent on reminding her of what was likely the most traumatic event of her life. I owed Lori my best expository powers.

"That's just the right way to put it," I said. "Ozone is generated as a side product in a lot of industries. Arc welding is one of the main culprits. The ozone is created in the high voltage of the arc."

Lori shook her pen at me. "We're looking into a welding company. So it would be great if I can get this straight. I know that ozone has three atoms, and it's not very stable — it wants to give up one of the oxygen atoms, to take it back to a stable two-atom state."

"You're halfway there," I said. "The ozone is ready to react with anything in its way in order to return to that stable state."

"And if it happens to be our lung tissue that's in the way, ozone will eat it up." Lori snapped her fingers.

There went a lung, I thought.

"You certainly are a quick study, Lori," I said, and meant it. "Was Amber able to help at all with this? Did she have a technical background?" Not to be too subtle.

"No more than I did, with our liberal arts degrees. You know, chemistry for journalism majors. No physics at all, I'm afraid. Not required."

"You're breaking my heart."

Lori gave me a comic sheepish look and turned the page in her notebook. She'd maintained a neutral expression through my attempt to bring Amber into the conversation.

"I'm thinking of doing only the ozone workplace exposure issue and not the CFCs this time around, but I'd still like to go over what happens with CFCs. They're tougher for me to understand."

"An excellent idea, to stay with one issue at a time. People can get mixed up otherwise."

"I'm glad you agree," Lori said. "Show me the CFC problem anyway."

"In case I'm not in New York City when you do Part Two."

She smiled. "Right."

"It's the chlorine atoms in the CFC molecules that cause the damage. When the CFCs reach the stratosphere, the ultraviolet radiation from the sun causes them to break apart, into two separate atoms, which then are free to react with the ozone. This starts the chemical cycle of ozone destruction." I made rolling motions with my arms. "One chlorine atom can break apart tens of thousands — I don't know the exact number — of ozone molecules."

Lori looked up from notes she'd been taking while I talked. "Wow. That's as clear an explanation as I've ever heard."

"Thanks. Of course, it's more complicated chemically. The meteorological conditions have to be just right — or just wrong, I guess — for ozone depletion to occur. It has to be very cold, for one thing, which is why the worst cases are near the poles. But, generally speaking, the mechanism is that simple."

Lori grew quiet, and I thought I'd lost even a student who started out eager to learn.

"I know you want to talk about Amber," she said. "Uncle Matt's told me about you."

I straightened my shoulders. My stiff "He has, has he?" brought a laugh.

"In a good way," she said. "How you love to investigate and all. But it's just too soon for me."

"I understand."

"Amber and I —" Lori stopped and stood suddenly. She kissed my cheek. " 'Bye, Gloria," she said, and was gone in a flash, leaving tufts of red and orange yarn behind her on the table.

I sat, skimming a tiny spoonful of foam

from my cappuccino. I felt like a failure, unable to find out anything useful about Amber.

Except that Lori seemed to know a lot more about Amber than she'd let on to us yesterday. Not close, she'd said, just colleagues. Yet she'd been to the Keenan farm and had *a thing* for Amber's brother?

I swallowed the rest of my cappuccino, put on all my layers of outer clothing, and headed out into the cold.

Maybe the meeting hadn't been a waste after all.

CHAPTER SEVEN

After a ride in a mercifully modern elevator — no wobbly accordion door, no worn-out, sticky buttons — I found Room 903, with TINA MILLER, PRIVATE INVESTIGATOR stenciled on a frosted glass window.

I opened the door to a young woman in stiletto-heeled boots, bent over a low file credenza. From the bottom drawer she'd just pulled a snazzy, sequined purse — not just for formals anymore, I knew from my thirty-something goddaughter.

I thought of my file cabinets in my old lab. They were chiefly a storage place for small equipment, meters, calipers, cables, and a general assortment of spare parts. No purses, and very few files.

"Dr. Lamerino? Dee Dee Sanders," she said, extending a hand. Close up, I saw that Dee Dee's purse had a sparkly outline of a horse-drawn sleigh bearing Santa and a pile of gifts.

"I'm glad you could fit me in," I said.

She waved her hand and clicked her tongue. "No problem. Have a seat — there's some brochures right in that rack — and Ms. Miller will be with you in a sec. And help yourself to some candy." Dee Dee pointed extravagantly first to the row of dull, padded chairs, then to a stack of pamphlets, and finally to a candy dish on her desk. "And if you don't mind? I'm leaving to have lunch with my boyfriend."

"Thanks, I'll be fine," I said.

"Oops, here he is," she said, fluttering toward the doorway, where a dark-haired young man in a business suit with stubble-by-design on his face gave her a big smile. "Zach, this is Dr. Lamerino. Dr. Lamerino, Zach."

"Hey," Zach said, not making eye contact with me. He sported a nonchalance that said I was one of a million clients he'd met in this office.

Dee Dee grabbed two pieces of candy, gave me a quick wave, then sped out of the office with Zach, her sweet perfume trailing. For some reason — their ages or their manner or recent events in my own life — I pictured an occasion in the near future with small white napkins bearing the words "Dee Dee and Zach Forever" in script lettering.

I fished through the candy dish, shaped like Santa's boot, for something not peppermint and found a chocolate kiss wrapped in red foil. Not See's chocolate Christmas balls, the California delight, but it would do.

I flipped through a brochure on the agency and its services. Testimonials from satisfied clients filled sidebars in the booklet: Words from CEOs and human resources directors lauded the Tina Miller Agency, claiming that it was "more efficient and effective than our company could have hoped for."

One of Miller's services was premarital screening. I wondered if this had anything in common with the old Pre-Cana conferences that were mandatory for Catholic couples when I was in school. Neither I nor any of my friends had been to Pre-Cana, but we'd heard rumors about the sessions — couples promising to have "as many children as God sent" and to bring them up in the strict Catholic tradition, and signing papers to that effect. Papers that were sent directly to the Holy Father in Rome, it was said.

The agency list included executive, corporate, and celebrity protection; preemployment verification; spousal surveillance; individual background profiles; assistance in civil liability and personal injury cases; missing persons cases; insurance claims and fraud; and child custody and protection cases. Tina Miller handled workers' compensation, medical malpractice, automobile accidents, and slip and fall.

I thought it curious that "slip and fall" was its own category, unlike, say, tumbling down stairs or being hit by a test tube flying out of a centrifuge.

I was glad I had a trouble-free life. My only lab accident had been too much exposure to a germicide lamp, requiring hours of sitting in darkness to reverse the effect.

The walls of Tina's outer office had the same neon glow as those of our hotel room. I imagined a widespread sale on yellow in Manhattan paint stores, which led me to wonder where Manhattanites bought their paint and home improvement supplies. A hardware store was the one business I hadn't passed in the seven blocks between Coffee And and Tina's building.

Ten minutes after I'd finished reading the brochure and browsing through the latest issue of *Technology Review,* which I'd brought along, I sat across from the PI herself.

At a glance, I guessed that Tina Miller was

about my age and shopped in the men's department. She wore a long-sleeved polo shirt and brown corduroy pants. An image of a cowboy astride an unruly horse sat at her waist on a large bronze belt buckle. Was she from Colorado? Montana? All the licenses and framed certificates on the walls bore the seal of the State of New York.

One more guess and I'd have said Tina had worked against her name all her life, trying to be a Maxine or a Sydney. She had a wide mouth, free of lipstick, and a loud voice.

"So, Dr. Lamerino, I'm glad this timing worked out. What is it? A malpractice case? I've done a few. Doesn't usually take long to smoke out fake limps or whatever. You'd be amazed how quickly a guy will shed his back brace if you offer him a tee time at Mansion Ridge."

I gave her a questioning look. "Mansion Ridge?"

She leaned back in an upholstered swivel chair that could have used a duct tape repair and opened her arms, as if to embrace my ignorance. "The Jack Nicklaus signature course up in Monroe. Not a golfer, huh?"

I shook my head. "Not a golfer and not a physician, I'm afraid. The 'doctor' is an academic degree, in physics, and retired at that."

Tina plopped forward with a thud. "Ah, clever," she bellowed. Her voice had the volume I wished for in my Revere High classroom visits. "Did you think I wouldn't agree to see an untitled client, or a mere scientist?"

I shrugged, a bit embarrassed, and looked past her at the ninth-floor view of West Fifty-seventh Street. More office buildings, more Christmas garlands, and a Lladro store that Rose had spent a good deal of time and money in over the years.

"Maybe you wouldn't have agreed to see me so quickly," I said. "I'm sorry —"

She held up her right hand, decorated with four rings, all of them silver with various ornamentation. Only her index finger was bare. I felt my fingers itch at the density of metal Tina carried around. It had taken me long enough to decide to wear one ring, a thin, plain platinum band.

"Don't apologize for a little pretense," Tina said. "Deceit is the core of my business. And I have nothing against scientists. I started out as a chemistry major, believe it or not, downtown at NYU, but then Martin Luther King was shot, and then Bobby Kennedy, so I switched to sociology, you know, the better to help humanity. Imagine my surprise when no one was hiring people to save the world."

"I always assumed a physicist would save the world."

"Yeah, well, you may be right. Now I try to bring equity to the universe at large by catching one little cheater at a time."

I thought of nobler causes, but who was I to judge? Besides, I guessed flattery would get me more cooperation.

"I'll bet it wasn't easy for you, either, in a man's field, especially a few years ago." *Oops.* Another false start in my so-called interview. Maybe being technically on vacation had slowed down my brain. "Not that you're old . . ."

Tina's laugh was loud and hoarse. "I'm not in denial about my age. Kind of proud of what I've done, in fact. It took a while to build this business up. People tend to think women can't do this job. You have to be sneaky, and nosy, and persistent. You have to be willing to take risks to learn other people's secrets." She picked a pencil from a generic black holder on her desk. She managed to doodle and keep eye contact with me at the same time. "I say, who better than a woman?"

Another show-stopper. It was clear who

was in charge of this interview.

"Who indeed?" I asked.

"So what does a physicist want with a PI firm?" Tina asked. She nodded toward my only ring. "Looks new. Trouble already?"

I had a fleeting idea of claiming that I needed her services to track down my low-life husband, who'd betrayed me after only a few months, but in the back of my mind I heard a voice: *Don't con a conner,* or something like that. I opted for the truth.

"I was a friend of Amber Keenan's," I said, "and I work with the police."

Well, mostly the truth. I was fewer than six degrees of separation from Amber, and I did work with a police department only a ninety-minute plane ride away.

Tina cocked her head, her countenance turning sad. "I heard about Amber on this morning's news. Awful. She freelanced for me now and then. I didn't know her very well."

So far, apparently, no one did.

Tina continued, maintaining a mournful look. "I didn't know you were her friend. I'm so sorry."

Here I was, claiming friendship with Amber, a woman I'd seen only once, in the throes of death.

"I wonder if you'd be willing to tell me

what Amber was working on recently," I said.

Tina put the pencil down and folded her hands, a pose that signaled the delivery of bad news. "I'm sure you're aware that I can't release that information."

I nodded, creating an expression of sympathy with the rules of confidentiality, combined with disappointment at not being able to help in the worthy effort of finding Amber's killer. Tina's file cabinets, in various wood grains, stood around the room, their gold metal handles tempting me, like an elusive password behind which was hidden data. "Maybe you have a few minutes to tell me in general what Amber did for you?" I spread my hands, a helpless gesture. "Or just what kind of things you do here?" I hated my dumb-little-girl voice, but I hated more the idea of leaving Tina's office empty-handed.

Tina picked up the pencil again and tapped it on her desk-blotter calendar. Her desk and bookshelves were noticeably free of photos or memorabilia. "Sure," she said. "I don't mind sharing a bit of the gossip, in an anonymous, hypothetical way, of course."

"Of course."

"Well, I just finished a premarital screening case. I'm trying to move away from those, but they pay the bills. Rich men never trust their fiancées. Which is fine with me. Keeps me in business. So we dig a little, and we find out the woman was a stripper in a past life." Tina held up her hands. "I'm just saying hypothetically."

"Of course. But how fascinating. You must have a million of these stories."

She nodded expansively. "The sad ones are the missing persons, especially when it's kids. But, okay, here's a good one for you. There's this guy who dresses up in a tux, goes to weddings — no one he knows — and robs the money basket. You know, where guests put the envelopes for the bride and groom. Everybody thinks he's an usher or something. You'll never believe how he got caught, how stupid he was. He —"

Rrrring. Rrrring.

Tina checked the caller ID box attached to her phone.

Rrrring. Rrrring.

"I better take this. Dee Dee's out to lunch. Are we almost done?" Tina looked hopeful as she lifted her telephone receiver.

"Almost. But I want to hear the end of the wedding thief story."

Tina smiled, indulgent. "Sure. You can just have a seat outside. I won't be too long."

The waiting room was still empty. I

90

couldn't help checking out Dee Dee's small desk, which was practically on my way from Tina's office to the square, understuffed chairs of the reception area.

A metal file organizer with several horizontal trays, stacked like the floors of a skyscraper, took up one corner of the desk. Neatly printed labels sat in slots along the side of the frame; smaller labels were along the edges of the legal-size folders in each compartment. An organized woman, Dee Dee.

I could hear Tina, though not clearly, on the phone in the inner room.

"Okay . . . Saturdays or Sundays, got it . . . I'll have to check . . . city hall."

I hovered around Dee Dee's desk. The office was quiet except for Tina's muffled voice and the sounds of footsteps from the corridor outside. The steps were too rapid and not clicking enough to be from Dee Dee's stiletto heels, rather like a rush of people on their way to the elevator for a trip to the street-level restaurants. I tilted my head down and craned my neck until the labels in the file organizer were in focus.

ANDERSON, B.; NAZZARRO, L.; MILBANK, A. I read conscientiously, as if the folders held a clue as to what got Amber killed and what Lori was hiding from us.

My digital camera was in my purse, but I doubted I had the dexterity to whip it out and capture images in the style of a genuine spy.

"Keenan, Keenan," I mumbled, half to myself, scanning the folders. In my new career as police consultant, I'd become good at reading sideways and upside down.

"Listen, Charlie, there's another thing . . ."

Tina's voice. Not signing off yet.

I read on. JANSING, L.; SASSO, K.

K. Sasso? What a coincidence. Rose's daughter-in-law — Robert Galigani's wife — was Karla Sasso in her professional life. Rose and Frank had had breakfast with her parents yesterday on the Upper West Side.

It couldn't be the same person.

I took a deep breath.

"I don't think . . . why in the world?"

Tina, still on the phone. There was more time. *To do what?* I asked myself. *To snoop?*

Apparently so.

I tugged at the Sasso file, which was on the thick side, pulled it out partway from the stack, and lifted the corner. I could make out the printing on a thin strip of the top piece of the paper. Just enough to see the bright blue letterhead.

KARLA SASSO
HOPKINS, SARCIONE, AND SASSO
555 THE FENWAY
BOSTON, MA 02115

I grunted. Not what I wanted to see. I wished I could go back to the time just before the Sasso label came into view, though I didn't know exactly why I was so disturbed.

Why couldn't Karla, a Boston divorce lawyer, have business with a New York City PI who listed spousal surveillance in her brochure? Not unusual, or suspicious, I told myself. Except that this was no ordinary PI firm. It was the one where the late, murdered, Amber Keenan had worked.

Dee Dee wasn't back from lunch, but I knew Tina wouldn't be on the phone forever. It was now or never. In jerky, two-handed motions, I yanked the Sasso folder from the slot and riffled through the pages. Letters, forms, expense sheets, and then more of each. I caught glimpses of legalese — heretofores and whereupons — and subject lines like *Carter v. Carter* and *Lasky v. Lasky*. The standard phrasing for divorce proceedings. What was I looking for, anyway? I shook my head, mentally slapping myself back to rationality. I hastily straightened the pile of papers, balancing the folder on Dee Dee's short row of dictionaries and reference books. A flurry of eight-and-a-half-by-eleven pages, smaller than legal size, fell to floor.

"I guess that's it, then . . ."

Tina's call was coming to a close.

I scooped up the pages and stuffed them into the folder, then squeezed the folder into the slot. I knew I'd messed up Dee Dee's order, but there was no going back. What was worse, there was one piece of paper still on the floor, half of it under Dee Dee's desk.

I heard Tina's footsteps approach the door between her office and the reception area. My breath caught. All my blood seemed to rush to my face. The door opened as I lifted the errant paper from the floor and shoved it into my thankfully large, deep purse. Rose's tiny, hard-leather numbers might be chic, but in situations like this, only the soft, tote-style purse I always carried would do, I thought, never one to miss an opportunity for going off on a tangent.

I brushed my pants of bits of dust. "I keep dropping my gloves," I said, showing Tina one I'd deftly pulled from my pocket.

Tina used both hands to make an ushering motion toward her office. "Shall we continue?"

As much as I wanted to hear how the wedding bandit was caught, I needed to get out of the building. I looked at my watch and muttered a *tsk tsk.* "Look at the time. It's later than I thought, and I need to be downtown in about fifteen minutes." I opened my palms to indicate how sorry I was to have to run.

"Another time," Tina said, shrugging, in a meager show of disappointment.

I searched Tina's face for signs of awareness that her office was now a crime scene, but I saw primarily relief. Plus a bit of a questioning look at my abrupt change of heart? That might have been my imagination. I struggled to keep myself from looking at the disheveled file in the metal holder or at my purse, where a single sheet, hot as it was, seemed to be raising the temperature of the lining.

We shook hands. Mine were sweaty from the exertion of chasing the papers and from nerves. I imagined Tina dusting her own hand for my fingerprints, then comparing them to the prints on her folders.

I walked to the frosted glass door as quickly as I could without alerting Tina to a problem. I fell in with a crowd of workers carrying paper bags and plastic takeout boxes. A mixture of smells floated through the hallway. I identified hamburgers, salad dressings, and a reheated Mexican dish, probably from a small office microwave oven. I hoped Dee Dee wasn't part of the gang. I couldn't face her. With luck, it would be a busy afternoon, and a horde of clients would pass through the office before the messy file was noticed.

It could have been any one of twenty people, I imagined Dee Dee saying, though not a single client had darkened the door in the whole time I was there.

The elevator to the street was crowded with workers I assumed were from the many law firms and CPA offices I'd seen listed on the menu-like lobby directory. My mind was in chaos, swirling with questions. What was Karla's letter to Tina Miller about? I hoped it was a routine legal missive and my inadvertent theft was useless. Shameful, but not disastrous. Surely its loss wouldn't be a problem for the Miller agency: I was positive twenty-first-century offices had multiple copies, hard and soft, of every piece of correspondence. Dee Dee wouldn't be chastised and I wouldn't be found out. It would be a close call, but no harm done. Most important, I would have nothing to explain to my husband or to my best friend, K. Sasso's mother-in-law.

On the other hand, if there was something to the letter, something that was relevant to Amber's murder investigation, then what?

By the way, what was the penalty for stealing a letter? Had I committed a felony? The envelope had been opened already, so it wasn't like stealing from the U.S. mail, a federal offense. I pictured myself asking Matt the question.

Honey, suppose a person lifted an already-opened letter from a file organizer?

I made my way through the lobby, past a large Christmas tree with oversized, colorfully wrapped packages underneath. The boxes were empty, I figured. Deceiving. Like me. I imagined every pair of eyes looking at my purse, and a corps of NYPD waiting outside on West Fifty-seventh Street.

I exited the building — not a cop in sight — and picked up speed, nearly running away from Tina's office, perspiring in spite of the low-forties temperature. I wrenched my scarf from under my coat and jammed it into my purse. On top of the letter.

I'd never done anything like this before. I tried to think of a word other than "theft" to characterize my rash behavior. Borrowing? Temporary custody? Obstruction of justice also came to mind. Not an improvement.

When I thought I'd walked far enough from Tina's neighborhood, where Dee Dee might be picking up lunch, I ducked into a bookstore café and ordered the largest cappuccino on the menu.

I sat down and pulled the letter from my purse, keeping it low on my lap. The sheet was wrinkled from being crammed into my bag. I was relieved that it had no creases at the one-third points as an original might, from insertion into a business-sized envelope. *This means it's a photocopy,* I thought, *or a scanned color copy to preserve the letterhead.* I breathed easier, by a nanohair.

I decided to keep it hidden on my lap until my drink was delivered.

I felt deceitful enough to start my own PI firm.

CHAPTER EIGHT

Lori walked from Coffee And to her building, crossing her fingers, saying every prayer she could remember from first grade, making promises to God to donate more to charity. Okay, to *start* donating to charity. Until now she'd considered *herself* a charity, but that would stop, she vowed.

She needed to get into her apartment.

The breakfast meeting with Gloria — she wondered if she was supposed to call her *Aunt* Gloria — was a disaster. The woman should have been a cop herself, the way she got Lori to say things without thinking. She had that soft, pleasant voice that misled you into thinking everything she asked was innocuous. Lori knew she'd blown it this morning, talking about Amber's Midwest home and family. God, she'd even mentioned the crush she'd had on Amber's brother, Billy Keenan.

She turned the corner on West Forty-eighth. Halfway down the street, Lori could see a cop on her stoop, a short flight up from street level. He was young and cute — but so was she. She'd at least give it a try.

"Hey," she said, mildly flirtatious.

The cop had been shifting his weight from one foot to another, the keep-your-blood-moving dance of winter. When he saw Lori, he stopped and swung his club, like a baton, at his hip.

Lori knew how to lift her dark eyebrows just enough to express intensely personal interest: *You have captured my attention,* they said. She knew she had the best haircut to show off her high cheekbones and delicate chin, and she took advantage of the new styles to accentuate her petite figure. The short black jacket and bright scarf she wore today gave her a jaunty, sexy air she wasn't above using to her advantage. Not exactly what Greer, Friedan, and Steinem advocated in her women's studies texts.

"Hey," the cop said.

Lori noticed the curly red hair under his cap, and how tightly his jacket fit across his chest.

"Wow, that stick is awesome," she said.

The cop smiled and blushed. *Good.*

"How you doin' today, ma'am?"

"I'm great. Did you see the tree lit yet?"

Lori couldn't tell if he wore a wedding ring under his heavy gloves. *Please don't let him show me pictures of adorable red-haired children.*

"Yeah, I was down there last night, on my trusty steed." The cop straightened his shoulders and held his arms in position to hold the reins of an imaginary horse.

"Wow, you're a mountie, too?" Lori asked, fishing her keys from the front pocket of her tight-fitting pants. She moved closer to the door. The front entrance had been redone recently, with metal framing, and from the outside the rust-brown edifice looked like a doorman building, though it was far from it.

"What floor?" the cop asked.

Lori winked. "Wouldn't you like to know?" She reached for the door handle.

The cop stepped between Lori and the door. Still smiling, but not as malleable as Lori had hoped. "Actually, I have to know. Part of the building is off-limits."

Lori gave a hopeful look, though she felt it was a lost cause. "I'm on four."

Oops, why hadn't she lied? It wasn't as if she was the most honest person around these days.

The cop shook his head and wagged his finger. *No go.* "New York's finest are still

101

working up there."

Lori put her hand on her hip. One last effort. "Just for one tiny minute?"

The cop took off his hat and scratched his head. "You know I can't do that."

At that moment, uniformed officers — an entire crew of them, it seemed to Lori — opened the door from the inside and marched out, carrying boxes of stuff. Her stuff, she could tell. She saw one of her flowered pillows sticking out of a carton.

Her stomach rolled. It might as well have been her life passing before her, and then out of her hands.

She wondered how carefully they'd go through everything. She could ask Uncle Matt, but she hesitated to bring up anything about the case, especially with his wife nosing around. Not that it mattered. The money was in plain view.

"You can come back in an hour or so. Then maybe we can grab some lunch," the redheaded cop said, jerking his head toward the low-end diner on the corner.

"Yeah, maybe," she said.

"Some other lifetime," she mumbled to herself, and walked down the steps to the street.

Work was the only thing that would bring

some sanity back into Lori's life. Whatever else was going on, there were still ozone issues to deal with for her video, and maybe doing something that made a difference to the world would give her perspective. Wasn't that why she started Pizzano Productions in the first place? She'd wanted her parents to be proud of what she did with the money they'd left her. If she couldn't double or triple her inheritance, the least she could do was use it well.

She'd thought of producing something more immediately profitable, like the exercise videos and food-show DVDs some of her classmates turned out, but she couldn't get rid of the investigative bug. *All the President's Men* had unduly influenced her, Uncle Matt used to tell her.

Lori ducked into a store, found a quiet spot in men's shoes, and checked her Black-Berry. She scrolled through dozens of e-mails, mostly junk, but stopped at one that was only a half hour old, from an interviewee on her list for the ozone video. Rachel Hartman, the public relations officer for Blake Manufacturing, had agreed to see her ASAP at Rachel's West Forty-sixth Street apartment, to spare Lori a long subway ride downtown to where the facility was. ASAP was fine with Lori, who was only a few blocks away and in need of a distraction.

Rachel's apartment was on the corner of Ninth Avenue, on a block called Restaurant Row, and above a bistro that was one of Lori's favorites. As she climbed the steps to the third-floor, Lori could smell the vinegar peppers, the garlic bread, and the salami and cream cheese rolls they served on their antipasto plate. She'd had nothing but a couple of sips of coffee and two nervous bites of a croissant with Gloria this morning, and she was hungry. After the interview, she'd treat herself to a late lunch at the bistro.

Rachel led Lori into her spacious, well-appointed living room. Lori gave a fleeting thought to switching careers, except she doubted PR paid this much, either. A benefactor, Lori figured, or a rich husband was behind this. A beautiful Tiffany-like (or was it genuine?) tulip vase on a low glass coffee table was one of many lovely objects of art in the room.

Tall and strawberry blond, with legs long enough to fill one of those five-story ads for lingerie, Rachel could have had her pick of sugar daddies.

"I'm home sick today," Rachel said, with the slight lisp that came with an overbite.

"But don't worry. I'm not contagious. I'm taking a mental health day. Translation: Christmas shopping. My sister's in town from Los Angeles. Anyway, I thought if we did this interview, I wouldn't feel quite so guilty."

Rachel turned to give Lori a conspiratorial grin. The way her hair bounced, she could have been posing in a photo shoot in front of Macy's.

Lori smiled and took a seat as Rachel indicated, on a beige leather couch. A tea service was already on the coffee table. Rachel poured a fruity-smelling brew from her seat across from Lori. Rachel, who was dressed in a light brown that complemented her décor, was either well organized or well staffed, Lori thought.

"I'm sure this won't take long, and Bloomie's is open late for the holidays," Lori said.

Rachel pointed to a handwritten list of stores and times, on the light oak end table next to her. "Believe me, I know, but my sister likes to hang around the Village. She's staying down at one of those places with arty suites. She thinks midtown shopping is too upscale."

This apartment surely is, Lori thought. "The Village is a great place to stay," she said, playing it safe.

Rachel rubbed her hands together as if the apartment were chilly, which it wasn't. "So. Questions?" Rachel asked.

Lori was happy the schmoozing was over. "We already have the footage from your Tenth Street facility," she said. "I just need to clear up some points for the narration."

The footage was from Amber, of course. Lori remembered the day Amber had left the studio and headed to Blake Manufacturing. She'd made some comment about how boring it was to shoot scenes of guys in Darth Vader helmets and thick, fireproof aprons.

"They made me take a picture of some drawing they've done showing a close-up of stuff welded together, like on a valve or a wheel. How exciting." Amber had stopped to mimic yawning. "Who's going to stay awake during those scenes?"

"I guess you don't get the same thrill as when you're crawling in the bushes snooping on some guy who has a wife and two mistresses on the side," Lori had responded.

"Definitely not."

Lori suspected that Amber wouldn't have lasted too much longer at her job with Pizzano Productions. Eventually she'd have been able to afford her own facilities and would have gone with Tina full-time or found some other sleazy way to make money. Now Lori needed a new camera-person anyway, a little sooner than she'd thought she would.

"The narration?" Rachel asked, apparently not for the first time.

Lori came back to the present, to Rachel's couch and blue toile tea set. "Right, what I'll be saying in the voice-over."

"So you won't be showing me saying anything?"

Lori tried to determine whether the beautiful PR lady did or did not want to be seen in the video. "What are your thoughts, Rachel?" she asked. She could practically hear Professor Moore in his class on interview techniques: *Whenever possible, let the subject feel part of the production process.*

Rachel put her lovely fingers to her mouth, avoiding direct contact with her lipstick. Lori figured it was just as likely she was reviewing her Christmas list as thinking about the documentary. Lori had the feeling Rachel had already decided not to be seen. She wouldn't be surprised: People, especially PR personnel, didn't want to be held to what they said in interviews, and it was easier to deny quotes if there was no visual documentation.

"Oh, let's leave me out of this," Rachel

said finally. "It's not about me. It's to showcase the company."

"Fine, but I'll tape this conversation if you don't mind."

Rachel raised her eyebrows. "I don't know . . ."

Lori waved her hand and talked quickly. "It's for my own reference, I promise. Because I don't have the greatest memory." Lori touched her head. *Duh,* she implied, showing Rachel where her memory cells were weak. "This way I won't have to keep bugging you with questions."

"Okay, then."

For a few minutes Lori asked Rachel for general information about Blake Manufacturing. She'd get to the tough questions once the PR lady was relaxed and trusting. She took diligent notes as Rachel talked about the management of the company (the owner was a certified journeyman tool and die maker and accomplished mechanical designer, blah blah blah), the overall organization (the employees profited from a system where they were allowed to grow professionally and at the same time have a variety of learning experiences, blah blah blah), and other employee-friendly policies (Blake welcomed union welders and had a commendable retirement plan, blah blah blah).

Rachel had her own messages ready, no matter what Lori asked, and slipped them in wherever possible. "We manage all phases of the customer's project, from material specifications to welding and machining to the finishing process to the final assembly and inspection. Our goal is to exceed our customer's expectations, whether they've ordered a custom bicycle or a staircase or a ——"

"This is all good stuff," Lori said. *Is that a direct quote from your Web site?* She wanted to ask.

Rachel, apparently encouraged, went on. "Everything's changed so much with computers," she said. "We do a three-dimensional model to evaluate designs before a costly fabrication process. The customer can see the concept graphically at all stages."

"Can you tell me a little about who's responsible for the oversight of federal regulations for the company?" Lori asked.

Rachel cleared her throat. "Of course, but I just wanted to add a bit more about this three-D stuff, because it's fascinating. We now offer three-D animations that can be packaged with a product. You know, more and more vendors are including videotapes or DVDs with the product, showing how to assemble the pieces, or even mass-mailing them to attract new buyers."

Lori nodded, mumbled, "Good," and made it look as if she were taking it all down in her notebook even as the tape recorder ensured she wouldn't miss a word.

"The reason I'm asking about the regulatory oversight is that, from public records, I see that Blake has had to pay a lot of fines for violating OSHA rules for ozone exposure in your workplace."

Lori didn't add that last year Blake had paid more fines than any other company its size in the Northeast. She knew that for many businesses, it was cheaper to pay fines than to institute the changes or upgrades necessary to follow the regs.

"Yes, there was the occasional fine, but Blake is only one of four companies run by our parent in New Jersey. I wouldn't know, overall, how those infractions were distributed."

"Infractions" sounded so much more benign than *"violations,"* Lori noted. But, wouldn't you know, Rachel had brought up a possible loophole. New York was very restrictive in many regulatory and legal matters, often more than federal mandates for the

same issue. If its parent company was in New Jersey and not New York, this might let Blake off the hook. Lori made a note to check with her friend at DEC, the New York State Department of Environmental Conservation.

"I'm sure you're aware that arc welding is considered to be one of the highest-risk occupations," Lori said, "because of the elevated levels of ozone that may be generated unintentionally. I've also seen data that indicate Blake workers are getting sick at a higher than normal rate. Can you comment on that?"

Rachel uncrossed her long legs, pulled her short brown skirt forward, and leaned in toward Lori. While Lori was admiring Rachel's gold ankle bracelet, Rachel pushed the OFF button on the tape recorder. "Blake has such a generous benefits package that sometimes there are abuses, if you know what I mean. Employees tend to take advantage of our lenient policies regarding sick leave and disability. But you did not hear that from me." Rachel paused to zip her lip. "I mean, who doesn't have symptoms like itching eyes or a sinus inflammation now and then. It doesn't mean you've been overexposed to anything but the normal atmosphere."

"Which isn't that great, either," Lori said. She pushed RECORD again, trying to hide her annoyance. She shifted a bit and caught a view out the west window onto Ninth Avenue. Lights were liberally strung around the wrought-iron fences on balconies at all levels of the buildings across the street, giving the overcast sky the romantic, comforting look she usually loved. Now she wondered how she was going to get through the season.

Rachel cleared her throat and made a show of looking at her watch. Lori needed to move fast if she was going to get anything out of this meeting.

"Do you have any company memos I could look at, like communications issued from management, detailing how Blake implements OSHA requirements?"

"I'm not sure what you mean."

Lori wondered if Rachel knew what "implement" meant.

"Well, there might be notices or directives to the foremen, for example, or whoever, on what the ozone exposure limits should be and how to enforce the regs to keep the workplace safe. Also, there should be records on what kinds of filters or detectors are used in the fabrication areas. As I'm sure you know, once ozone is created in the welding arc, it can drift through the air for a long distance. If it's not diluted by fresh air, you can have a hazard, like, way across the shop, really far from where it was generated."

Lori was glad she'd done her homework.

Rachel looked flustered, as if her personal shopper had just shown her a wardrobe meant for a much older, larger person.

Lori continued, keeping control of the conversation. "So all your employees are at risk of suffering severe lung injury if they work in areas that have inadequate ventilation. Maybe there's a company newsletter with communication about safety and safeguards? I believe the current regulation is that ozone exposure in the workplace should be no more than point-one parts per million."

"I'm not a numbers person, you know," Rachel said, "but I do believe there's a range, from point-one to point-two, depending on how long the employee is exposed. But don't hold me to the ppms."

For not being a numbers person, Rachel knew how to quote the most lenient guideline, Lori noted. She made two or three more attempts to get definitive answers from Rachel: What measures are you taking? Who's in charge? Are your inspection reports on file?

Rachel held fast to her position that Blake was exemplary in following regulations. "I know you'd like to find something a little more sexy, like rampant disregard of government rules, but you're wasting your time."

Lori decided to give it up. At least she had it on record that Blake's official liaison did not think there was a problem with occupational ozone exposure. She'd find a way to juxtapose that with a graphic of employee complaints and treatments for ozone-related ailments for the last three years.

"That should do it, then," Lori said, packing up her recorder, notebook, and pen.

"I'm so glad this worked out," Rachel said, her tone more relaxed now that the recorder was disabled. "When I heard about what happened to that girl who works for you, I thought you might not get back to me."

Lori's mouth went dry. She searched for a response other than shaking her head.

Rachel apparently took her silence for confusion. "You know, that pretty girl who came out to the facility to take pictures last week."

"Amber Keenan," Lori said, in a soft voice. The name stuck in her mouth.

"I can't believe she was murdered," Rachel

said. "I've never known anyone who was murdered. Supposedly, New York leads the nation in effective crime fighting, and I was just reading in the paper how the murder rate in the city is way down, the lowest in forty years." Rachel uttered a *tsk tsk* sound. Lori thought she'd scream if she heard the word "murder" one more time. "Anyway, it's supposed to be safer than ever around here."

"For some people, I guess," Lori said, picking up her jacket.

"But, you know, that girl *was* a little stubborn," Rachel said. "She wangled her way into areas that weren't on the list we gave her. She kind of barged her way past some barriers and had to be called back by security." Rachel inspected her fingernails. "A girl can make enemies that way. I was wondering if you'd had any other complaints?"

First, Lori was surprised that Amber had taken her assignment that seriously, given her boredom with the topic. Lori was also annoyed. "Are you saying that's why she's dead?"

"No, no. I just want you to know we tried to be very cooperative. But if she was always upsetting people . . . well, never mind. I guess we're finished here." Rachel stood and straightened her skirt. She reached into a magazine holder and pulled out a large manila envelope. "Let me just give you this. It has our recruiting brochure and other FAQ sheets that might be useful."

"Thanks," Lori muttered. This was where ordinarily Lori would stand and shake the hand of the person being interviewed, tell her what a pleasure it was to meet her, and how she hoped they'd see each other again. At this time of year, there might even be a friendly question. *Where are you going to spend the holidays?* Or, if there were Christmas decorations in the apartment, which there were not, she might venture a *Merry Christmas to you and your family.*

"Anything else?" Rachel asked.

"We're finished," Lori said, thinking how Professor Moore would disapprove of her rudeness. She put on her jacket and walked to the door.

Outside the apartment, Lori raced down three flights of stairs and onto the street.

The smells in the hallway had turned sour, and she passed up the bistro.

CHAPTER NINE

I wasn't much of a reader, except of technical magazines and scientific biography — the newest one on Marie Curie was back in my luggage in our room. Though I wouldn't think of picking up fiction or a general nonfiction book, I liked the new trend of combining bookstores with coffee shops. It gave them both a bit more class, I thought, and increased the number of espresso makers in the world.

That said, I wished I hadn't inadvertently sat facing the true crime section of the bookstore café I'd wandered into. I needed no reminders of my legal status.

I hadn't intended to steal Karla Sasso's letter from Dee Dee's tray. That fact should be worth something, I hoped. Maybe the difference between a misdemeanor and a felony. Not that I could prove I didn't enter the office for the purpose of taking the paper from the file. I knew it mattered that

I didn't lift a proprietary item. Say, the secret formula for the next-generation New York cheesecake. I remembered a case Matt told me about, a theft of files from a commercial nursery in Revere. Because the papers contained details of growing a new variety of peony, the crime escalated in seriousness, and the thieves ended up charged with the theft of tens of thousands of dollars.

That wasn't likely to happen in my case. Still, I was aware that even if I'd taken my own medical record from my doctor's office without permission, it would be considered a theft, and it would be up to the DA to — I could hardly think the phrase — *arrest me,* or not.

I wondered if I could make surreptitious restitution. I could return to Dee Dee's office and slip the letter back into the file. Or under the door: Let her think a breeze had wafted it across the room.

Whatever penalty awaited me, I needed to read the letter. I looked over both shoulders. Most patrons were dressed in business attire, briefcases at their feet, eating premade sandwiches from the refrigerated case under the counter. They seemed too wrapped up in their own conversations to bother about me and my confiscated eight-and-a-half-by-eleven sheet.

Fumbling under the table, I unfolded the letter. My fingers were cold from the weather and slippery from my nervous state. I adjusted my reading glasses to focus on my lap and read.

To: Tina Miller Agency
Re: Fielding v. Fielding
I received your report dated December 1, regarding your asset search and surveillance. Thanks very much for your work.

As it happens, I plan to be in New York in the next couple of weeks. I'll give you a call when I arrive so we can arrange to speak about the results so far and our next steps in this matter.

Sincerely,

It was signed: *Karla Sasso.*
Fielding v. Fielding. Not *Keenan v. Someone.* Not *Someone v. Keenan.* This letter was not remotely connected to Amber Keenan's murder, I mused, and convinced myself that what I'd pulled truly represented the rest of the folder. Making a judgment from a sample of one — a first for me.

This was good news. It meant Rose's daughter-in-law simply, coincidentally, had legitimate business with Tina Miller — and why not? Lawyers and PIs interacted all the time, and Karla was a New Yorker, after all. For all I knew, she and Tina had been neighbors for years and now shunted business to each other whenever appropriate.

All that fuss for nothing.

I looked out onto the street, somewhere in the West Fifties, and saw a sight that cheered me: a hot dog wagon dressed for the holidays. Every city wraps greenery, fake or otherwise, around telephone poles and lampposts at this time of year, but how many had festive garlands streaming from portable hot dog ovens and pretzel wagons? I grinned in spite of my plight.

I ran my fingers over the paper on my lap and considered my options. How could I get the letter back into Dee Dee's file?

Not that it would work here, but I smiled as I remembered a trick my grade school teachers used. I could hear Miss Johnson's voice: *Let's close our eyes, boys and girls, and cover our ears, and the student who took the colored chalk from the tray can come up and put it back.*

I sighed, half wishing for the simple life at the Abraham Lincoln School in Revere. One big difference was that I was never the one guilty of the theft. Joey Di Luca took that chalk, and another time Connie Benedetto snatched the package of bright green construction paper and slipped it into her desk. I never stole supplies and always got an *A* in conduct.

That was then.

Now I was faced with my adult theft. A more realistic plan was to mail the letter to the Miller Agency in a plain brown wrapper. With the density of services in midtown, it would take no time to find an envelope, a stamp, and a mailbox. I'd add a stop at St. Patrick's to light a candle. I'd be spared. No one would have to know how close I'd come to incarceration.

The disadvantage to this plan was that it would bring the theft to Tina's and Dee Dee's attention, and I had no idea how they'd respond. If I hadn't messed up the entire folder, they might think the letter was misfiled. That wasn't likely, given the condition I'd left the Sasso file in, not to mention what I felt was my suspicious sweaty-handed leave-taking.

What if the agency had fingerprint-lifting equipment and online access to a database? My prints were on file, from the many security clearances I'd had during my research years in California. My stellar record as a physicist who could be trusted with national security secrets felt like a lump in my throat.

The plan to return in person to the agency seemed risky also, the odds of my finding myself once again alone in Dee Dee's office being very low.

I imagined placing an anonymous phone call telling Dee Dee to go alone to locker number such-and-such at Penn Station.

Ridiculous.

I needed more options.

Blip blip blip. Blip blip blip.

The tinkling ring of my cell phone. I dug it from my purse and checked the caller ID.

Matt! Had he followed me? Had Tina contacted his NYPD friend already?

My hand slammed into the drinking straw that was sticking out of my water glass. If the tumbler hadn't had a base large enough to support a skewed center of mass, it would have fallen over.

I looked past the coffee shop to the stacks of books, as if I'd heard Matt's voice from there. I imagined he was standing near the true crime section, scowling, his arms across his chest, ready to deliver scathing remarks about my behavior. Irrational notions flitted through my head: that Matt had followed me to Tina's office and to the bookstore café, that he'd had one of his NYPD friends tail me, that a camera had caught me lifting the file in Dee Dee's office (maybe this one was not so paranoid) and Tina had called the police.

Blip blip blip.

I could let it blip one more cycle and go to my voice mail, but eventually I'd have to face Matt and explain my whereabouts or my unavailability. I heaved a sigh and clicked TALK.

An attractive young Asian couple stopped by my table, meant for four, and asked if they could sit on the other side. I nodded and turned a bit to shield my conversation from them. They piled layers of clothing and packages onto the extra chair and then unwrapped two thick sandwiches. They began to speak, in Chinese I thought, in normal tones, but it sounded to me like the loud clinking of lab glass. As if I didn't have enough distractions.

"Hi, Matt. How's the conference going?"

"Terrific. Can't wait to tell you about smart guns."

"Can't wait to hear."

"I also have some tidbits from Buzz. I have a Yogi Berra quote — I wrote one down this time — and some news in the Keenan case."

"What's the Yogi Berra quote?"

A long pause. "When you come to a fork

in the road, take it."

Much too appropriate for my situation. I uttered a nervous laugh. "Funny," I said.

"I was kidding, you know, telling you that first. Didn't you hear me say I have news about Amber Keenan?"

"Oh, Amber," I said, my mouth dry. "I'm glad." I cleared my throat. "Where are we eating tonight?"

Matt was silent for so long I thought we'd lost our connection. Then, "Are you in trouble?"

"No." Was my voice really as high as it sounded to me? Was I mimicking the Chinese rhythm on the other side of my table? "Why would you ask that?"

"Only because you've never been so blasé about the skinny in a murder investigation. And there's that thing in your voice."

"What thing?"

"The nervous thing, like when you're on the edge of putting yourself in danger, or you've done something questionable, legally speaking."

I wondered if he knew how right he was. I couldn't tell him that I was in a quandary about the Keenan case. On the one hand, I felt the only way I could make restitution for my theft was to withdraw completely from any Amber-related involvement. On the other, the only way I could make up for turning my back on Amber was to find her killer. And I used to think quantum paradoxes were baffling.

"I'm fine, Matt. You said yourself, this is New York and I have no authority here. Not that I actually have authority in Revere." My mouth was impossibly constricted. I took a sip of water.

"Okay, now I am worried. Where are you?"

"No, no, nothing's wrong. I'm just having a coffee, and there's a problem hearing you because it's very crowded in here." I turned toward the young couple at my table, this time hoping Matt would catch a bit of the animated Chinese conversation across from me.

I saw myself dressed in gray cotton, if they had jumpsuits big enough to fit me, sitting at a long table with other inmates, our plastic trays touching.

"And you're not wildly interested in the Keenan investigation?"

"Not *wildly*, and only if you are."

"This is not my honey. Tell me where you are or I'll have a BOLO on you in no time."

I uttered a half-laugh, half-cry, and realized how much I needed to see Matt.

Not that I could ever tell him what I'd done.

"What were you thinking?" Matt asked, scratching his head. He'd walked to the bookstore café from his conference at the Hilton, a few blocks away, in record time. His face was flushed from the cold and, I guessed, distress at my behavior.

The young Chinese diners were still at the table, sipping from large plastic cups, and I wondered how much English they understood.

"I just wanted to help. I felt I'd let Amber down, and I thought if I could figure out why she was killed it might help the police." I threw up my hands.

Matt sat on a chair from the table next to mine, so close our knees were touching. It had taken me all of three minutes to tell him what I'd done, how badly I felt, how afraid I was of the consequences.

I hated that I'd caused him pain. He'd never caused me a moment's anguish, except when he was diagnosed with prostate cancer. Nothing Matt ever did made me lose sleep or look as concerned as he did now.

"I should be able to handle this," he said, as if coming back from a tough legal battle with himself. "You didn't break in or hurt anyone. You saw something that had personal interest for you, Karla's letterhead. You were curious."

I swallowed. Matt sounded like a defense lawyer. Did I need one?

Matt went on, as if he were rehearsing for an arraignment. "You're a model citizen. You haven't done anything like this before. Not that they know of, anyway."

He gave me a look I knew was meant to remind me of all the lesser infractions I'd committed working with his department in Revere. A little extracurricular snooping here, a little white lie there, a bluff or a pretense now and then, but all in the name of justice.

"I have *never* stolen anything," I said. Keeping the record straight.

He patted my knee. "I know that. Now you need to promise me that you won't pursue this case. It's not Revere. It's not safe. Do I need to make a speech?"

I shook my head. "No."

"I need you to step away from this while I talk to Buzz," he said, taking out his cell phone. "Do something to distract yourself. Do you think there's anything in New York City, the Big Apple, to interest you, besides police work?"

I tilted my head from side to side. *Maybe.*

"Rose?" Matt said into his phone.

Rose? Not Buzz? "Why are you calling her?" I whispered.

"Gloria's ready for some sightseeing," he said into the phone.

I breathed a sigh of resignation and gave him a sweet smile. Cooperating. Behaving. All the while feeling like a kid whose parent had to go and straighten things out with the school principal. I reminded myself that Matt and I had convinced the Galiganis to take the trip with us so we could enjoy the sights together. At the time, I'd fully intended to let Rose lead me to the places that interested her, to broaden myself in ways other than dress size. It was time to live up to my promise.

I took Matt's phone. "It's me."

"I can't believe you're up for something fun, Gloria," she said.

"What do you feel like doing? I'm all yours, Rose," I said, as much for Matt as for my shopaholic, sights-obsessed friend.

I put a chipper note in my voice. Maybe Rose would choose the planetarium, I thought, hopeful. Rose had been there once, though, and had already informed me that was enough. She wasn't even swayed when I told her the upgraded facility on Central

128

Park West was called the Rose Center for Earth and Science.

My favorite tour would have been to Brookhaven, the national laboratory on Long Island. I'd have given a lot for the inside scoop on their upcoming special conference where two experimental groups, dedicated to the Tevatron and the Large Hadron Collider, would share data and techniques.

I hoped Rose had already covered the Christmas windows at Lord & Taylor. I wasn't sure I could *ooh* and *aah* to her satisfaction. I didn't relish another trip through Saks or the gold-inlayed Trump Tower shops, either.

You'd think I'd have been less picky, that I'd have been grateful just to have been acquitted.

CHAPTER TEN

Rose and I had covered all the main tourist attractions in our youth. The Statue of Liberty. The Empire State Building. Grand Central Station. The New York Stock Exchange. The United Nations Headquarters. I'd even jogged (more like walking a little faster than usual) with Rose in Central Park. We'd had tea (with the tiniest sandwiches I'd ever seen) at the Waldorf and lunch at the Plaza (with the largest vase of flowers in my youthful experience). Rose had also managed to educate me on the then-new Lincoln Center for the Performing Arts.

What was left?

"Ellis Island," Rose said now, calling my cell phone from Bloomingdale's. Matt and his cell phone had left, and Rose and I were completing arrangements directly. "I've been meaning to go down there, but I still haven't done it since they reopened."

How could I refuse a trip to the spot where so many of my relatives, including all of my grandparents' families on both the Lamerino and the Circelli sides, had entered the country?

We decided to take separate cabs and meet at Castle Clinton, where the ferry tickets were sold. Easier said than done. New York was cleaner than earlier times I remembered, and I'd read that crime was down, but what hadn't improved was the availability of taxis. It seemed harder than ever to commandeer a cab. Lori had explained the complicated system of lights on the roofs of the cabs: When just the center bar is lit, highlighting the cab number, the cab is available. When the center and the side lamps are lit, the cab is off duty. When no lights are lit, the cab already has a fare. Sounds efficient, but as far as I could tell, the drivers were not scrupulous about setting the correct lighting. I saw heads in the backseat of every cab that passed me, whether its light was on or off.

Lori had also taught us the finger signal. A nice, G-rated finger signal. If you were going only a short distance and not taking a homebound driver out of his way, you used your thumb and index finger to indicate "little." This tactic would not work for the ride from midtown to Battery Park, however, and it took twenty minutes to capture a taxi.

Reluctantly, I gave the driver an address that took me away from the investigation that had captured my attention.

Rose was excited to meet me. She'd already bought our tickets and memorized an Ellis Island pamphlet.

"Twelve million people landed here," she told me. "Today their descendants — that's us, Gloria — account for almost forty percent of the United States population. Imagine."

"I must say, that is interesting," I admitted to Rose. "Maybe there's something to this sightseeing thing after all."

Rose showed me her palms, indicating she'd always known as much. Buoyed by my comment, she went on. "The rich passengers were processed on the ship and sent straight to wherever they were going, but the ones in the lower classes or in steerage were detained on the island for medical checkups and paperwork. They were kept in the main hall, which is on the tour."

We knew that detention must have been the fate of our grandparents, all of whom started life in America with little more than one battered steamer trunk and a dream.

I wondered if Amber Keenan had been among the descendants of immigrants (Irish? Welsh? I was no good with names that ended in consonants) to Ellis Island. I had no idea how many of them made their way to the Midwest. Something to ask Rose the next time I needed to keep her busy.

The ferry ride from Lower Manhattan to Ellis Island, on the waters of New York Harbor, was truly a vacation moment as Rose and I talked about the old days. She was always happy to reminisce, and I was grateful not to be responsible for thinking up topics other than her daughter-in-law's letterhead, which was at the front of my mind. I had to struggle to keep from feeling I'd betrayed her, also, by taking Karla's letter.

Thankfully, Rose hadn't been inquisitive about why Matt foisted me on her for the afternoon.

Once on the island, we spent a while cruising the exhibits and the cases of artifacts from the turn of the twentieth century.

"These might have come from my own house," Rose said, pointing out collections of crocheted doilies, wedding dresses, christening outfits, and embroidered hankies. "Isn't this fun, Gloria? See what being a tourist can be like?"

"It's fun, but let's not make a habit of it," I said.

Rose laughed, clearly taking my comment as more of a joke than I meant.

The Ellis Island Immigration Hall put us both in a contemplative mood. We made our way to the dormitories that our grandparents may have slept in. Bunk beds — thin, lumpy mattresses, more exactly — were stacked three high, two such units to a room, in a space that was barely ten by ten.

"And we think our hotel rooms are small," Rose said.

"I feel extremely petty complaining about the size of our closet when I see this," I said.

By unspoken agreement we stood there in silence. I knew Rose was praying, and I thought I was, too.

But my mind had been wandering away from Ellis Island, to a precinct in Manhattan, where Matt was pleading my case to Buzz, if that's what he was doing. I wondered what favors he'd owe as a result of my indiscretion. More indicative of my lack of willpower was that I was dying to know what Matt had learned. He'd mentioned some "skinny" he could share on Amber Keenan's case. I didn't dare ask him while he still held my freedom in his hands.

Anyway, I was off the case.

"Gloria, did you hear me?" Rose asked. "I'm suggesting we get in line for the next ferry back, since it will take a while to catch a cab uptown once we're in Manhattan."

"Good idea. Oh, by the way, Rose, do you know if Karla does any business in New York?" Off the case, but not off the curiosity.

"She certainly does. It's nice to be able to claim a business expense when you're visiting parents, right? Not that the IRS should worry," Rose said, giving me a poke in the arm.

"She lived here in New York through college, didn't she?"

"Yes, all her life until she graduated. She was on vacation in Boston one spring and drove out to Revere to see her cousin Edwina. You've met Edwina. She's the one with the charming pixie haircut. Nice young woman. Well, Edwina's brother was a friend of my Robert's, so they were introduced, and the rest is history."

The history was that Karla Sasso relocated to Revere, went to Northeastern Law School in Boston, and married Robert, who was now in partnership with his father, running the Galigani Mortuary. Their teenaged son, William, was Rose's only grandchild. Rose always gave her children equal time, so I was surprised she didn't launch into the history of her other two children: John, a journalist for the Revere newspaper, and Mary Catherine, MC, my godchild, an ex-research chemist and now a high school teacher.

"I hope we'll be able to see Karla this week. Unless you think she'll have too much business?" I said.

"Oh, didn't I tell you? I talked to Karla this morning. I wanted her to know we'd still be here, so we can all hook up at her parents' for dinner some night. You and Matt are invited, too, of course. She mentioned having to follow up on some work with a private investigator."

I gulped. "A private investigator here in Manhattan?"

"Yes, and I wish she'd forget work for a while and relax. She's seemed so stressed lately."

I mulled this over, but before I could pry further, Rose turned her back to me. "Let's not miss that view, Gloria. Isn't that the perfect skyline?"

Looking over Rose's shoulder, I had to agree. The beauty and the density of the buildings were overwhelming. Rose snapped a few photos, but I couldn't bear to limit the view to a tiny four-inch-square screen, and my camera stayed in my purse.

I wondered in which building *Fielding* lived, and why Karla was stressed. *It's nothing,* I told myself. *What lawyer isn't stressed?*

After nearly a half hour of stepping on and off the curb at Battery Park, taking turns sticking our arms out, bouncing up and down to keep warm, Rose and I garnered a cab to our hotel. We settled in for a tinny-sounding "Let It Snow" blaring from the back-door speakers. Once we were warm, Rose made another pitch for a wedding reception for Matt and me, just a simple party at her home, to celebrate our marriage.

"A party for the new Mr. and Mrs. . . . Oops," she said. "I mean, the Lamerino-Gennaro union. Really, Gloria, I don't see why you didn't change your name. Aren't you happy to be married to Matt?"

A straw-man fallacy if I ever heard one.

Then, as if to make up for her biography of Karla and Robert on the ferry, Rose related anecdotes about John (he took his girlfriend, Suzanne, to a wedding last weekend, and that could be a sign he's thinking of getting married himself) and Mary Catherine (she finally got rid of the couch I left in the apartment above the mortuary and bought her own).

I took in enough of the stories to pass a quiz, but in the back of my mind was Amber Keenan and her short life. I knew Matt was out there bailing me out with the NYPD, and I'd promised not to meddle again, but how was I supposed to pretend Amber's terrible death hadn't happened, right in front of me?

In the hotel elevator, Rose pushed the button for the sixth floor.

" 'Bye until dinner, Gloria. Thanks for a wonderful, wonderful afternoon."

All I'd done was show up. Rose had suggested the trip to Ellis Island, bought the tickets, and narrated the tour. If she weren't so easy to please, we wouldn't have been friends this long.

I wondered if Rose noticed that I hadn't pushed the button for my floor, three above hers. Now alone in the elevator, I pushed *L* for lobby. I didn't know if Matt was in our room, and I didn't want to know, until I'd done one more errand, even though it was already past daylight.

On the street again, I rewrapped my old-fashioned, plain wool scarf around my neck and headed north to Lori's building on West Forty-eighth. Matt had told me Lori was going to spend another night with her friend in Queens. I had no intention of going up in her elevator, but I wanted another look around the outside area, without Lori, and without a uniformed sentry.

Rounding the corner from Eighth Avenue, I could see that there was no cop outside. I walked up the street, nearly as deserted as on Sunday morning since there were few theatrical performances on Monday evenings. I surveyed the building. When I got to the alley, I slipped in.

And someone else slipped out, knocking me into the brick wall. No apology, no *'scuse me.* Whoever had been in the alley didn't want to share it with me. I caught only a shadowy glimpse of the person, the impression of someone tall and not too heavy. He or she had been close enough to leave a scent. Not the odor you'd expect from an alley dweller, however, but a fruity perfume. A woman? If so, a lady who worked out. I rubbed my shoulder where it had been smashed against the wall.

No time for nursing wounds, however. I had work to do.

I fished around in my purse for the small flashlight I always carried and tracked the edge of the alley closest to the building. Where the police might have missed a centimeter or two, I told myself. In my daydreams I saw a piece of incontrovertible evidence pointing toward the killer. A piece of his jacket with his name stenciled at the neck, the way we used to identify our lab coats. A gun or a knife (so what if Amber wasn't shot or stabbed) with fingerprints matching a known killer of young women. A date book or a cell phone with fingerprints the same as above.

That was my imagination. In reality, all I saw was several bits of bright tinfoil, in red, gold, and green. From wrapping paper? *This is dumb,* I told myself, stuffing one tiny red scrap into an outside pocket of my purse. Maybe just not to leave empty-handed.

Or maybe I needed something to fill that empty spot where Karla's letter had been.

Matt and I sat in our tiny hotel room, in what had become our conversation positions: Matt partly on the windowsill, partly on the heating and cooling unit, me on the bed. It was dark, and I could see into an office across West Forty-fifth Street where what appeared to be a holiday party was going on. Trays of food, bottles of wine or champagne, and everyone wearing red

Santa hats. I had a flash of nostalgia as I remembered parties from my lab life around this time of year, when the chemists from the next building would whip up a nameless pink brew with a "secret" ingredient that we suspected was denatured alcohol. Old Rad (for radiation) Lab, it was called, and *drink at your own risk* was the operative greeting.

"We're all set," Matt said, magnanimously including himself in the problem that needed to be settled in the first place.

I took a breath that seemed to start at my feet and flow smoothly through my body. It was as if I'd been holding my breath for the whole day, and now pure oxygen was free to move around inside me. My stomach muscles, sore from tension, relaxed. *This must be what it feels like to hear a not-guilty verdict,* I thought. *Even though I am guilty.*

"Do I want to know what you had to go through to make this go away?" I asked Matt.

"You do, but you're not going to." Matt seemed calm, so I guessed he hadn't had to sell his soul, at least.

"I understand." I figured Matt didn't quite trust me not to do something like this again if I thought there was a simple procedure to get me off the hook.

I had so many questions for him. Was the Tina Miller Agency going to get its letter back? Matt had taken it from me in the bookstore café. I wished I'd made a photocopy, although I realized that went against my firm purpose of amending my life. I was dying to know if the police would tell Tina it had been stolen, and who stole it.

Chasing all my unanswered questions for Matt around my brain, I wasn't ready for one from him.

"Would you be willing to talk to Buzz about ozone?" Matt asked.

I blinked hard and stared at him. "Ozone? Me? I . . . talk to Buzz? Your cop friend?" I couldn't have stuttered more if my lips had been swollen from some bad calamari at Zio Giovanni's.

Matt laughed and slapped his thigh. "I thought that would get you. Only because I know you, I'm taking that as a yes."

After what I'd put him through, he deserved a "gotcha" moment. He'd not only kept me from a trip upstate to Sing Sing, he'd gotten me a gig doing what I love to do: talk science to an audience who cared — or, at least, needed to know.

"How did you manage that?" I asked.

"Oh, yeah, well, as I told you, I had some news about Amber's case. A couple of things. First, it's looking like Amber was involved in some kind of blackmailing scheme. Buzz might tell us more, but it's kind of simple, really. Instead of reporting back to the PI agency with her photos or what-have-you, Amber turned around and blackmailed the people she caught."

"Wouldn't the agency get suspicious, unless they were in on it?"

"Not if she spread things out, I guess, and chose her victims wisely. It's not clear yet how clean the agency is."

I pictured Tina Miller behind her desk. She seemed no-nonsense, honestly working hard to make her business successful. So she ran a very clean agency, was my guess, but I didn't want to dwell on that phase of the case.

Matt continued. "The second thing is that the uniforms found a letter when they searched Amber's apartment that could have something to do with ozone. They need some help deciphering what Lori's video is all about and what Amber may have learned. They're not about to ask Lori because . . . well, she's not completely ruled out, since it was her loft and all." He waved his hand. "Not that's she's a viable suspect."

"No, no, but she might not know all the technical details of what Amber could have uncovered."

"Exactly. So I told Buzz about the work you do for the Revere PD, and he thought it was a good idea to talk to you."

"Really? The NYPD?"

"You act as though it's a promotion."

"No, I —"

"Just because they're about thirty-nine thousand times bigger?"

I leaned over and kissed him. "They don't have you."

The revelers in the office across the street were toasting each other. I thought I also saw a couple by the water cooler in an extra-long mistletoe embrace. I wished I'd brought mistletoe for our room, but it turned out we didn't need it.

CHAPTER ELEVEN

I fingered the NYPD VISITOR badge dangling at my waist and wondered if I could keep it as a souvenir. Yesterday, as a potential felon, I'd dreaded the idea of facing the NYPD; today, as a science teacher, I relished it. Matt and I sat at Buzz Arnold's desk in his precinct house. I guessed Matt gained a new appreciation for his semi-private office at the Revere PD. Buzz's desk was one of six in a room meant to hold three comfortably.

A young woman who appeared to serve as secretary sat by the door at a gray metal desk, much like the government-issue furniture I'd written my lab reports on for decades. She wore a nubby yellow-green sweater with a strangely skewed collar. The buttons started just above her left armpit, ran across her throat, and ended close to the right shoulder. The sweater was open most of the way, causing the buttonhole placket to drape to her chest. Studying New York fashion for a few days, I'd come to the conclusion that symmetry was out this year.

Buzz, short and stocky, looked enough like Matt to be his brother, except for his haircut, which I supposed had given rise to his nickname.

I was introduced to several other nicknames — a Flip, a Bones (not a skinny man, leading me to all kinds of gruesome images of how he earned the soubriquet), and a CJ — and one plain Greg, all of whom continued to work on phones, computers, and fax machines in the busy office area. From the position of our chairs, Matt and I could as well have been meeting with Flip or Bones, so close were we to their desks.

The precinct's general run-down condition — peeling paint, battered furniture, scratched linoleum floor — matched that of Matt's RPD building, but his department had recently qualified for a Massachusetts state grant for physical improvements. I thought this precinct would qualify if New York had such a program.

"Dr. Lamerino. Very pleased to meet you," Buzz said. *Meetcha.* I wondered if the stereotypical New York accent was for the benefit of visitors. I knew Buzz was originally from Revere.

"It's Gloria, please. And thank you for inviting me." *For not arresting me.*

"Yeah, I'm hoping you can fill me in on this ozone-oxygen thing. I figure I should find out about this stuff before I have to drag a tank of it around with me, huh?" Buzz paused to laugh at his remark. "So, start from the beginning, okay?"

Music to my ears, in whatever accent.

There was no desk in our hotel room, and the tiny nightstand didn't have space for anything as big as letterhead stationery, so I'd stopped at a big Duane Reade drugstore after dinner and picked up a pad of paper and a package of markers.

I had to decide how much I could get away with as a tutorial on oxygen. When I was in school, the atomic weight of oxygen was used as a standard of comparison for each of the other elements. Now the carbon-12 isotope was used. I didn't think Buzz would care about standards set by the International Union of Pure and Applied Chemistry, though, so I skipped instead to a few basic properties of oxygen.

Buzz had pulled a flat slide-out panel from his desk to give me a writing surface. I flexed my fingers and started with an *8*.

"Oxygen is number eight in the periodic table." I tried to keep the textbook sound out of my voice. Hard as it was to acknowledge, I realized no one in the NYPD came to work in the morning looking forward to a science lesson. "It's a gaseous element, colorless, odorless, and tasteless, and forms about twenty percent of our atmosphere." I wrote *20%* and paused. "I don't want to repeat things you already know. Is this sounding familiar? From high school chemistry, maybe?"

"Yeah, yeah. I mean no, no, but go on."

"What we care about here is one particular form of oxygen, called ozone, which is really just three oxygen atoms connected like this."

I drew a picture of the ozone molecule, using a traditional ball-and-stick approach. I uttered a silent apology to my scientist friends who spent their lives trying to introduce newer, holistic models, which were more accurate but not as easy to sketch.

"The black circles represent oxygen atoms."

"Got it."

"Unlike oxygen alone, ozone has a strong and irritating odor — the word 'ozone' comes from a Greek word meaning to smell — and ozone is corrosive and toxic."

"Not good. So why do we care if it's

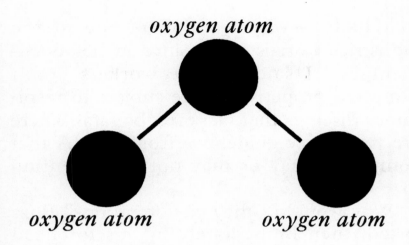

oxygen atom

oxygen atom   *oxygen atom*

depleted, as they say?"

"Here's the funny thing about ozone. It's not good if we're breathing it in down here at ground level, but up there" — I pointed in the general direction of the stratosphere — "it acts like a shield protecting us from ultraviolet light from the sun. Also, up there it occurs naturally. Down here, we have to make it. Any kind of electrical discharge in the air will turn some of the oxygen to ozone."

"Like lightning?"

"Yes, lightning produces ozone, and so does a discharge from arc welding. For the arc welder, she or he is close to the source of the ozone and likely to breathe in harmful amounts unless proper ventilation and safeguards are used."

"Got it."

"Which is why welding is one of the industries Lori is going after in her documentary," I said. "If the workers aren't protected properly, they're subject to respiratory diseases that can even be fatal. There are regulatory guidelines from OSHA that companies may or may not pay attention to."

"Why wouldn't they pay attention?" Buzz asked, then immediately hit his forehead with the palm of his hand. "Never mind. Stupid question. Let me count the ways companies can get around laws of any kind."

"Right. This is not that different from any other abuse of workers or the environment. Lori hopes to target companies that don't have safeguards in place, or ones that pay off an inspector, or . . . well, I'm sure you know this end of it better than I do."

"Okay, this is getting clearer," Buzz said. "But check this out. See that?" He waved in the direction of a device, less than a foot wide, mounted near the ceiling, in a corner of the room. "They tell me it's an ozone generator to purify the air. It was put in a while back when some of us were still smoking, and there was also this mold buildup in the building. We still keep it there, because, you know, we don't attract the most hygiene-conscious individuals."

Matt laughed, apparently reminding Buzz of his presence.

Buzz pointed an invisible gun at Matt. "Present company excluded, huh, Mattie?"

Mattie? This was the week for new nicknames. First honey, then Mattie.

"You bet," Matt said.

"That baby cost more than a new Beretta, with ammo." He turned and pointed to another metal box mounted on the ceiling a few feet away. "Okay, now see that? We have a second unit to make sure there's not too much ozone coming from the first unit. See what I'm talking about? Now you tell me, this ozone, if we need to monitor it, why are we pumping it in, in the first place?"

"It's a tricky balance."

"Like a lot of things, huh?"

Oh-oh. Was this a warning to me that I'd better keep my distance from police work? I was being overly sensitive to the close call I'd had over Karla's letter. I needed to focus on the lesson.

"Let me sketch out how ozone cleans the air," I said, "which is what the first unit does."

I looked around the office area. In a flight of fancy I thought I might have the attention of Flip and Bones and all the other officers present, but in fact they'd all moved out of the room. I hoped it was just coffee break time and nothing I'd said. In my dreams I was standing at an easel, lecturing to the squad, using the little laser pointer that was another staple of my purse, taking the place of lipstick and powder.

I needed to be satisfied with my audience of two.

"Because of its chemical structure, a single atom of oxygen is unstable — that means it wants to combine with something else. It's almost always found in pairs, what we call a diatomic form, where it's more stable.

"So ozone, with three atoms, is also not very stable. It wants to return to the paired state by giving up an oxygen atom. That's the property that makes it a good disinfectant: It's called oxidizing. It kills undesirable microorganisms in water or air. Think of it as burning up the foreign particle."

Buzz nudged the pad closer to me. "Show me."

One of my favorite requests from a student. I drew an irregular shape next to one of the ozone atoms.

"Suppose this is a dust atom," I said, "or a particle of smoke." I drew an arrow from the ozone atom over to the pollutant atom. "The ozone molecule wants to be stable, to go back to being just diatomic oxygen, so at

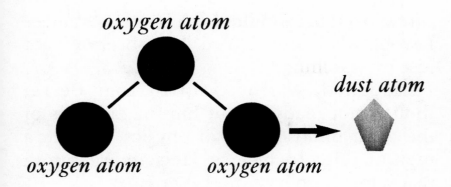

oxygen atom

dust atom

oxygen atom   oxygen atom

the first opportunity, it joins the pollutant atom, and they essentially destroy each other, and that leaves just the diatomic oxygen molecule, which is stable and pure and —"

"Thus you have rid the air of the smoke or dust particle," Buzz said.

I loved when my students interrupted me with the right answer. "See how easy that was? You can see how great ozone is as a disinfectant. Better than other cleansers or treatment options, like bleach, because the ozone molecule essentially vanishes without a trace."

"Why didn't my high school chemistry teacher explain it this way?" Buzz asked.

"She probably did," Matt said. "Only you had your mind on other things."

Buzz took out his invisible gun again. "Right you are, Mattie. Hey, Gloria, I think I have just the right Yogi quote for you." He threw back his shoulders. A baseball stance? I wouldn't know. " 'You can observe a lot just by watching.' "

I laughed, warming up to Yogi Berra, though not ready to put him in the class of the great philosophers of physics. I made a mental note to have a Heisenberg quote ready for the next time I met Buzz.

"Just to finish up," I said, after a decent interval, but not about to abandon my lesson. "What that first unit up there does is generate ozone, through some application of high voltage. But you have to monitor just how much ozone you produce —"

Buzz held up his hand. "You don't want to produce more ozone than you can use — say there's not as much dust in the room as you thought — and have it lingering in the air, breathing it in."

I smiled at Buzz and Matt. "My work here is done," I said.

"So I get an *A*, teach?"

"She's an easy grader," Matt said.

"Okay, let's see if we can relate this to your niece's project, Mattie. She's basically looking for companies that aren't following the guidelines for how much ozone can be in the air down here, right?"

"As I understand it, she's working both ends of the problem," Matt said. "The *down here* part and the *up there* part." He put quote marks in the air around the two parts. Then he made a gesture to me to continue his thought.

"Eventually Lori will produce a video on CFCs and the depletion of the ozone layer." I pointed *up there.*

Buzz sat back, put his hands behind his head, and frowned at me, as if I'd tricked him and he might now have to give back the excellent grade I'd awarded him.

"We can do that another time," I said.

It might have been my imagination, but as soon as I put my pad and pen away, the other detectives wandered back into the room.

"Okay, it's Mattie's turn to educate me." Buzz reached over to a stack of papers and pulled out a clear plastic sleeve with a sheet of paper encased on one side and an envelope on the other. The package that precipitated this meeting, I assumed. "Give me your take on this letter. It's the one we found in Amber's desk in her apartment."

The letterhead on the paper was bright blue in part, and for a moment I thought he'd brought out Karla Sasso's letter. My heart skipped. It was a trick! Buzz — and Matt? — had lured me to the police station by promising me an opportunity to teach

155

science, but he really meant to arrest me! Fortunately, the idea was fleeting, and I felt no one was aware of my brief nightmare.

I looked across Matt's shoulder. The letterhead read FAMILY SUITES, a regular hotel or a residence arrangement, I figured. From the street name I could place it only in Lower Manhattan. The colorful logo seemed to be a stylized nuclear family, with stick figures of a woman, a man, and a child between them.

The letter seemed hastily written, by hand. I'd have thought a person writing an incriminating or threatening note would use something other than his own penmanship on local hotel stationery, but, as Matt always said, there really are no smart criminals.

Matt smoothed out the plastic to eliminate the reflecting bubbles and read the letter out loud, adding underlines where they appeared.

Ms. Keenan, I've left several messages for you, and now I'm trying to reach you by this note. I urge you <u>not</u> to act on the footage you have in your possession. It will do more harm than good, especially to <u>you.</u> You <u>must not</u> expose this. You know how to contact me.

The letter was unsigned. Matt turned the sleeve over and pointed to the address on the envelope, which was that of Lori's apartment.

"Amber's workplace, not her home," Matt said. "So if this is Amber's killer, it means he didn't know where she lived and had to wait for her to show up at Lori's, and preferably when Lori wasn't there."

"You got it," Buzz said. "Looks like this is work related, one way or the other. Either the ozone companies or the marks she was blackmailing. I'm figuring the ozone only because it was sent to her ozone place of business, so to speak, and not to her home or to the Tina Miller Agency. So we won't spend a lot of time on people Amber hung out with in bars. We're running some prints, checking out this hotel. We might get lucky."

"Case solved?" I asked. I hadn't meant to sound disappointed, but I'd hoped to be of more use. I realized I needed to add to my list of New Year's resolutions: reevaluate priorities. Finding Amber's killer should be higher on the list than whether or not I'd been of any assistance.

"We wish. It's just barely a lead, but it'll keep us busy for a while."

Buzz stood, and Matt and I followed the cue. Both men reached for my jacket. In a

157

police station, the chivalry felt appropriate, but I plucked it from both and dressed myself.

"We appreciate you coming down," Buzz said, addressing me but slapping Matt on the back.

"My pleasure. Shall I leave this?" I asked, pointing to my ozone sketchpad.

"Oh yeah," Buzz said. "Thanks."

I envisioned his sweeping the pad into the wastebasket by his desk as soon as I was out of eyeshot.

The three of us left the room and entered the hallway, ready to walk down to the street level. At the top of the stairs, I turned to Buzz. "Can I ask you something?"

"Gloria —" Matt said, eyebrows raised, a worried look on his face.

Did he really think I was going to quiz Buzz on the disposition of Karla Sasso's letter?

"No, it's okay, Mattie. Shoot, Gloria."

"I've been wondering, why didn't the killer finish . . . I mean why did he leave Amber alive?"

Buzz cleared his throat and looked at Matt, who nodded. "We think he heard the elevator."

I gulped. "Me." I said in a weak voice. Not that I hadn't thought of it myself, but hearing it from an NYPD detective made it more real. And more frightening.

"We have some evidence that he went out the fire escape."

The noise toward the back of the room, by the window. For a brief moment, I'd shared the loft with a killer. I shivered at the thought. The vision of Amber, on the floor, bleeding, exploded in my head.

"And the blood?" I asked, determined to have the information in spite of the queasy feeling taking over my body.

"Her nose was broken."

I reached for the newel at the staircase landing and leaned on it for a moment. I had one more question.

"Amber's body?" I asked. Not a complete sentence, but not bad, considering I was struggling to keep my mental and physical balance.

"It will be shipped to her parents out west as soon as the ME's done. In a coupla days."

"Thanks." I smiled at the notion of Kansas, barely one-third of the way across the country, being called "out west." I figured Buzz used that term for any town west of the Hudson River.

I took a deep breath, feeling some closure. I'd been able to contribute a little to Buzz's background for the case; they had a viable

159

suspect in the author of the threatening letter; and I had answers to nagging questions. I felt connected to Amber and was happy to know the disposition of her remains.

I was almost ready for more sightseeing. We had a date to meet Rose at Rockefeller Center, where she planned to ice-skate and I planned to take her picture doing it.

"A minute, Buzz?"

I turned to see that Bones had caught up with us.

Bones pulled Buzz aside and leaned into his ear. I thought I heard the name Pizzano. I didn't like the expression on Buzz's face, the way he looked over at Matt.

There went my sense of balance and closure.

After a short time, Buzz turned back to us, scratching his head, a pained look on his face.

"They've gone through your niece's things, Matt." *Matt,* not Mattie anymore. Not chummy or teasing. "Something's turned up."

Though I'd already bundled up for the street, a chill came over me.

The case wasn't closed, after all.

CHAPTER TWELVE

Lori separated two slats of the blinds on her window and looked down on her street.

She could tell an unmarked police car a mile away.

She dealt with the NYPD a lot during location shoots all around the city. The beat cops were always very cooperative, putting up their wooden horses to close off streets where she needed space or a special backdrop.

There was also that brief fling with Bernie from the Sixteenth Precinct, the romance that had lasted just long enough to celebrate his making detective. As sure as Bernie's wife had turned up at his promotion party unexpectedly (Bernie had deleted the *M* word from his dating résumé), the beige four-door double-parking in front of her building right now was a cop car.

She let the slats click back into place and moved away from the window.

Lori had come home from Queens a couple of hours ago, before Cindy talked her into a permanent move. Uncle Matt had arranged for a cleaning service to go to work on her place as soon as the cops were finished. The loft looked clean enough, but there was a definite creepy feeling about it, and she could have sworn she smelled blood.

She'd watched the overflowing boxes leave her building while she was flirting on the landing yesterday. They'd found her records — she'd seen the edges of the big ledger she foolishly kept up to date, and she was pretty sure there'd been an envelope full of cash from Amber practically blinking *Find me* near where Amber's body had been.

Lori's photos were all slightly off where they should be on her shelves. She straightened the large, silver-framed photo of her grandmother Loretta, whose wedding dress hung in Lori's closet.

"For that special day," Lori's mom had said.

Next to Loretta's picture was a black-and-white of her parents, shot by Lori herself when she was eight years old and documenting family reunions. Lori thought how ashamed they'd be at this moment. They'd raised her to value honesty and integrity over money.

She wondered if Uncle Matt knew anything yet about her scurrilous dealings with Amber. When her mother died, he'd been there, supporting her all the way. Her own father had all but disappeared and emerged with another woman, who must have been waiting in the wings.

She looked out the window again. A plainclothes cop stood by the sedan, leaning on the banged-up front fender. She couldn't hear him, but his lips seemed pursed, and she thought he was whistling. Maybe this was the end of his shift and he was going home to his wife and kids, or his domestic partner. Maybe he'd reached his quota of pickups for the month and would get time off. She envied his apparent good mood.

Lori heard the creaky old elevator. Amber always hated the elevator, insisting someone would get hurt in it someday. Lori heaved a sigh. Amber was beyond hurting. A year or so ago, before Amber churned up everything, they'd had some good times. Hitting all the great spots of the city, talking endlessly about the advantages of digital over film (Amber) or film over digital (Lori). They'd covered the city, attending film festivals, gallery openings, book fairs, and lectures at the Ninety-second Street Y.

It didn't seem right that Amber would never show up again. She'd wanted Amber out of her life, but not this way. Just not around to tease and cajole Lori, to challenge her values, to ridicule her when she caved in to Amber's scheme.

More sounds of gears straining, metal scraping metal. It could be that the cops were bringing the rest of her stuff back.

Who was she kidding?

Lori knew all the clicks, grinds, and thumps on the wobbly trip from the street to her loft. The cage had reached the second floor.

Lori angled her rocker toward the door, sat down, closed her eyes, and waited.

She let her last scene with Amber flash before her.

It's Sunday morning. Lori has a date with college friends for breakfast and ice-skating at the Wollman Rink in Central Park.

Bzzzz. Bzzzz.

Her alarm goes off at six thirty. Way too early. She hits the snooze button. She can sleep a lot longer and still be on time.

Bzzzz. Bzzzz.

Lori thought she missed the snooze button, groaned, and slapped it again.

Bzzzz. Bzzzz.

Not the clock, the stupid doorbell. It had to be Amber. She wished she hadn't taken away Amber's key, so she wouldn't have to get up now. But she needed to have control over who came and went in her studio now that it was also her home. Real estate in Manhattan wasn't that easy to come by. Lori had been lucky to get her loft at a time when she had the money to renovate and then had been able to work it out so she could live here, too.

Amber had promised to look harder for a place for herself. At the moment she was crowded into a small apartment with three roommates and didn't even have her own bedroom. A couple more transactions, as Amber called them, and she'd be able to afford her own setup.

Lori could hardly wait — who knew what little sideline Amber would come up with next? Lori's special loft could become the central meeting place for pimps or drug dealers, at the rate things were going.

Lori put on her sweats and paddled to the door. She checked the peephole. Amber, with a big grin, waving a check. She had half a mind to ignore her and go back for another snooze session. On the other hand, this would be a perfect time — while she was sleepy, before she could talk herself out of it again — to confront Amber and be done with her once and for all.

She unhooked the chain, flipped the locks, and opened the door.

"Hey," Amber said, shedding her outer jacket.

Another new jacket and purse, Lori noted, and most likely not knock-offs from the street. Lori wondered how such a beautiful face could look so disturbing, how a friend from her earliest days at Columbia, the innocent farm girl, could have turned into a schemer who took advantage of people's weakest moments.

Moralize away, she told herself, *as if you're not part of it.* An image of her mother came to Lori, as it often did when she felt she was not living up to the values she'd learned as a child. She'd tried to get out from under Amber's game but never managed to stay strong.

This time felt different. Maybe because she hadn't had enough sleep. Or maybe being with Uncle Matt again brought it home more clearly: She had to get out of the blackmail business.

"We need to talk," Lori said. She followed Amber to the darkroom at the east end of the loft. Apparently Amber was in her film phase again.

"I know we said I shouldn't come before seven at the earliest, but I have a whole bunch of film here, and it's going to take forever to dry. And . . ." Amber smoothed the check out on an end table and held it in front of Lori's face. "Look what I have for you. I know you prefer cash — so do I — but this has to do. Next time there might be a little something extra since old Mr. Fielding —"

Lori's stomach turned over. Too much spaghetti in Little Italy last night, followed by that whole cannoli Gloria had talked her into. Too little sleep. And a sick, sick, person waking her up, standing in her loft. Her home.

"It's more than that," Lori said, nearly screaming. "More than you're too early, which you are. I'm done with this, Amber, and you should be, too."

"Dial it back, Lori. It must be that time of the month, right?" Amber picked up the check and tucked it into the diagonal slit pocket of Lori's sweatshirt. "Another five K, Lori. How long would it take you to earn that selling one DVD at a time through your little network of buddies in the video stores?"

Lori removed the check and threw it on the table. "I don't want this," she said. Then she went to her desk drawer, pulled out a stack of bills, and tossed them next to the check. "I don't want this, either. I mean it, Amber. And you have to stop, too. You have to stop this, or I'll turn you in."

"*I* have to stop?"

Amber is laughing. The sound tears through Lori's brain.

Lori is marching off to her bedroom, behind the new Japanese screen she bought with money from an Amber payment. She wants to knock the screen over, to throw it out the window, down four stories to crash on the street.

She gets dressed. It's early, but she'll walk in the park, then go for breakfast. Later she'll pound the ice, stay away from Amber, and feel better.

Amber is already in the darkroom; she's turned the sign on the door to read STOP. *She's singing a Christmas song:* He knows if you've been bad or good . . .

Lori bangs on the door. "I don't want to see you here when I get back," she shouts.

Sitting on her rocker, teary eyes closed, Lori heard the elevator reach the third floor, where it hit that jagged piece of metal a few inches from the gate.

She got up and went to her closet. She

took her black leather jacket from the hanger and then put it back. Too nice. She pulled on a fleece-lined parka with a button missing.

By the time the cage bounced onto the fourth-floor threshold, Lori had her scarf on and her gloves ready. She turned off the lights and looked out at the amazing array of buildings. New York was the best city in the world for making films, she thought. She remembered the first rule of New York film-making: When in doubt, cut to the skyline. She imagined the lines in a teleplay:

Young woman leaves brownstone with uniformed officers. [Cut to skyline.]

She waited until they rang the tinny bell. She opened the door.

"Lori Pizzano?"

She felt a jolt of fear, then drew a resigned, almost relaxed breath.

"That's me," she said, and followed New York's finest into the caged pen.

CHAPTER THIRTEEN

Matt and I walked arm in arm up Sixth Avenue toward Fiftieth, where we were to meet Rose for ice-skating (her) and spectating (us). We'd already seen the Rockefeller Center tree, illumined by Rose's detailed knowledge of it. She knew exactly how many lights (thirty thousand) adorned the spruce, and how big the tree was (seventy-one feet tall, weighing nine tons). And just as she was the historian of Revere, she'd recounted for us the tree's lineage, grown this year by a family in Suffern, New York. How she did all this research without the Internet, I couldn't fathom.

Neither Matt nor I was in a mood for holiday cheer, and as we strolled amid happy faces, I found the plethora of twinkling lights — in store windows, on lampposts, and draped around buildings — nerve-wracking, though I was sure the merchants paying the utility bills were hoping for a different response. The bulbs that blinked on and off, as if their fuse boxes had gone haywire, seemed to mimic my state of mind.

Buzz had said only a few words about why they were bringing Lori in for questioning. Something about her financial records and an unusually large amount of money in the loft had set them on the path of connecting Lori to the blackmail scam Amber was running.

"It could be nothing, Matt, so I don't want to get you all riled up," Buzz had said. "We're doing a routine questioning, based on what's turned up. Take your bride here and go about your business."

It was not the time to react to his designation of me — retired, and never having worn a long white dress and veil — as a bride.

Matt wrote his cell phone number on one of his business cards and handed it to Buzz. "I'd be glad if you'd keep me in the loop."

Buzz slapped Matt's back. "Will do, buddy."

"Buddy" was good, I thought. Not the term you'd use with a guy if you were ready to throw the book at his niece.

"Blackmail," Matt said to me now, as we crossed West Forty-ninth Street. "I just can't get my head around it. That Lori was getting a piece of . . . whatever kind of scam Amber had going."

"I guess that's what she was holding back on us the other night," I said. "That sentence she wouldn't finish. Lori will just explain everything to the police, and we can all unwind and have a good time. Maybe they asked Lori back because her apartment was the crime scene and they have more questions about it."

I talked on and on, hoping to find the right phrase to relax the muscles in Matt's arm.

Matt squeezed my hand, his touch barely noticeable through two pairs of thick gloves, his and mine. "I know the buzzwords, no pun intended, and Lori's already had her *routine* interview, on Sunday." He blew out a breath against the cold air and seemed to watch carefully as the fog he created drifted away. "When a cop says 'something's turned up,' he means the person has gone from being a witness to being a suspect."

"But not for *murder*," I said.

Matt shrugged and breathed heavily. "I don't know."

"But what about that letter Buzz showed us, sent to Amber at the loft? Didn't we agree that whoever killed Amber probably didn't know where she lived? Why would

Lori kill Amber in her own apartment?"

No answer forthcoming.

Blip blip blip. Blip blip blip.

Rose, calling my cell phone. I found it under several layers of warm knit and clicked TALK, becoming part of the large fraction of pedestrians holding phones to their ears or talking into headsets.

"Are we late?" I asked her. "I hope they didn't run out of skates for us to rent."

Rose had gone to see Frank off at La Guardia for his trip home, and she was ready to skate, the next thing on her to-do list for this vacation. I was ready to take her picture doing it.

"Funny, Gloria. I know you two have no intention of skating. Did it go all right with the NYPD Blue?" One of Rose's favorite rerun shows on television. "Did you get to teach and draw pictures of little atoms?"

"I might have helped a little, but . . ." The qualifier was out before I knew it, along with a little catch in my voice that I knew Rose would pick up.

"What's wrong?"

It was hard to talk with the hubbub of shoppers and traffic on Sixth Avenue, so I kept it short.

"Matt must be upset." I heard the concern in her voice and in the clicking noises she made while she thought of a way to help. "Well, we'll have to distract him. I'm already in a queue to get my skates. The line was long, long, long, so I decided to get in it right away before you came. I'm wearing my hat, so you shouldn't have trouble finding me. I've been reading a magazine and also that hotel brochure while I'm standing here. Did you know the star on the tree this year is covered in twenty-five thousand crystals and has a diameter of nine and a half feet?"

"Amazing. All that math."

"It's the only math I like."

"I know."

In what other century, I thought, would we be bantering this way, cell phone to cell phone, in real time? I reverted to my soapbox, lecturing to myself, advancing my theory to an internal audience: If only the so-called sciences of psychology and the human spirit had advanced as much as technology, Amber wouldn't be dead, there wouldn't be war, and we wouldn't need the NYPD Blue or any other army.

Short as she was, we could pick out Rose in the long line for skate rental. She wore a bright red chenille hat she'd bought from a street vendor for five dollars, along with a

Gucci-like wallet for ten dollars and a set of watches that was three for twenty dollars. So far, other than dinner and snack food, I'd bought only an Ellis Island Christmas ornament, in case Matt and I put up a tree when we got home to Revere.

Without warning, the line of people waiting to enter the rink was halted, and the ice cleared of skaters. The music changed, and a figure skater in a green and red outfit and a Santa hat entertained us for a few minutes. I had a better shot of Rose without the crowd of amateurs in the way, so I snapped a picture of her in line. I hoped she'd see us and wave, but it was crowded at the street-level viewing area and I doubted she'd be able to locate us, especially since both our hats were black.

Behind us, a group of impromptu carolers bravely started singing "The Twelve Days of Christmas." It was hard to ignore their spirit, and Matt and I joined them. We were all a little shaky at the higher numbers, where about twenty weak voices sang, *eleven mumbles a-mumbling, ten la la la-ing* . . . and then belted out, *five goooold-en rings* . . .

By the time we turned back, Rose in her fiery red hat was back on the ice and waving indiscriminately to the crowd. For a few minutes, I forgot about ozone, Amber, and a Pizzano in trouble.

Not counting ourselves among those who skip meals when under stress, Matt and I talked Rose into stopping at a deli near our Times Square hotel. We sat in a booth and checked out the framed caricatures hung edge to edge on the red-painted walls. We called out the names of celebrities as we recognized them. Matt and I were good at the classics — Sammy Davis Jr., Barbra Streisand, Dean Martin, and Frank Sinatra at different ages. Rose had a better grasp of pop culture and was able to identify a couple of young actresses and singers whose names began with Jennifer or Jason or Ashley.

"Do you have anything small?" Rose asked the waiter.

The young man, a caricature himself with his facial hair landscaped in curlicues, shook his head. "Sorry. We're known for our big."

When our sandwiches came, we understood what he meant: We were each served approximately a pound of meat between two slices of rye bread. I could hardly wait to see how big the cheesecake portions would be.

Matt looked tired, a consequence of Lori's plight, I knew.

"You still haven't told us about yesterday's conference," I said.

Not to be too obvious. I might as well have asked, *How can we get your mind off your niece?* I was hoping that a Christmas miracle would happen back at the precinct and Lori would be free and clear before we finished our carnivore meal.

"We heard all about smart guns," Matt said, squeezing the last drop of mustard from the container onto his bread. I'd won the no-mayonnaise battle, an effort to get his weight down as his cancer doctor had ordered. Matt was too much a gentleman to suggest what I should do to achieve the same.

"Like smart bombs?" I asked. "With sensors to guide them to their targets?"

"Nope. It's smart at the other end. The gun recognizes its owner from a thumbprint or some other pattern. It will function only in that person's hand."

Rose dropped the small piece of turkey she'd pulled off the edge of her sandwich. "Amazing. Of course! So if the kids find a gun in the house, they can't use it. I like it."

"The guy who breaks into your house can't use it, either," I said. "Brilliant concept."

Matt shook his head while he finished a

large bite of pastrami. "Not as good as it sounds. Most of us didn't like the idea."

I wondered if this were more of the Luddite syndrome, named in honor of those who reject new technology just because it's unfamiliar and therefore, they reason, probably unnecessary and unsafe. Certainly unwelcome. I thought of my older cousin Mary Ann, who was convinced it was Matt's cell phone that caused his prostate cancer.

"How come you're not thrilled with it?" I asked, in a neutral tone.

"What's not to like?" Rose asked, every day sounding more like her teenaged grandson. *Oops.* Karla Sasso Galigani's son, I thought, before I could rein in my associative powers. I set up an instant dilemma, ridiculous beyond words, where I was a one-woman jury, having to choose between Karla and Lori — my best friend's daughter-in-law and my husband's niece — as Amber's killer.

"To me, it's a computer, not a gun," Matt said. "It's got this little touch pad on the handle, like an alarm panel."

"Or the ATM machine," Rose said. "There's Milton Berle," she added, pointing across the narrow aisle between the two rows of booths.

"And Lucille Ball, two up from Uncle

Milty," Matt said. "You're right about the keypads on the ATMs, in the department stores. I had to key in my Social Security number at Macy's last week. Codes and PIN numbers are everywhere. I just don't want them on my gun. Some of these new models store all this data about how strong your grip is and what angle you hold the gun at. It's called a personal something."

"Personalization technology," I said. "That's one of the new terms in consumer products."

"It's nuts."

"You're thinking the gun's going to fail, like a computer, and you'll be stuck there, essentially unarmed," I said.

Matt shrugged his shoulders, holding on to the second half of his sandwich. "Yeah, what do you say to the bad guy? Hold on a sec, I have to reboot?"

I laughed in spite of myself, at his comment and at our different technology thresholds. Whenever possible financially, I was an early adopter. I wasn't negatively affected by the obvious disadvantages of getting the first products on the market: My first cell phone was bigger than the land phones of the time and weighed my purse down more than my flashlight, and the purse-sized laser pointer I bought ten years ago had fewer features and cost ten times more than the one I carried now. As for Matt, he'd only reluctantly allowed me to introduce a microwave oven into our home.

"You'd have loved that session, Gloria," Matt said. "They were demonstrating all these new electronic weapons. There's even a gun that gives you two choices. You can switch instantly between two barrels. One has beanbag rounds, the other has bullets. You can stun or kill."

"What will they think of next?" Rose asked. She took a small bite of meat. "I wish Frank were here to help with all this food." She had a hopeless, overwhelmed look.

Rose had eaten about one-half of the one-quarter sandwich she'd cut off. Matt and I had consumed a good portion of our meat, combining the leftovers into a single half sandwich that we'd take back to the hotel. We'd left room for dessert but decided to delay it until later in the evening.

Chirp chirp. Chirp chirp. Chirp chirp.

Matt's distinctive cell phone ring. The one new technology he couldn't do without. We were midway through pulling on vests, coats, scarves, and hats, but Matt had kept the phone handy through the meal.

He looked at me, and I knew he was thinking *Buzz,* as I was.

I would have been completely focused on Matt's side of the phone call, except for Rose's next maneuver. Under her coat was the magazine that had kept her company in the ice skating line: *New York City Today.* Now she put it on the table between us while she dressed for the outdoors.

Staring up from the cover was Tina Miller. I leaned over for a closer look. The cover design was a collage of the year's ten best, from clubs to galleries to books. There was no doubt — one of the little squares framed Tina's face, more made up than when I'd seen her. Under her image was the caption: MEET NYC'S TOP SMALL BUSINESS-WOMEN.

I wouldn't have been surprised to read a subcaption: LETTER STOLEN FROM LO-CAL PI OFFICE. THIEF A TOURIST FROM REVERE, MASS. I surreptitiously fished around in my purse, as if Karla's letter were still there and Rose could see through the black leather.

At the same time, I heard Matt's voice. "Are you charging her?"

If I didn't know better, I'd say my dizzy feeling was from too much roast beef.

CHAPTER FOURTEEN

It wasn't easy for me to sit in our hotel room while Matt was at the precinct. He'd convinced me that it would be better if he went alone to deal with Buzz, Lori, and an assistant district attorney who was called in to talk about Lori's case. Exactly what the case was, we still didn't know, except that it involved a potential blackmail charge against Lori. Buzz had told Matt over the phone that Lori wasn't yet free to go and that he'd called in a "friendly" ADA.

Fortunately, I had the latest issue of *New York City Today* to peruse.

Rose hadn't given the magazine up right away.

"You never read this kind of thing, Gloria," she said. She fanned out the glossy pages of the periodical as if it were a children's flip book, like the one I'd given her daughter when she was a little girl that pictured the spinning planets. "Look at this.

The feature articles are on the hot new dance floors, the ten best places to buy wine — you didn't even drink champagne at my wedding. Speaking of weddings . . . we'll come back to that. Remember, you gave your toast with iced tea?" She turned a few more pages of the magazine. "Then we have Broadway show reviews, ten cheap tours you can take around the five New York City boroughs —" She slapped the pages closed. "This is not you."

I realized she was trying to spare me wasted time, lest I be searching the slick publication for news of the New York Academy of Sciences.

"I need something light and distracting," I'd told her, then felt guilty when she acquiesced. Under normal circumstances, I would have admitted what drew me to the magazine, but I didn't want to call her attention to Tina Miller, someone I'd recently ripped off, nor to the nature of the stolen item.

I was off the hook when Rose's cell phone rang near the end of this negotiation. It was Frank, calling to say he'd arrived home safely, and by the time she was off the phone with him, the matter had faded to the background.

"Okay, then, I'm going down to my room

and make some calls. William has a cold, and I want to check on him. Also I need to talk to Karla because I forgot which one of us is supposed to get him the iPod for Christmas. MC had a teacher's meeting, and I want to find out if they discussed a field trip to the mortuary — there's a lot of chemistry to this business, you know." Here Rose winked at me. "And John thought it was over with him and Joyce, so I'll see how that's going. Robert is swamped without Frank and me for a few days. He might need me for something. They're helpless with the records in my office, since Martha's on vacation, too. I'll give Martha a call, to confirm the date she returns."

I was exhausted listening — that was more phone calls than I made in a week. I wished her well with the project as I locked the door behind her.

I sat on the less-than-comfortable bed, more like a futon, wearing very fuzzy purple socks Rose had given me at dinner. A sale at Strawberry, which she happened to drop into, and they'd come in handy, she'd said. She was right. The room was chilly even with the thermostat as high as the forced stops would allow.

I envied the ease with which Rose shopped, all year long, building up an inventory of gifts and merchandise that would be distributed as occasions arose. She always had something on hand for a birthday or anniversary, expected or unexpected, or for a host and hostess. For my part, I was having trouble figuring out a Christmas present for Matt and the fewer than half a dozen other people that made up my list.

On my lap was the magazine with Tina Miller on the cover. I checked the table of contents and went right to page thirty-two, NEW YORK CITY'S SMALL BUSINESS-WOMEN OF THE YEAR. I zipped past Katy the florist, Melinda the copy shop owner, and Leslie the veterinarian, each of whom had a page devoted to an interview and photos.

Tina's full-page spread was impressive. The graphics people had been creative. A PI agency didn't have the allure of flower arrangements and cute puppies, but the photographer had managed to make Tina's file cabinets and the certificates on her wall look interesting. Of course, unlike Judy the deli manager and Patricia the jeweler, Tina couldn't parade her clients in front of the *NYC Today* camera. Instead, the shots of her and her office were taken at odd angles for artistic appeal, and close-ups emphasized a miniature car collection and other objects on her bookshelf, which I hadn't noticed during the few minutes I'd been in her office. I wouldn't have been surprised if the magazine had supplied the props.

The article was written in Q-and-A style with questions about how Tina got started (her older brother asked her to spy on a younger sister to see if she was stealing his chewing gum) and what her goals were (to be the biggest and best in New York City, of course). Strains of *if I can make it there, I'll make it anywhere* went through my head, linked to the caricature of Frank Sinatra on the deli wall.

"I want to move people from the idea that the PI is the person slinking around in the bushes with binoculars and a telephoto lens trained on your bedroom window. Sure, we do some of that, but really the business of private investigation these days is very sophisticated. It's computer based and depends on intelligence and resources as much as canniness. We need to know about alarms and codes and remotely operated devices, not just lock picks."

Tina talked to the interviewer about her rise from being a one-woman enterprise to heading her current operation, with consultants and a worldwide network of data to tap into. In some ways, the story reminded me of the articles I wrote — and profiles written about me — during my short stint working with classified data at a government-funded lab. We could speak in general terms only, giving no particulars: "A device was tested," we might write, or "Our theoretical predictions matched experimental data." Photos would show the outside of a laboratory building against a clear California sky. No real information was given up.

Here, the pictures displayed that Tina had rows of file drawers, but no names could be shown, no investigative techniques described meaningfully, no resources revealed. I guessed I was among the few who'd seen one of her files up close. I cringed at the memory.

Blip blip blip.

In my haste to find my cell phone, Tina Miller toppled to the floor.

"We're waiting for a decision from the ADA," Matt said. "But it's looking hopeful."

"Hopeful how?"

"I'll give you details in person."

"When?"

"I'll be there as soon as they make a final determination."

I hung up. Matt's phone call had been

another information-free zone.

I barely had time to hide *New York City Today* under our mattress — you might call it an extreme way of avoiding Tina talk — when the little hotel room was crowded again, with Matt, Lori, Rose, and me.

Matt's look of relief told me what I needed to know. Lori was out of the woods — at least for now. I felt that until Amber's killer was found, the reprieve was tenuous.

"I'm so ashamed," Lori said. "Believe me, nothing any of you say or do can make me feel worse."

"We're not going to try," I said.

Gone was Lori's sharp, New York City chic look. She wore a jacket more suitable for hiking in the hills of Berkeley, California. (Not that I'd ever done that in thirty years of living there.) Her face was drawn and pale, and she seemed on the edge of tears.

"Nice that you have friends on the NYPD, Matt," Rose said.

I had to concentrate to remind myself that Rose was referring to Matt's helping keep Lori out of jail. She couldn't have known about my own foray into the life of crime.

"A lot of things contributed to Lori's not being charged," Matt said. "She has no record, of course. It was clear that she wasn't heading up the scam herself, she never approached the mark, and the kickback she received from Amber wasn't completely out of bounds."

I wondered what "out of bounds" meant in terms of blackmail. Something like petty larceny versus grand larceny? If I ever thought the law was black and white, my tenure with the Revere Police Department had taught me otherwise, and my experience with the NYPD was even more variegated. All of which had worked to my advantage.

Rose tried to foist food on all of us, especially Lori. She'd brought trail mix, bagels, potato chips, brownies, and bottles of water from a deli right off the hotel lobby. Her hostess skills had never been more challenged, I thought, not even during the years she made valiant attempts to help me serve guests in style in my ill-equipped mortuary-apartment kitchen.

"All I can say is, I fell for it," Lori said, her voice cracking. "Easy money. No one gets hurt. All the slogans you hear on TV dramas. You never see yourself being that stupid, but just like in those scripts, you can always rationalize. I needed to upgrade my equipment, my rent was being raised, I wanted to try some new packaging for distribution, go international, and on and on."

Lori paused to take a raisin from the trail mix Rose had poured into a hotel glass. I'd already shared a brownie and a bagel with Matt.

Lori went on, relaxing a little as she unburdened herself. "Amber was very persuasive. She convinced me that as long as I wasn't using the money to take a cruise to Bermuda — although that's exactly what she had in mind for herself — it was okay. I don't think she even saw that what she was doing was a crime."

"I've been thinking about that," said Rose, plucking a single cashew from the glass. "Why is blackmail a crime anyway? I mean, gossiping, or just telling a secret you found out, isn't illegal, unless, you know, it's government secrets you're selling to the Russians." I noted that Rose was a little behind in her designation of the current evil empire. "Asking someone for money isn't illegal, either, so why is it illegal when you put the two together?"

It was hard to tell if Rose really believed this or if she was trying to make Lori feel better, but I'd also given some thought to victimless crimes. Strictly speaking, nobody involved in them was an unwilling participant. Blackmail, insider trading, prostitution — all seemed matters of individual choice, and harmless for society as a whole, compared to violent crimes. So what was the point of criminalizing something like blackmail? To protect us from being exploited? People take advantage of each other in many ways all the time without the law intervening.

"If the reverse were to happen — if someone were to offer to pay me to keep his secret — that wouldn't be a crime, either," I said.

"I read that eliminating most victimless crimes would double the available jail space and greatly reduce the load on the judicial system," Rose said.

"The law's the law," said the lawman among us. As flexible as Matt was, sometimes his training and long career in the administration of justice came to the fore. "And until it changes, we follow it."

So much for shades of gray.

He spoke matter-of-factly, so only those who knew him well would hear the uncharacteristic stiffness in his voice. No one dared bring up civil disobedience and other ways of changing the law. Since Matt had gotten two of us out of legal jams in the last twenty-four hours, I supposed he deserved a little respect.

I wondered if the ADA who decided not to charge Lori with blackmail had given as much consideration to the long-standing ethical debate as we did. I hoped so.

"I'm not arguing here, Matt," Rose said. "But what if Lori claimed the money was a generous Christmas present from Amber? Or a contribution to her production company?"

"Sure, that's how a lot of blackmail money is buried — donations, contributions of one kind or another — but that ploy doesn't work forever. Eventually the truth comes out, usually when someone gets hurt. Like this. In this case, we're pretty sure that once the forensic accountants have a chance to go over Amber's books in detail, they'll find her victims." He swiveled his head back and forth between Rose and me. "We still call them victims, if that's okay with you."

Rose and I both nudged him. One advantage to the small room: Everyone's elbows were within reach of everyone else's.

Lori had been quiet while we debated legal philosophy. I figured she was still processing everything — her own apartment's being the scene of Amber's murder, behavior she was ashamed of, needing her uncle to intercede with the NYPD, and

192

ultimately not being charged with a crime.

"You told them everything, right, honey?" Matt asked, taking Lori's hand.

"Yes, I swear, Uncle Matt. They already knew I was home the morning Amber was killed and that I'd let her in. I'd taken the key away from her because I didn't want her to have free access to my place once I moved in. I lied because I was afraid —"

Matt nodded and interrupted, making his voice more soothing with each response. "I know. They didn't find the key to your place anywhere among Amber's effects at the scene, so they figured that out. Well, once your friends corroborate the time you joined them at breakfast, that part will be over."

I hoped it would be that easy.

"I never knew exactly who was being blackmailed, except sometimes Amber showed me photos." Lori shuddered and zipped her jacket higher, until I thought her chin and tiny mouth would be swallowed up. "But I told the cops exactly how many times I'd profited, how Amber got her marks, everything." Matt patted her hand. *Good girl.* "I . . . I did it three times."

Shades of confession at St. Anthony's Church. *I lied three times,* we would say to old Father Benedetto. Or *I cheated once on my spelling test.* A few prayers — or rosaries

for the big sins, like impure thoughts —
seemed to cover everything. I almost joked,
*Say three Our Fathers and three Hail Marys
and make a good act of contrition,* but I
didn't want to risk offending Rose.

"I got five thousand dollars each time,"
Lori continued. "I didn't even spend the
last two payments. There was a cash payment still in my desk drawer, and one time
Amber wrote a check. I guess that's how
they knew something was up."

"Eventually they would have gone through
your records anyway," Matt said. "Once
they saw your name in Amber's accounts,
even just for rent money, they'd have come
around to examine your books, see what
your recent purchases have been."

"I thought blackmail was a cash-only
transaction," I said.

"Not if you want to be able to spend the
money freely," Matt said. "It would take too
long to use up that many hundred-dollar
bills getting your groceries for cash at the
Stop & Shop."

"But you can deposit up to ten thousand
dollars in cash legally."

"Not week after week. It's a flag. Unless
you have an obvious source of where it's
coming from, which Amber didn't."

"I see. It's not as if she was operating a

hot dog stand."

"Did you want a hot dog?" Rose asked. "There's a wagon on the corner."

Lori sniffled. "Amber even had lawyers on her payroll," she said, still on her track of telling all.

"Lawyers?" I asked, my voice catching.

"Yeah, she'd get referrals, like, if a couple was breaking up, Amber would find out through one of Tina's lawyers — Amber said Tina knew nothing about this, though — and then if one of them was rich, she'd try to get something on them."

From Tina to lawyers who worked with Tina to Amber to blackmail. I tried to stop the links my mind was constructing. It felt like the times I'd be checking one thing on the Internet and it would take me around a whole string of sites I didn't know were connected. I filed away the links, as if I were bookmarking them on my browser, for later reference.

"Do you think they suspect me of killing Amber?" Lori asked her uncle.

Matt shook his head. "If they thought that, you wouldn't be sitting here. They'd have held you for the blackmail until they had something for the murder."

I saw his reasoning, but I knew the only way to clear Lori once and for all was to find Amber's killer. I bit my lip. This was not my jurisdiction. Not that I *had* a jurisdiction, but since we were here anyway, guests in the city that never sleeps, I might as well do something useful.

Eighth Avenue traffic rolled by, with the occasional emergency vehicle blaring. I wondered if the number of ambulances was thirty-nine thousand times greater in New York City than Revere, like the relative number of cops.

I needed to get serious, to get back to my routine when I worked with (using the word "with" loosely) the RPD: make lists, connect the dots, and work out the case. The flowchart was shaping up even now in my mind. I saw two groups of likely suspects: Amber's blackmail victims, and Lori and Amber's documentary subjects. If there was a stray ex-boyfriend or a random killer of young women out there, he'd have to wait until my next cut.

My next chore would be to locate the prime suspects.

"You need to be careful, honey," Matt said. I glanced up, happy to see that he was addressing Lori, not me.

"Why are you saying that, Matt?" Rose asked.

"Do you think Lori's in danger?" I asked Matt.

"You know, I thought of that," Rose said. "How maybe Lori was the one they were . . . oh, no, no, never mind."

"It's not out of the question," Matt said, looking at Lori. "I don't want to scare you, but, as I said, be careful. Let's keep in close touch, okay? Let me know — anything out of the ordinary."

Lori nodded and gave him a long hug.

I searched his face, as if I'd be able to quantify exactly how worried Matt was. Routine concerned-uncle worried? Well-thought-out worried? Homicide-cop worried? All of the above, I guessed.

For me, I felt on-the-case worried.

CHAPTER FIFTEEN

Lori couldn't believe the close call with the police and the ADA. If it hadn't been for Uncle Matt, she might be . . . well, who knew where she'd be spending the night? Probably not in her own apartment.

She walked there now, after doing a few errands — returned a pile of movie videos, picked up her dry cleaning, and bought a quart of mocha java ice cream. The chores made her feel her life could be normal once again.

She kept her head down against the cold wind. The temperature was uncomfortably low, the wind chill factor bringing it below zero, but the clear, dry air sparkled and seemed quite in concert with the jingle bells on every corner, either from a Salvation Army worker or a toddler's shoes. The silver-bells thing did nothing to lift her spirits beyond simple gratitude that she wasn't in jail.

Her keys were ready as she rode up to her floor in the shaky old elevator. Lori crossed the narrow entryway and was inside her loft in record time. She flipped the locks on her huge metal door and slid the dead bolt over. She traced the pin all the way to the bracket and down into the notch, hooked the chain in place, and then put Uncle Matt's cell phone number on speed dial on her land-line and her cell phone.

Until now it hadn't hit home that she might be in danger. She'd been so anxious about her involvement in Amber's scheme, it overshadowed the idea that she might have been the one the killer was looking for in the first place. Lori had assumed that since Amber was the one living on the edge, she'd been the target — but the murder had taken place in Lori's loft, after all, and now she wasn't sure.

Lori hated the feeling that came over her now. It had begun when she was nine years old. For most of her life she'd felt vulner-able, expecting disaster at every turn. Her thirtieth birthday was a milestone, not for the usual reasons her friends celebrated the big three-oh, but because she'd reached an age denied her mother.

Enough of that.

She had piles of work to do — interview

tapes to transcribe, videotapes and DVDs to look through, storyboarding to complete, paperwork to catch up on — but she had no energy for the tasks. From the table near the door she picked up a pile of mail. This she could handle. She leafed through the envelopes, sorting junk from bills and correspondence. She wished she could chuck her credit card bill — the one that confiscated cash was going to cover, until the cops took it. The next thing she'd do, once the ozone narrative was complete, would be to send back the new amplifier and a few other things she'd bought. She didn't need any reminders of her transgressions. Good thing she'd put the old stuff in storage in the basement.

One envelope caught her eye, hotel stationery. The logo, name, and address had been crudely crossed out, but she could see part of the logo and she could tell from the ZIP code it was in Lower Manhattan. There was no name or other address.

Lori opened the envelope. The top few inches of the paper had been torn off, obviously to get rid of the letterhead. She read the handwriting:

I urge you <u>not</u> to act on the material you have in your possession. It will only bring you harm. Enough people have been hurt. <u>Do not</u> expose this.

A shaky feeling came over her, a slight dizziness and a chill across her shoulders and down her spine. She sat on her couch, then jumped up when she noticed a red spot on one of the pillows. *Blood!* She let out a small scream. She walked toward the other end of the loft, the work end for the most part, although the lines were blurred. She took a breath and focused. From a distance she could see better: The spot was only a rose petal, one of many strewn freely throughout the flowery design of the upholstery.

Another breath and she felt her pulse slow.

Lori had been clutching the letter. Now she turned the hotel paper over in her hands a couple of times — no other writing, no special feel to give her an idea what it meant. What else could this be but a mistake? She was overreacting to everything. Understandable after what she'd been through the last couple of days. She tossed the letter and envelope in her wastebasket with the other junk, some of it not necessary to open, and fluffed the pillow.

What she needed right now was company. *Go for it,* she told herself.

Lori punched in Craig Daly's number.

We're way past even the nineties, she thought. Nothing wrong with a girl asking a guy she liked out for dinner. It wasn't a date, really, anyway. Just a warm body to help her through this trauma.

Craig never needed accolades like some of the other crew she worked with. He'd never aspired to be in front of the camera, and his ego was practically nonexistent. Amazing when you thought about it, given how much power editors had over the final look of the film. The editing could make or break a production, Lori mused, waiting for Craig's voice and his big *no thank you.*

She imagined his telling her he had plans with his girlfriend, some cute young twenty-something named Melissa probably. Lori didn't know for sure, but from some info she had on his college years she thought Craig was younger than her thirty-one years. People told her she looked no more than twenty-five, however, so maybe Craig was fooled, too.

Or maybe he had plans with a bodybuilder named Biff, which was quite possible, since Craig was one of the few guys who'd seemed to resist Amber's charms. Well, one way or the other, at least Lori would know soon.

"Hey, Lori," he said. "What do you need?"

Caller ID, of course, but Lori was always

startled when someone knew she was calling. She didn't like the *What do you need?* greeting. It emphasized the fact that they never called each other spontaneously, just to chat, but only if there was a reason, like she needed something specific. *What's new?* or *How's it going?* would have been better, indicating they had ongoing communication that wasn't necessarily work related.

God, here she was analyzing to death Craig's four-syllable greeting, as if she were back in her high school cafeteria with her girlfriends: *Buddy said, "See you later," so do you think that means he's going to call, or come over?*

"Just checking in," Lori said. "Getting caught up after, you know . . ." *Groan.* She certainly hadn't meant to start that way.

"It's pretty awful, isn't it?" Craig said. "I still can't believe Amber's dead."

"Neither can I. The police have a lead or two." Lori had no idea why she exaggerated. Maybe to make Craig feel better. Maybe to hasten the end of the topic.

"Really? Yeah, they came to talk to me, too, but I couldn't tell them very much."

Craig was born in Brooklyn and had the accent to prove it. "Talk" came out *too-alk;* "all" was *oo-all,* with a smooth sliding sound from the *oo* to the *all*. Lori loved it. Much more interesting than the Boston accent she'd worked hard to get rid of.

"Actually, I . . . uh . . . got your message yesterday and . . . uh . . . I was down at the precinct for a while. I'm sorry it took so long to get back to you." This was not how Lori had intended the conversation to go.

"Oh, it was nothing critical," Craig said. "I've got some good shots here of two welders at Blake's and another one at Curry's looking pretty dismal before they put their helmets on. Caught unawares by the inimitable Amber." Craig cleared his throat. "Sorry, I'm not used to her being gone. So do you want to let in the part where the welders look disgruntled, or do you just want the welding?"

Lori knew what Craig was asking. She pictured one way it might go: The voice-over would be about the employee complaints. Lori would say something like "Ventilation at Blake's is poorer than at any other manufacturing plant in the triborough area, exposing employees to ozone levels that cause everything from discomfort to severe respiratory diseases." At the same time, the picture on the screen would be the face of the gloomy welder, the implication being that the welder is despondent because he knows he's in an unhealthy environment.

How legitimate was that? The welder really did make that face — no phony Photoshop expression — and the narrative was accurate, but putting them together was an editing choice, and a statement. It reminded her of the discussion Rose and Gloria started about blackmail, how two things might be separately okay, but the juxtaposition produced another entity entirely. Maybe someday blackmail wouldn't be a crime. All Lori knew now was that she'd never felt so guilty or so remorseful in her entire life.

"Let's not do that, Craig," she said into the phone. "The facts speak for themselves."

"I thought you'd say that, but I wanted to be sure."

Lori took a deep breath. "Have you had dinner yet?"

"Uh, no. I was just going to grab some pizza."

"You want to go somewhere?"

"You know, I better not. I'm taking an Italian class to get ready for my trip to Italy, and I have to study if I'm going to get anything out of it."

"Oh, sure, sure," Lori said, glad that Craig couldn't see her face getting redder and redder. "I forgot about your art cruise with the Met. When is it again?"

"Not until April, but there's a lot to learn. All I know so far is *Dov'è la sala da bagno?*" While Craig laughed at his bathroom reference, Lori tried to figure how to end the call.

"Well, I have some work to do, too," Lori said. "I have some footage from Blake's that I haven't looked at yet."

"Oh, I thought I had all the Blake and Curry tapes and DVDs here."

"You have most of them, probably. I think these are from shoots you didn't go on. Amber must have done her own sound on those days." Why was Craig prolonging this conversation? Lori was ready to pull the old you're-breaking-up-I-can't-hear-you routine, but she'd called his landline.

"I plan to have everything out of my inbox before I leave for the cruise. Next time I see you, we can go over my list."

"Good idea," Lori said. "Or should I say, *fa bene?* Oops, I think I have another call."

"Okay, see you."

Lori hung up. *That went well,* she thought, rearranging herself on the sofa. Next time she'd offer to help Craig with his Italian homework instead of inviting him to dinner.

She looked across at the framed prints on

the long, exposed brick wall along West Forty-eighth Street. Her college graduation present from her father: a two-week trip to Italy and a print from a local artist in every city they visited. She didn't have many pleasant memories of Dr. William Pizzano — a surgeon too preoccupied with his patients to give his healthy daughter much attention — so she clung to these mementos. Before the pictures were back from the frame shop, her father was dead of a heart attack. Lori scanned the wall. The Trevi Fountain in Rome. The Duomo in Florence. A view of Lake Maggiore from Lombardy. Country churches in Assisi and Sorrento.

When she found herself wondering what the CFC and ozone regulations were in Italy, she decided she might as well do some work. The police hadn't returned all her DVDs and videos yet, but she had two or three DVDs that she hadn't watched in her tote bag. She always kept a few with her in case she was stuck somewhere, and lately she'd been going to Starbucks or Timothy's with her laptop, to avoid being in the loft at the same time Amber would be working there.

Lori blew out a breath. No more of that, but why did there always have to be bad news with good?

She needed to recoup something from the day. Plan A — dinner with the adorable Craig Daly — had failed. There was still a chance for Plan B: popcorn with Blake Manufacturing footage.

On her way to the cabinet for the air popper, to the kitchen for tea, to her armoire to get her robe, to the media rack with the DVD — every time Lori passed by her door, she glanced at the security chain, relieved it was still hooked across the jamb, wondering if she'd ever feel safe again at home.

Lori changed into her old velour robe and took up her usual position for watching videos. She plopped on the couch, feet on the coffee table, notebook and pencil on her lap, a large bowl of cheddar popcorn and a mug of tea within easy reach. She pushed PLAY on the remote.

"Roll film," she said with a smile to the empty room. An expression from an earlier time that she and Amber had playfully used with each other.

Blake Manufacturing came into focus on her TV. A gray cinder-block building with few windows, a common enough sight in Lower Manhattan. Amber had kept the camera on as she walked into the front entrance, checked herself in at a security post, and made her way down a narrow passage with a Blake employee leading the way.

In the welding area, Amber had shot the camera up to the ceiling, catching the ozone monitors in the high corners. She'd managed to zoom in on the model number of one unit so Lori could check catalogs on the Internet and see what kind of equipment Blake used. Good work, Amber. Whatever else she did, Amber got her job right. She'd also found the one female employee Blake listed as a certified welder. Lori watched as a woman with a long, curly ponytail, wearing what looked like serious oven mitts, maneuvered around a brilliant arc.

Colorful but deadly, Lori thought, remembering how ozone was created in the sparks. She was so pleased with the phrase that she jotted it down. She decided this would be the spot to insert an animated graphic to show how ozone was created by the high voltage across the two pieces of metal. She had a few minutes to spare now that she'd decided to leave the ozone-CFC issue for Part II (which, due to the critical acclaim that Part I was sure to receive, would be a snap to get funding for). She could ask Gloria to help with a sketch, maybe even accompany her on the follow-up visit to

Blake's — but first she'd need to think of how to establish limits. Lori had the feeling Gloria could go on forever about science. Now that she had nothing to hide from her, though, it might be a more pleasant interaction.

Lori refilled her popcorn bowl and ate through a segment that showed a dark-skinned man wielding something he called a welding tip. Lori made a note of the funny alliteration for possible use as comic relief. "This provides concentrated heat for better puddle control," the man said. The sound was so muffled, Lori wasn't sure she'd be able to use this piece. She remembered now that Amber had insisted on going down to Blake's that day even though Craig couldn't make it. As a result, there was no boom mike, just a lavaliere that Amber had clipped to her subjects. Eventually Craig would get this material and take it to an editing studio in Chelsea. Lori made a note to ask if he'd be able to beef up the sound then.

Lori shifted and pulled her robe down around her ankles. She cued up a Curry segment and was tempted to fast-forward through a guy talking about how robots were taking over the big production jobs. A tough-looking woman showed the camera the details of her helmet: lens, inside and outside protection plate, headband, sweatband, and accessories that made Lori yawn.

No wonder Amber was bored. Even though some of the guys were cute — one in particular, waving a long narrow rod around and talking about low-voltage welding. "Putting on the finishing touches is more like art," he said, clearly enjoying his few minutes of fame. "This pencil tip is conducting the heat. You've got an eighth-inch weld here, not like the big globs you see on your bridge pieces." Lori scanned forward. An older guy talked about what a shame it was that bikes were now mass-produced overseas, and, finally, a very old guy — Uncle Matt's age, she thought — said these young guys should be grateful Curry still had a department for arty-farty welding.

These must be Amber's happy takes. No disgruntled workers here. Lori hoped the rest of the material had something juicier. Such was the life of a documentary filmmaker — you never knew what you were going to come home with. Not like the fun short shorts she did in school, where she was in charge of her story, start to finish. She missed that sense of control, designing a storyboard and shooting, knowing what you were going for. On the other hand, sometimes documentary subjects came up with surprises. Lori wished for that one little gem that would have PBS begging to give her airtime.

Back to Blake's and more talk of structural pieces, brackets for construction, beams, rails, and titanium. Lori decided she had time for a bathroom break without pausing the disk. So what if she missed a couple of minutes of a dark room with sparks flying, she thought, shuffling off.

When she came back, the dark room had been replaced by a brightly lit office filling the TV screen. She saw jerky shots of a desk, file cabinets, a woman's foot and ankle, all the way up to midcalf, and then no image, as the lens was blocked.

Lori scanned back and forth a couple of times, but nothing clearer emerged. Maybe this was just the end of Amber's self-defined shift, and she'd forgotten to turn the camera off.

Lori scanned back to get one more look, left the player in pause, and headed for another refill of popcorn and tea. Some dinner.

Thump! Creak!

Lori stopped short, a little past her door. The elevator? Hopefully just old Wa Tant on three, home from his late shift at the bakery.

The elevator passed two, then three. There was no mistaking the bumping, clicking sounds as the cage ticked off the floors, making its way through the tight, grimy shaft. Lori pulled her robe around her body, shook off her slippers, and walked barefoot to the peephole. She looked around the apartment — the nearest thing to a weapon she saw was Amber's tripod. Unless you counted the rose-petal pillows. Lori shivered at the memory.

She stood at the door, giving up the idea of arming herself. She simply wouldn't open up. The door was metal and two inches thick, with industrial grade hinges. She was safe. Trembling, but safe.

Lori peered out into the hallway. The cage stopped; the accordion gate opened.

A guy with a blue-and-white striped Yankees cap, carrying a large, flat box, stepped out.

Craig. With a pizza.

Lori turned her back to the door and looked at herself in the full-length mirror bolted to the brick wall a few feet away. Her oldest robe, no makeup, her hair not brushed once since this morning, barefoot, her left hand sticky from buttered popcorn.

Great. *Might as well start off with no pretense,* she thought, and opened the door.

"Hey," Craig said. "I figured we have to eat, right? And maybe you can help me with some Italian."

Lori was so sorry she'd changed out of decent clothes. As the smell of pizza — with the works, she could tell — reached her nose, making her feel slightly ill, she also wished she hadn't eaten so much popcorn.

"This is great, Craig. *Ho molto fame.*" She couldn't believe she'd said it — back to dating tricks she thought she'd abandoned years ago, telling a guy she was starving when she had no interest in his pizza.

But so what? He was here, she had company, and that was good.

Craig stepped in front of the TV, where a woman's lower leg and foot, partway behind a desk, had been captured in freeze-frame. "What's that you're watching?"

"Oh, nothing, it's the end of some stuff Amber shot at Blake's."

"Dude, look at that. Someone's having fun in an office."

"Yeah, I think Amber forgot to turn the camera off."

Craig picked up the remote. "Do you mind?"

"Knock yourself out. I'll get some drinks." *And put on some clothes.* "Beer okay?"

"You bet."

Lori came back into the area she defined as her living room wearing jeans and an NYU sweatshirt.

Craig had switched to a sports channel that Lori didn't even know was part of her package. He'd dug into the pizza.

"Dude, you need a new TV."

"Dude" again. What generation was this guy? *How come I don't notice this language while we're working together?* Lori asked herself. It must be the curious expectations of a date, which this almost was. "A new TV. Right," she said, not bothering to hide the sarcasm.

"No, really. You should get that new hundred-and-two-inch flat screen they showed at Expo. What I wouldn't give to see *Spider-Man* on that set."

Lori raised her eyebrows. She felt herself losing interest with every new revelation of the off-duty Craig.

Bzzzz. Bzzzz.

Her tinny, irritating doorbell. The basketball game, which Craig had on way too loud, must have drowned out the elevator noise. Lori went to the peephole, hoping not to see an NYPD uniform.

She stared at the distorted view of a guy with straw-colored hair sticking out around a Pacers cap. Another guy carrying a pizza box.

Lori opened the door.

"Billy Keenan!" she said, and fell into his arms.

Finally, she was able to cry about the loss of Amber.

"I'm okay," Billy said, after his own bout of tears. "It was just that first impact of seeing where Amber died." He slammed his chest with his fist and choked up again.

Craig distracted Billy with questions about life on the farm. The two guys hit it off immediately — one who'd lived in Brooklyn all his life, a professional film worker in a dark turtleneck, the other a Kansas farm boy wearing a plaid flannel jacket and a clean white T-shirt. Lori wondered if Craig really cared how many acres the Keenans had (like asking one's yearly salary, Lori had heard) or whether this year's weather was good for the crops (did Craig even know what a crop was?).

Lori served beer and two kinds of pizza: Craig's with the works, Billy's with the works plus anchovies.

"Wouldn't this game look great on one of those big flat screens?" Billy asked Craig.

Lori heaved a sigh and remembered the

trade-off to having guys around. *"Mangiatevi, ragazzi,"* she said.

CHAPTER SIXTEEN

On Tuesday evening, I had an opportunity to work on my notes and lists. Unfortunately, the paper I was writing on was very small, the lighting poor, and the conditions cramped.

I was in seat A101, front mezzanine, of a Broadway theater. Rose had gotten us tickets for a long-running musical with an animal in the title.

"You need to relax, Gloria," she'd said, surprising me. I thought she knew me better.

I'd been told that I didn't know how to relax, but, in my opinion, it was all relative. At work I'd relaxed when my experimental data fit a theoretical curve, when my xenon flash lamps were in good working order, and when there was a calculator nearby for some fun with arithmetic.

In retirement, I relaxed when a killer was identified and brought to justice.

I gave my two suspect groups — Amber's blackmail victims and the ozone documentary subjects — a column each. I'd leave it to the NYPD to cast a broad net. I knew they were interviewing Amber's roommates and her ex-boyfriend. They'd continue to comb her financial records for suspicious charges and probably go door to door in her and Lori's neighborhoods. They'd cover her phone logs and e-mails, broadening the horizon. For me, I needed to narrow the scope to make the problem seem manageable.

Matt glanced down at my busy lap and grinned. I wasn't trying to fool either him or Rose. I'd asked for the aisle seat so I wouldn't disturb any of the other theatergoers. I hoped they'd think I was a music critic taking notes.

I used the new ballpoint pen Rose's grandson, William, had given Matt on his birthday in October. The pen lit up as soon as the tip hit the paper. I'd gotten so excited when I saw it that Matt generously handed it over to me.

"I'll get some free ones at the conference," he'd said.

He was right. He'd come back to the hotel every day with giveaways — pens and pencils with advertising from companies selling training classes, ankle holsters, tactical vests, and other gear I didn't want to think about. Plus a complimentary roll of tamperproof evidence tape.

The old building was beautiful, I had to admit, one of many densely packed into the theater district. The dark red, plush interior and elaborate sconces throughout the theater were reminiscent of an earlier day. Rose had recited its refurbishment history on the cold, windy walk from our hotel, telling us the date it opened (1925?) and the seating capacity (approximately six hundred, down from one thousand, for more of a sense of intimacy, Rose said). There was no elevator in the building, but it was worth the hardship of climbing first up three long flights and then down one short, steep flight to our seats to be closer to the ornate paneled ceiling. My exercise for the month. I wondered how they moved freight and equipment without motorized aid, then realized I was probably confusing theaters with labs.

The ambience of a remarkable old building might be all I got from the evening, I realized. I'd done nothing but doodle. I remembered the companies Lori was featuring in her documentary and wrote their names in the ozone column: Blake Manufacturing and Curry Industries. I made a note to check on the Internet if necessary, for their CEOs and HR directors, but I felt Lori would give me the information. I knew we'd had a rocky start, but I deemed that to be because I'd pushed too hard on talking about Amber when she was trying to hide their illegal business dealings.

I drew a star next to the idea of taking a little trip to the Blake and Curry facilities on the pretext of being a science teacher at Revere High. I had hardly any qualms about this, since I did give occasional lectures to the science club at the school. I penned in an arrow to point to my note *faulty ozone monitors recalled?* and a question mark next to *slip away from Matt and Rose.*

Finding Amber's blackmail victims would be harder. I knew it was hopeless to try to enlist Matt's help in pumping Buzz for information. It would have been hard enough for me to find a way into this part of the case in Revere; in New York City, it was probably impossible.

Not that I'd stop trying.

I adjusted my coat over my lap and continued doodling — the better to think — and drawing stars on my notepad here and there as I listed possible avenues of research.

Every now and then I remembered that I was in an excellent seat at a widely acclaimed Broadway show and looked across the orchestra to the stage below. I saw humans dressed as animals, dancing and singing. One time I saw creatures wearing large hats the color and shape of a thatched hut.

I went back to my notes.

I'd commuted to college from Revere to Boston, fewer than ten miles away, but more than an hour on buses and subway lines via the limited public transit routes of those days. I did my calculus homework on the MTA, the one Charlie was famously lost on in song. If nothing else, the experience was good preparation for doing mental work in the midst of noise and hubbub.

Here in the theater I was able to concentrate on the pieces of the puzzle that was Amber's murder. I was unbothered by the stampeding dance troupe or the thunderous orchestra.

Neither was I making any headway.

"How do you like the performance, Gloria?" Rose asked at intermission.

I knew how hard she'd worked to garner tickets at the last minute. After all, we were supposed to be back in Revere this evening. Playing our usual canasta game, albeit in the hotel room, would have been good enough for me, but I didn't say that.

"This is wonderful," I said, waving my glass of lime-flavored mineral water in a toasting gesture.

"Good to multitask by?"

"I'm getting all there is out of the drama, complex as it is."

"Shall I give you a quiz?"

Matt shuffled his feet and bit his bottom lip. A nervous gesture, one I'd seen in the past when he thought Rose and I were arguing seriously. But I could read all of Rose's different smiles, and the one she wore throughout this interchange was her good-sport smile. She didn't mind my not showing overwhelming gratitude for all her work getting the tickets. In fact, she probably saw my willingness to even attend the performance as a sign that I might someday become cultured.

"Just don't ask me to name the animals in the jungle," I said.

Matt, still not completely attuned to the decades-old patterns Rose and I had built up, broke in.

"Time for some police humor from the precinct?" he asked. "I have a couple of those how-stupid-can-they-be stories that cops tell about the bad guys. Buzz swears these are true."

Matt started in, before we could shake our heads no or start another round of flippant teasing. "Here's one: The cop asks the suspect, 'How old is your son, the one living with you?' The guy says, 'Ten or eleven, I can't remember.' Cop asks, 'How long has he lived with you?' Guy says, 'About twelve years.' "

Rose rewarded Matt with a good laugh. "Congratulations, Matt, you've got the attention of me and your wife." She paused. "Hmmm, your wife. Funny, I don't have much recollection of the ceremony. Oh, that's right. You didn't have one."

Matt cleared his throat and looked at me. "Please," he said.

"Okay," I said, and Rose knew at once that she'd been given the go-ahead to have a reception for us. If arranging a party — invitations, cleaning, ordering food, then milling around, chatting, and more cleaning afterward — would give her pleasure (as evidenced by her immediate, though discreet, clapping when I agreed), who was I to deny her?

At my request Matt had stepped aside to check his phone messages before the gongs signaled us back to our seats.

"Maybe Buzz called to say there's been a

breakthrough in the case," I'd said.

"Don't know that I'd be the first to know, but will do."

Now he came back from a corner of the mezzanine where there were at least a half dozen other people on cell phones. I didn't like his frown or the anxious look on his face.

"You were right in a way," he said.

"A new lead?" I asked, though I knew better. I'd seen his new-lead look, and this wasn't it.

"Not exactly."

A chill went through me. "What?"

"A message on my voice mail. There was a mugging on a jogging path in Central Park."

So what? I thought. A response that embarrassed me when I considered it later.

"How awful," Rose said. "Imagine the poor family, and around holiday time."

Not that it was news to me, but I marveled that my friend could care so deeply about an anonymous mugging victim. Surely this wouldn't make headlines in New York City. Why would Buzz leave Matt a message about a mugging?

Unless . . .

I held my breath. Lori? No. Uncle Matt would be much more distressed. I looked again at his face, for reassurance.

"A woman named Dee Dee Sanders. She worked for Tina Miller, the PI that Amber Keenan —" Matt paused. "Well, you know who she is."

The one you robbed, I heard in his voice, but it might have been my guilt picking up a nonexistent nuance.

For the second time in a little more than two days I'd thought Lori was a victim, and it was another woman instead — and I'd failed to revive one of the victims and I'd stolen from the other.

I had a lot more to think about during the second act but gave it up when my tiny notepad became too overrun with stars, bullets, and arrows. I leaned back and tried to enjoy the music.

Matt reached over and took my hand. "Now that it's available," he said.

"You should have asked."

We wrapped ourselves in our layers of wool and knit and elbowed our way past theatergoers waiting for taxis. Our destination was just around the corner, a bistro on Eighth Avenue, where dessert beckoned.

We were so close to our hotel, it felt like we were sitting in an extension of our lobby.

"This is okay," Rose said, pushing away the long-stemmed glass that held her zabaglione. "But I still miss Rumplemeyer's."

I, too, longed for an amazing brownie sundae from the restaurant that once graced Central Park South. However, that didn't stop me from finishing the dessert in front of me — a decent affogato all'amaretto. This lack of discrimination on my part, where desserts were concerned, was one of the reasons I outweighed Rose by many kilograms.

Instead of eating, Rose was surveying the rest of the after-theater crowd. She eyed a young woman wearing a fur pom-pom scarf and leaned over to me. "Fifteen dollars," she whispered. "On the streets."

"Is that good?"

"I'm going to pick one up for MC. I was waiting to see how many people were wearing them around here."

I wondered what MC's high school chemistry students would think of the pom-poms, and whether it would matter to MC that her mother had arrived at the purchase through a statistical fashion analysis.

When the discussion came around to Dee Dee, it was brief enough, since we had no information besides Buzz's message. It was hard to explain to Rose how I knew Dee

Dee without having my face turn red thinking of my inadvertent lifting of her daughter-in-law's correspondence.

"Remember yesterday . . . I told you I'd be doing some research. I was in that office. Do you want to taste this gelato, by the way?"

Rose, stirring her espresso, gave me only half her attention, training the other half on the scarves entering the bistro. That suited me perfectly. "Maybe a little, if you don't finish it." (She was kidding.)

"Do you think Buzz will call again tonight?" I asked Matt.

"I left a message for him. If he checks in, he'll find it and get back to me. Otherwise I expect it will be sometime tomorrow."

"Is your phone on?" I asked. I gave Matt my sheepish look, so he'd know I'd wanted to resist checking but couldn't.

He gave me a pity look, which I took for a yes.

"I almost forgot," Matt said. "There was another message at intermission. From Lori. Billy Keenan, Amber's brother, is in town from Kansas. They had trouble locating him, but he's here now to officially ID his sister's body and escort it home when they're ready to release it."

"The poor guy" was Rose's first comment.

How can I meet him? was my first thought.

"Lori's inviting us to her place for lunch tomorrow if we'd like to meet him, to offer our condolences, make him feel welcome," Matt said.

Meet Billy Keenan *and* get into Lori's loft without conniving? A double coup. "Tomorrow?" I asked. "That's Wednesday, right? I was hoping to catch a matinee."

My penance for my facetiousness was to help Rose blot out the espresso she spilled on one of her new scarves. That's how hard she'd laughed.

Every night in New York our small bedside table was crowded with Matt's and my cell phone chargers and the docking station for our digital camera. This evening I checked the phones to make sure they were on, though usually we charged them in the OFF position.

"Buzz isn't going to call in the middle of the night," Matt said, coming out of the bathroom as I was making the switch. I had intended my obsessive-compulsive behavior to go unnoticed.

"You never know," I said. "He might also be OC."

Buzz didn't call, though, and I drifted in and out of sleep with images in my mind of

Dee Dee in her high-heeled boots, her pleasant demeanor as she offered me candy, her free and easy manner, her flowery perfume.

I sat up on one elbow. The clock read 12:30 A.M. Perfume? The perfume I'd smelled on the person who'd bumped into me leaving the alley by Lori's building? I looked over at the luminous purple bar on the camera's docking station. Foggy bits of conversation crept into my head: Matt telling me about a new instrument called RUVIS, for reflectance ultraviolet imaging system, a technique where you just shined ultraviolet light on surfaces to collect fingerprints. No more annoying black powder. I'd also read about smell-capturing technology, but it wasn't widely available. I imagined a simple RUVIS-type scope that let cops retrieve the last odor left at the scene of a crime.

That silly idea put me to sleep, until another one intruded. This one was a candy connection. I'd picked up crinkled foil paper in the alley. Not wrapping paper, as I'd thought then, but candy wrappers. Like the wrappers in the candy dish on Dee Dee's desk.

I almost woke Matt to give him the news about the perfume and the candy — and my brilliant conclusion that Dee Dee must have been in the alley the night I went snooping. The killer returning to the scene of the crime? Dee Dee had just been mugged. Not one to believe in coincidences, I had to believe the attack on her was somehow related to Amber's murder.

Did all this make Dee Dee a suspect or a victim? I needed to talk to Matt about the dilemma, even though it meant copping to my nosing around in the alley on West Forty-eighth.

I shifted and moved from side to side in bed, hoping to "accidentally" bump Matt awake, but he was fast asleep. I thought of turning on the TV, but I realized that if the street noises, still considerable in the middle of the night, didn't wake him, the TV wouldn't, either.

It would have to wait until morning. By then I might have more inane ideas to add to these.

CHAPTER SEVENTEEN

Blip blip blip. Blip blip blip.

My cell phone. I peered at the clock. One in the morning. Buzz? It's a good thing we left the phones on, I told myself and my sleeping husband. I wondered briefly why Buzz would call me and not his friend Mattie.

Blip blip blip. Blip blip blip.

I reached over, dislodged the phone from its charger, and clicked the TALK button.

"This is Gloria." My semiformal phone greeting in spite of the hour, though softer than usual.

"Hey, I'm sorry to call this late." Lori's voice.

"Is anything wrong?" The universal question when a phone rings in what some think of as the middle of the night.

"No, no. I wanted to know if you'd be interested in coming with me tomorrow morning. With all that's going on, I completely forgot until two minutes ago. I know Uncle Matt wouldn't want to come, but I have an extra ticket."

Ticket? What was I missing here? I'd barely recovered from the ticketed event on Broadway a few hours ago. I carried my cell phone into the bathroom, though Matt was a very sound sleeper. "You know, Lori, I'm also a little distracted and forgot — what are these tickets for?"

"Oh, duh, I thought I told you. I belong to a small businesswomen's group, and there's a special breakfast meeting tomorrow morning. Oops, I guess that would be *this* morning. It's called — ta da — The *New York City Today* Magazine Power Breakfast."

"The magazine that featured Tina Miller."

"Yeah. They're going to give plaques to her and all the businesswomen featured in that issue. It would be a chance for you to . . . you know . . ."

"Lori, you know me so well already."

"Thanks, Gloria."

I was happy for the bonding moment, except for the discomfort of sitting on a toilet seat cover. "When and where?"

"It's at the new MOMA. They're letting us use their café for this event. The bad news is, the so-called gala is at 8:00 A.M. Working women, you know."

"Not a problem. I might even be able to attend and be back here before your uncle wakes up."

"Okay, then. I'll see you there," Lori said. "I'm on the setup committee, so I have to be there even earlier."

I couldn't believe the good fortune. A chance to meet Tina again, as well as hobnob with those at the heart of the city's commerce.

A moment before signing off with Lori, I had an important thought. Rose, a member of a similar group in Revere, would never forgive me if I didn't invite her. Although a thriving business, the family-owned and -operated Galigani Mortuary was independent, and qualified as small. I knew Rose would give anything to participate in a power breakfast in Manhattan. She'd work the room and acquire enough material for a year's worth of anecdotes.

"Lori, is there another ticket available?"

"Uh-huh, I still have the two that are . . . uh, should have been . . . Amber's."

"Would you mind if I invited Rose?"

"Great idea. That means I don't have to give you the address for MOMA or tell you what to wear, right?"

I might have construed that remark as disparaging, but I knew Lori meant it in the most helpful way.

"As I said —"

Lori chuckled. "I do know you, Gloria. And while we're talking about that, thanks so much for your support this week. Maybe I didn't say it, but . . ." She choked up.

"I'm glad we were here, honey."

Of all the New York myths, one I hadn't heard was how the Big Apple turned everyone mushy.

I checked on Matt — still sound asleep. He couldn't blame *me* for not including him in my plans. I returned to the bathroom, choosing to sit on the edge of the tub this time, and used my cell phone to call down to Rose.

"You don't sound sleepy," I said when she picked up.

"I just got off the phone with Frank. He told me this funny story. You know how I told you our neighbor, Hunter, across Tuttle Street has been trying to see who keeps throwing trash in his driveway? Well, Hunter rigged a video camera — they're so small these days. He stuck it on his mailbox and — guess what? — it was the paperboy. He arrives around four in the morning, and almost every day he tosses a drink cup or a candy wrapper onto Hunter's driveway. No one else's, just Hunter's. Hunter thinks it's because he leaves only a small tip at Christmas."

"Kids these days," I said.

"Oh, Gloria. You're calling late and I didn't even ask. Is there anything wrong?"

"No, it's good news, in fact. I have tickets for an event."

"Now?" She sounded hardly surprised, knowing me, and also being always ready to move and shake. She was ready to go before she knew what the event was.

I briefed her on Lori's invitation.

She gasped. "Gloria, how exciting! I can't believe it. A genuine New York City power breakfast. And an awards ceremony. And at the new MOMA. It's a dream." A pause. "What were you planning on wearing?"

"Were" indicated that she was about to change whatever strategy I had, but I played along. "My burgundy pantsuit. I don't have that much with me to choose from."

I hoped Rose wouldn't remind me that she'd suggested I take more outfits in case of a wardrobe emergency. Rose had brought something for every possible occasion from a black-tie party at the Grand Hyatt to a test run of a laser shot in the Columbia physics department.

"I wonder what time the shops in the

lobby open," she said. "I saw an outfit in the window that would be perfect for you."

"Rose, I'm not going to buy a new outfit for an hour-long breakfast meeting."

"I'm sure it will run longer than that. Once everyone thanks their mother, their accountant . . ."

I sighed. It was too late to argue. And I doubted a clothing shop would be open at six in the morning when I'd be dressing. "By the way, do you know where the new MOMA café is?"

Silence. Then, "Yes, Gloria. I do."

Before Rose would hang up, she made me promise to let her choose my jewelry from her collection. I figured I was getting off lightly.

It was an easy walk from our hotel to the museum, on West Fifty-third.

One block over, on West Fifty-second, was the Museum of Television & Radio, Rose pointed out, reminding me of the time a couple of years ago that we'd used its comprehensive computerized database to watch an old Perry Como Christmas special.

Today's weather suited me perfectly. Another sharp, cold, overcast day, but no threat of rain. I'd often told whoever would listen that I'd had enough dry, unmitigated sunshine in my years in California to last a lifetime.

We stopped only twice — once to get coffees to go, and once so Rose could get an early-bird special at a sidewalk table. If we had more time, I would have taken Rose's picture in this typical scenario. This time she bought a bright blue evening purse with a rhinestone chain for Martha, her assistant at the mortuary.

"Her clothes are too dull, Gloria. Like yours." Rose said, tucking the purse into her tote. "This might inspire her."

Under her stylish black overcoat, Rose was dressed appropriately for getting an award herself, in a chic navy power suit with a cream-colored blouse that draped at the neckline. A circle pin that would have been a cliché on anyone else looked just right on Rose, holding a paisley silk scarf in place under her lapel.

She'd pinned an antique amethyst pin to my burgundy jacket in her hotel room, after pressing my jacket pockets and collar so they looked less floppy. I had to admit the brooch sharpened my image. Ordinarily my jewelry of choice consisted of a science-related lapel tack, my favorites being a set of small squares, each bearing a symbol of an element as it appeared on the periodic table. I hadn't brought any with me on the trip, however.

"Thank goodness," I'd heard Rose say when I mentioned it.

She'd denied making the comment.

As we approached the remodeled and re-designed museum, Rose came through with statistics. The new 630,000-square-foot space, close to three years in the making, had nearly twice the capacity of the former facility.

"When did you have time to look all that up?" I asked her.

"It's in all the guidebooks, Gloria. A Japanese architect named Taniguchi won the competition for the project."

"What's his first name?"

She raised her eyebrows and said nothing.

Lori had told me that we should use a side entrance to the museum and follow the signs to the café on the fifth floor. Thanks to the sweeping, airy design, some of the museum's collection was visible though the galleries were closed. I was impressed by the largest Monet I'd ever seen, a three-part mural. Rose was proud that I recognized a water lily painting, and she took full credit for my art education, as was correct.

Rose pointed out the wonders of the Sculpture Garden and Rodin's figure of Balzac. I was more taken with the building itself and wondered how they — whoever they were — managed to requisition all this open space in the middle of Manhattan.

The café was as crowded as close-packed molecules. Except for one or two holdouts in contemporary styles, the gathering of women was a testimony to power dressing. I'd seen so many unusual fashions this week, from the strangely slanted neckline on the NYPD secretary to the various wraparound blouses and abbreviated sweaters worn by women I'd observed around town. I'd wondered if anyone bought plain wool suits any more, or slacks that fit at the waist, or classic blazers.

And here they all were.

Lori found us in the crowd very quickly. I hoped it wasn't my travel-store burgundy knit that pinpointed us so easily. She'd succumbed to tradition and wore a brown gabardine suit with a knee-length skirt and a velvety lapel. Her plain, crewneck blouse was an off-white that reminded me of what Rose called her eggshell kitchen walls.

"The professional look becomes you," I told her.

She fingered her pearls. "My mother's,"

she said. "I dressed around them."

"Wonderful choices," Rose said.

Lori brought us to a round table near the podium. Our names had been printed in calligraphy on place cards in spite of short notice.

I was thrilled when Tina Miller took the seat next to me.

Lori's doing, I knew. Such was the prerogative of the setup committee.

"Nice to see you again, Dr. Lamerino," Tina said, though she couldn't have read my place card, which was turned away from her. She must have noticed my surprise and guessed the reason. She smiled. "It's my business to remember names."

"You're good at what you do. I read the wonderful article in *New York City Today*."

"They did a nice job. I was very pleased with it," she said, with a modest shrug.

"Congratulations on being chosen for this award. I'm sure you worked very hard for it."

"Thank you, and I did."

Tina's outfit looked like the same one I'd seen in the magazine spread — a tailored black suit and white blouse. I figured this was the only such suit in her wardrobe, as opposed to a broader collection of turtlenecks, corduroys, and belt buckles.

Despite Lori's good intentions, the seating arrangement did nothing to further my inquiry into the Dee Dee Sanders–Amber Keenan–Tina Miller connections. Our conversation was stilted and uncomfortable. It didn't help that it took place amid the din of waiters (the only males in the room) plunking down plates and pouring ice water and guests chatting, laughing, and shouting congratulations to each other across the room.

"How's Dee Dee?" I asked in a voice too loud to carry my concern. "Such an unfortunate thing to have happened to her."

Tina *tsk tsked.* If she was surprised that I knew so quickly, she didn't let on. "It's terrible that you can't even go jogging in the world's greatest park without being attacked."

"I thought the attack on Dee Dee was related to Amber Keenan's murder," I said.

Tina gave me a broad — if not quite sincere — smile. "I see you're still on the case, in a manner of speaking." She broke off a piece of her blueberry muffin. "Funny, I've been working with the NYPD myself for years and *I* haven't been deputized."

"Shall I put in a good word?"

One good dig deserved another, I figured, but my smart-aleck comment sent her away, mentally and physically.

"Could you please pass the butter?" she asked. Then quickly, "Is that Renee Duboscq two tables over? Please excuse me. I've been trying to reach her for days."

The next time I saw Tina Miller, she was behind the podium accepting her award. She never came back to her crepe and sausages.

On the other side of me, a young, attractive black woman was showing Rose a portfolio of her company: Alida's Personal Shopping and Custom Designs. Rose had made a friend.

I hoped Alida didn't do wedding receptions.

Before we left, Lori introduced us to several other women, some of whom I recognized from the magazine piece. Rose had kept busy giving and receiving business cards.

Near the coat check counter, Lori pulled us aside. "In the interests of your becoming familiar with people involved with the ozone issue, I want to point out Rachel Hartman." She nodded her head in the direction of a tall blond woman in a sleek black suit. "Pardon me for being catty, but she really shouldn't be here. She's the PR woman for Blake Manufacturing, which owns at least four facilities in the tristate area. Hardly a *small* business, but the rules have loosened up and now it's sort of — any woman with a job can join."

"And no PR person would miss an opportunity like this," Rose said.

"Everybody needs a little welding now and then," Lori said.

As we left the building I caught a glimpse of Tina Miller on a bench, changing from pumps to what looked like safety shoes.

CHAPTER EIGHTEEN

Still in my power breakfast clothes, I rode the elevator with Matt to my second of three special meals on Wednesday — Lori's luncheon. The third would be dinner at the Sassos' in the evening. I thought I was ready to face Karla without feeling as though I'd read her secret diary.

This trip was doing nothing for my weight control, but I reminded myself that another chance for a New Year's resolution to that effect was less than a month away.

Matt and I made a cozy twosome on the elevator in Lori's building, especially with our newly purchased, enormous poinsettia on the floor between us. I was glad the janitor had left his bucket and mop somewhere else this time.

"This is pretty small," Matt said, running his hand along the elevator's accordion door. Something I thought I'd made clear in my many iterations of that Sunday morning adventure, but I guess he needed the personal experience.

Despite an enthusiastic effort on my part, first thing in the morning, Matt had had no trouble shrugging off my ideas and questions about Dee Dee. In the very cold light of day, they'd faded into the back of my mind and began to seem preposterous to me, too. So I'd abandoned my circuitous reasoning and looked forward to lunch with Amber Keenan's brother. The least I could do was be nice to the family of a woman I'd failed in her last hour.

I suppressed a queasy feeling as the old box creaked its way up to the fourth floor. I leaned back against Matt. I'd hoped to ask the loft some questions, to see something missed by the NYPD forensics experts, but my secret euphoria at revisiting the crime scene was gone.

Rose had declined Lori's invitation in favor of meeting Karla's mother for shopping. They'd start at Trump Tower on Fifth Avenue and head north and east to Bloomingdale's, she'd said, as if I'd be envious. I knew that Grace Sasso would be a more appropriate shopping companion for Rose, and I was happy for her.

"I can't wait to tell Grace about your

upcoming wedding reception," Rose had said.

"I agreed to a *party*," I'd said.

"A party with a wedding theme," Rose had answered, picking a piece of white lint off my jacket. "I'll be keeping that in mind while we're shopping. Maybe I'll see something new in bride-and-groom decorations." Instead of responding, I busied myself searching for a foreign speck on her outfit. None to be found.

Lori was at the door to greet Matt and me, as if she'd heard the elevator and knew exactly when we'd be exiting. "I'm so glad you came," she said. She led Matt to a table where he could set the plant and then hugged us both, though I'd left her only a short time ago.

I assumed the tall young man following her was Billy Keenan. I had a strange reaction to him, imagining that he looked like his sister, though I'd never seen her full front, in an upright position.

Billy was a big man, with lighter hair than Amber's, worn in a bowl cut so that large strands of it fell in front of his eyes. I pictured him on his farm, his thumbs hooked in the straps of his denim overalls, his boots covered in who knew what. The result of my never having set foot in Kansas, or on a farm, I suspected.

"Billy flew in on Monday night. I wish he'd have called me then," Lori said. "Anyway, he'll stay here until . . . he has to leave." She ended weakly, then disappeared into the kitchen.

"I didn't want to be a bother," Billy said, shaking our hands in turn. "Nice to meet you all."

"We're all so sorry about Amber," I said.

"Anything we can do to help," Matt said.

"Thank you, ma'am." Billy's voice was soft, his manner respectful. He shook Matt's hand. "And, sir, there *is* something you can do."

Before Matt could ask what, Lori came in from the kitchen with another young man, leaving me to wonder what Billy wanted. Burning with curiosity as I was, you'd think he'd asked me for a favor instead of Matt.

"This is Craig," Lori said. "He and Billy got to know each other last night, so I thought it would be nice to have him over, too. Craig's the guy who does both the sound and the editing for me." She patted his back and shrugged her shoulders. "It's a small company," she said with an apologetic tone, answering a question no one had asked.

Craig uttered an enthusiastic "Hey" to

each of us and returned to kitchen chores. Before he left he assigned Billy the task of arranging chairs in a circle.

Lori's long dining room table, which looked also like a worktable, was laden with food: roasted chicken, pepper and olive salad, pasta primavera, and a basket of crusty bread. The smell of anise from the assortment of Italian cookies held its own against the aromas of garlic and vinegar.

I was curious about Lori and Craig's relationship, especially since he seemed to be playing the role of cohost. When Matt and I were assigned a task — to haul in drinks from an extra refrigerator in the back hall — I took the opportunity to quiz him.

"Is Lori seeing anyone special at the moment?" I asked.

"She just broke up with a guy she's known since before college," Matt said in a low voice. "Sean Mahoney. He wanted to move back to Boston, which he did, but Lori would never leave New York, and she wasn't interested in a long-distance relationship."

"What about Craig?" I whispered.

Matt shrugged and gave me a strange look, as if I'd suddenly taken over the role of Rose in our group. "I'm sure we'll find out."

I wasn't sure myself why I'd bothered to

ask about Lori's love life. I'd lived a few decades as an adult without a partner and certainly didn't think it odd or unpleasant for anyone to live singly, but Lori seemed very connected to social matters and to people.

"I'm just curious," I told Matt, answering his unspoken question. "I want everyone to be as happy as I am."

"I can't wait for the wedding," he said.

We reentered the main part of the loft laughing.

To keep myself from staring at the spot in front of the couch, now right side up, where Amber's body had been, I wandered around the loft. I estimated it to be at least sixty feet long and about thirty feet wide. I noticed that our gift was the first sign of Christmas to enter the loft and wondered if Lori had been having a particularly bad holiday season even before her home became a crime scene.

Decorative screens and draperies marked off space here and there. One of the few real doors, in the southeast corner, had a sign: GO. I assumed it was a darkroom with a STOP sign on the other side of the placard. The brick interior walls were a perfect backdrop for nicely framed prints and fabrics. Every few feet a painted white post dotted the high-gloss hardwood floors, ending at the ceiling. I hadn't appreciated the ideal chameleon space the first time I saw it, under less than ideal conditions.

There were fuzzy lines between Lori's work and living areas: Video and DVD cases were on both sides of the room, as were personal photos. Floppy disks were spread on the kitchen counter; a shoe rack sat on the floor next to the computer tower; and an easy chair upholstered in a mauve and red paisley fabric held a stack of clear jewel cases.

I took a leisurely look at the photos on Lori's wood-and-cinder-block shelves, artistically arranged against one of the short brick walls.

I wondered if Lori had moved the pictures around in the last day or so. One stood out, of her and a young woman with amber-colored hair, both smiling broadly. The backdrop was an image of a movie screen with the words TRIBECA FILM FESTIVAL. Another, showing Lori and Amber in the snow on the steps of the New York Public Library, brought home how much bigger Amber was than Lori. Amber and Lori were eye to eye in the photo, but two steps apart. At one time, it seemed, the two women were friends. I remembered how Lori at first denied knowing Amber well, and I assumed now that it was because she was trying to put distance between herself and Amber's blackmail operation.

If the photos were on display on the day of Amber's murder, I wouldn't have noticed. I'd been focused on Amber's body and my cell phone — and the sounds of a killer leaving the scene.

"You might want a closer look at this one," Matt said, coming up behind me. He handed me a five-by-seven photo in a light wood frame: a girl of six or seven with . . . I peered closer . . . her young, handsome Uncle Matt, in an Irish knit sweater.

It was always startling to see my husband in his earlier life, long before I knew him. In some ways I envied his niece and the people who'd known him so much longer. He'd been friends with Rose and Frank since his rookie days, when, according to them, he was a high-strung, stressed-out young cop. As much as Rose loved to talk about the old days, she hadn't told me much about the Matt-Teresa couple, only that Teresa had been the stable, low-key force in the family. Rose's diagnosis was that her death had brought Matt the perspective he needed and made him the calm, even-tempered man I married. Rose had the skills of a therapist in these matters, and I trusted her interpretation.

In a way, I was sorry I missed Matt's wild phase (Rose's term when he was around to hear it and blush). At the time I was hiding out in California, unable to deal with life outside my physics lab. The untimely death of my first fiancé, Al Gravese, a few months before our wedding seemed to set the course of my adult life, sending me across the country and away from relationships that might lead to the same horrible end.

Now I was part of this family, which included Lori, and I was thankful for every moment.

I looked at Matt, minus the Irish knit, but with the same droopy eyes and pleasant face.

"If I were the kind to lift things that weren't mine, I might stick this photo in my purse," I said. "Instead I'm going to ask Lori if she'll scan it for me."

You wouldn't think elbow nudging could be so sexy.

"Lunch is served. Please report to the buffet line. The left side is for loading only," Craig said, his voice like a documentary film narrator's.

My immediate judgment of him was thumbs up, in case Lori cared to ask.

"This is quite a spread, Lori," Matt said.

"Be impressed by Raoul, the cook at the deli on Forty-ninth," Lori said.

"Well, you made good choices, then." He held up a bottled water. *"Salut'."*

"Salut'. Thanks, Uncle Matt."

We sat in a circle with TV trays spaced conveniently at our sides.

"Have you been to New York City before?" I asked Billy when we'd all filled china plates with Raoul's offerings.

Billy put down his chicken leg. "Just once, ma'am, when Amber first moved here. I took that Circle tour, and I went to the top of the Empire State Building, but to tell you the truth, it was so crowded everywhere, I couldn't wait to get home."

If you want to be alone, try Lori's elevator on a Sunday morning, I wanted to say.

"That reminds me of a Yogi Berra quote a friend told me the other day," Matt said, "but I can't remember how it goes."

Craig jumped in. "I'll bet it's 'Nobody goes there anymore; it's too crowded.' "

Matt pointed his fork at him, and the three guys laughed. "That's the one."

Lori and I rolled our eyes. I made a note to arm myself with a science quote, soon.

"If you're in the mood for just walking around, Billy, I'd be glad to give you some company," Craig said. "I'm a native, remember."

"Thanks, dude. I could have used somebody who knows the ropes in all that rain. I had one heck of a time trying to hail a yellow taxicab downtown. I was soaked through. Lori said there are some rules about the lights on the roofs, but I didn't know about them."

"You should have taken the subway," Craig said.

"I didn't trust the subway, from all you hear, you know."

"It's perfectly safe," Lori said. "Craig and I take it every day."

"Next time," Billy said, his mouth not quite empty of pasta.

Chirp chirp. Chirp chirp. Chirp chirp.

Matt's cell phone.

I followed him with my gaze as he excused himself and walked away to take the call. I waited patiently as he finished the call, took a detour to the buffet table, and came back to his chair, next to mine, with more food.

"Buzz?" I asked. Softly, I thought.

"Buzz Arnold? Your cop friend?" Lori asked.

Matt gave a slight nod, clearly not wanting to pursue the topic. I felt as discreet as dry ice.

"Detective Matt, do you have any way to find out how my sister's case is going? I mean, I hate to impose on you, but if you have a friend on the force?"

At last, Billy's request. It made sense that he'd want to know more than he'd been told officially.

"I understand you'd want to know everything possible, Billy," Matt said. "I assume you've already talked to the people in charge of the case? I believe it's Detective Glazer in the lead?"

"Yeah, but he wasn't able to tell me much." Billy looked forlorn. "He wouldn't tell me why someone would kill her. But I guess this is New York, huh? And you don't need a reason to kill someone."

Craig bristled. "That's what I'd expect to hear from —"

Lori put her hand on his arm. I heard a soothing whisper, and Craig sat back.

I wondered how much the police ever told the relatives of murder victims — something I'd never had the occasion to learn from Matt. Would the NYPD describe Amber's blackmail business to her brother? Possibly, if they were sure it was connected to her murder. I doubted Lori had filled in those details for Billy.

"Maybe it has something to do with those ozone things," Billy said, still thinking about motives for his sister's murder. I hoped Craig would realize Billy was giving all possibilities equal weight and wasn't picking on Craig's hometown.

"Do you have any reason to think Amber's work on the video was connected to her death?" Matt asked. I was amused that he was not above doing a little ad hoc interrogation himself. "Did your sister tell you she was frightened, or concerned about the ozone project?"

Lori sat forward on her chair, her hand to her mouth. I thought she might be biting her nails.

Craig, too, seemed focused on this spontaneous police drama, and ready to defend New York City. I thought the mayor, whoever he was, would be proud to have Craig as part of a Visitors' Bureau staff.

Billy screwed up his face and raised his arms in surrender. "Amber wouldn't have confided in me. To tell you the truth, we didn't see eye to eye on most things. I never did understand my sister, you know." His voice grew louder, with an angry undercurrent, and he seemed to be addressing Amber herself. "She was never happy on the farm,

257

even when she was little. She used to dress up like the folks on TV and pretend she lived in a big city."

"But, as far as you know, she wasn't specifically worried about the nature of her recent work?" Matt asked.

Billy put his plate down and folded his arms across his chest. "I just think when you mess around with big companies in a megalopolis, you're asking for trouble."

Craig maintained his silence — helped, I was sure, by Lori's unobtrusively rubbing his back.

For me, I'd lost track of some of the back-and-forth between Matt and Billy. I had another problem.

"When did you say you arrived in New York, Billy?" I asked.

"Monday night, ma'am, kind of late. I checked into one of them motels out by the airport."

Then how did you get rained on? I wanted to ask. The rain was over by Sunday night, and it had been clear ever since.

Instead of speaking out, I pretended Matt was rubbing my back.

I had to stop thinking of every conversation as an interrogation, I told myself. Not everyone was obsessed with logic and consistency, day and night. Not everyone gave answers to questions as I did, to three decimal places. Rose and Frank chuckled when I said my average monthly phone bill was $116.38 or that I'd drop by her office at 1:12 P.M.

The inconsistencies in Billy's statements rattled me. Things got worse when I insisted on helping Lori clean up.

"It will be so much easier for you later," I'd said. "I'm sure you have work to do. We can at least take things to the kitchen, consolidate the trash." I'd held back on *Many hands make light work,* thinking it sounded too old-fashioned and not New York cool.

I made a trip around the circle of chairs, picked up papers and after-dinner-mint wrappers, and carried a load over to the only wastebasket I could see, by the small table near the front door.

"Is this okay for recyclables?" I called out, but high-amplitude sound waves from the TV filled the air between Lori and me, and I realized she couldn't hear me. I glanced down at the contents of the wicker basket and saw catalogs and pieces of mail. The right container, I thought. A few bits of paper fell in before I noticed a corner of an envelope. An envelope with the logo showing a stick-figure family. The letterhead on the threatening letter Buzz Arnold had shown us. The do-not-expose letter.

The killer's letter, as far as we knew.

I stopped short, holding the rest of the trash in midair.

My heart leapt. The air in the loft turned cold. I was as shocked as if Lori's wastebasket had become alive and wouldn't let me toss my handfuls of used paper goods into it. I bent down, trying to determine if there was a matching letter. In the top layer there were other envelopes and some unopened junk mail, but I couldn't see a letter with what I now considered an ugly design.

I looked around at Lori's luncheon guests, all of whom seemed to be occupied. Matt and Billy were watching a sports news channel on TV. I knew Matt was just being sociable; he couldn't tell one team from another. Unless Buzz's Yogi Berra quotes were rubbing off on him. I hoped not.

Lori and Craig were collecting plates and glasses. I heard phrases like "continuity errors," "establishing shot," and words that were more familiar, like "fade" and "dissolve." They were absorbed in their conversation — was Griffith's smooth cutting better than Eisenstein's overt "see the cut" method?

I wished I could cut everyone but me out of the scene. They were so close to me, I didn't think I could get away with sorting through the trash. It was surprising enough that no one seemed to notice the freeze-frame: Gloria standing immobile over the wastebasket with an assortment of rubbish.

I bent my head around one more time, to account for everyone. I felt another episode of theft coming on. I wondered if there was a special legal category: stationery larceny.

I pulled the envelope out of the waste-basket as I slid the refuse into it, and slipped the stolen property into my pants pocket. Smooth. I was getting good at this.

Rose would never own an outfit with as many compartments as my clothes had. "It ruins the line," she'd say.

"My lines are already ruined," I'd counter.

I liked a lot of pockets. They came in handy, like today.

Wide hips came in handy, too, sometimes. No one would notice the extra 0.185 millimeters (plus or minus 5 percent) on my right hip as I walked over to the couch.

"We should be on our way," I said to Matt. "Buzz will be waiting."

He gave me a strange look, but we'd learned to trust each other's signals. "Right," he said. "I'll get the coats."

We engaged in a round of good-byes that seemed endless to me, promising Billy we'd let him know if we found out anything new on the case, Craig that we'd check out a documentary on the Vietnam War that he judged the best of the decade, and Lori that we'd talk soon.

"Thanks for the plant," she said, hugging us. "I'm all inspired to put up my ornaments now. I sorted through them last week and separated the nice ones from the ones that I should never have packed up in the first place. I trashed quite a few."

It was all I could do not to ask for the contents of her current trash.

CHAPTER NINETEEN

Matt and I left the overheated lobby of Lori's building and went out into the cold. Temperatures in the thirties, I'd read. It felt like it. I hadn't planned to show Matt the envelope I'd recovered from Lori's trash al fresco, but there'd been no opportunity to talk to him alone in the loft.

"We need to see Buzz right away," I said.

"Well, you're half psychic, but not fool-proof," Matt said. "How did you know Buzz wanted to meet us? I didn't tell you what that phone call was about. However, you got the time wrong. He's not expecting us until four o'clock, and it's not even three."

I looked at Matt's peaceful expression — no frown lines, and the hint of a crooked smile at the ready — and regretted that what I had to show him would transform it. "I have my own agenda," I said.

"You think I don't know that?"

I smiled. My eyes lingered a moment on a

little boy approaching us on the sidewalk. I looked at him wistfully — skipping along, each mittened hand enfolded by an adult's, his parents, I assumed. His pale blue down snowsuit was so thick his arms stuck out almost straight from his sides. His red nose and eyes, framed in a fur-lined hood, were dripping from the cold, but the icy weather didn't affect his warm and uncomplicated laughter, making me long for a simpler stage of life. I considered turning as they passed and calling out a *Merry Christmas.*

My nostalgic mood and desire to interact with the family passed quickly, however. They probably celebrated something other than Christmas and didn't even speak English, I thought. The number of international accents I'd heard the past few days rivaled the number of different holiday tunes.

I pulled Matt into the doorway of a shoe repair shop. I chose it figuring there would be much less traffic in and out than for the card and gift shops in the vicinity.

"I have to show you something," I said, digging under my jacket, into my pants pocket.

A frown, and he hadn't seen anything yet. "Am I going to like this?"

"I doubt it."

"Buzz? Matt. Listen, we're still on target to meet you at four, but I have a favor to ask." The advantages of being a cop: immediate "service and protection" from your buddies.

I let out a long breath and felt marginally better. Buzz agreed to have a uniform, as I'd long ago learned to call regular police officers, go to Lori's apartment on some pretext and check out the scene there. A car would also be assigned to her building.

The call to Lori would be more difficult. Matt needed to explain that he had to have the letter that accompanied the envelope I showed him, and he had to get it without alarming her unduly. I heard only snatches of his conversation with her, since I was off on another branch of my logic tree.

With a slightly clearer head, now that Lori was about to be surrounded by the NYPD, I put together my version of Billy's true schedule: He came to New York City earlier than he claimed, probably a week ago, while his sister was still alive. He stayed at the hotel with the stick figures logo and mailed letters to everyone. Not to be prejudiced, but wasn't that what a farm boy might do? I asked myself.

Matt's voice came through a lull in my

thinking. "Just hold on to it, honey, okay? We'll come by and pick it up in a few minutes."

Billy had means (anyone could have hit Amber with a surprise blow, then smothered her with a pillow) and opportunity (Amber would certainly let Billy into the loft, and I was convinced he was in town at the time).

I needed motive.

"Not a big deal. I'll tell you when I get there, okay?" Matt was saying to Lori.

I considered having my shoes shined, both to breathe some warm indoor air and to repay the proprietor for not booting us (I smiled) from his doorway.

So, I asked myself, what was Billy's motive? Probably a difference in taste between urban and rural lifestyles wouldn't drive a brother to murder. At that moment, however, it seemed a possibility — gridlock at the intersection of Eighth Avenue and West Forty-sixth Street resulted in a crescendo of blaring horns. The cacophony was deafening, the situation compounded by a stretch limo that was double parked and an ambulance making its way north on Eighth. I wondered how Matt could carry on his cell phone conversation.

I ruled out lifestyle as motive for murder nevertheless and considered another: Billy might have been aware of Amber's lucrative blackmail scheme and wanted in on it. According to Lori, Amber wasn't the most discreet person, even about her nefarious behavior. Billy could have come to town to extort money from his sister.

The biggest problem with my theory of Billy as the killer was that the text of the letter, as I remembered it, didn't jibe with Billy as the author. I hadn't seen Lori's letter, but what I recalled of the one sent to Amber didn't fit a sibling. It was addressed to Ms. Keenan (too formal), at Lori's apartment (Billy would know his sister's address), and told Amber not to act on certain unnamed footage. If Billy wanted money, he wouldn't care about footage. Unless the footage was of Billy himself?

No, not the farm boy, I decided.

I hadn't been as close to solving the case as I thought. Still, there was no question in my mind that Billy Keenan had lied about when he arrived in New York.

"I think you should tell Buzz to pick up Billy for questioning," I said to Matt when he'd hung up with Lori.

"What? A new theory?"

We'd started our walk back to West Forty-eighth, our shoes unpolished. "It didn't rain after Sunday evening," I said. "It's been cold and cheer."

"You mean cold and *clear?*"

"Didn't I say clear?"

"You said cheer."

"I guess all this merriment is getting to me," I said. "Call me Scrooge."

I'd seen a greater volume of ornaments in New York City since Friday than in all my Christmases put together, I thought. Especially if you counted the pyramid of red balls on Sixth Avenue, each one the size of a seven-kilowatt home generator. Every third child wore jingling bells, either on his shoes, his mittens, or his zipper pull. Velvety gowns in shimmering colors adorned mannequins up and down the avenues. Christmas music poured out of every doorway. Fir trees and wreaths crowded the sidewalks outside the grocery stores and florist shops. Stollen, Santa cookies, and cakes decorated with holly filled deli and pastry shop windows.

Christmas had taken over my senses. I wondered how the natives stood the holiday buzz week after week between the Thanksgiving Day parade and New Year's Eve under the falling ball.

I supposed New Yorkers were used to a constant invasion of their home space. They lived with year-round tourism, tolerating I

LOVE NY on key chains, pencils, mugs, plastic bags, shot glasses — too many items to list — in shops all over town. I realized also that this kind of merchandising was becoming more the norm in all cities. The number of items with Revere Beach as a logo had grown from zero when I was a child growing up there to a catalog full this year. The little known Revere, Massachusetts, offered various paraphernalia with images of the now-defunct Cyclone roller coaster and other relics of the once-thriving Boardwalk.

Matt put his arm around me as we trudged up Eighth. "You need a vacation," he said. I gave him as warm a smile as thirty degrees would allow and felt bad that I'd required attention from him. It was *his* niece who might be in trouble. Who might, in fact, be entertaining Amber's killer. I picked up my pace and Matt followed suit.

"About Billy," I said. "He told us he got soaked waiting for a taxi. He couldn't have been rained on if he didn't arrive until Monday. It's been cheery *and* clear since then."

"I just don't see Billy for this. So the kid was exaggerating, making it sound like he had a tougher time than he really did in the big bad city. Or, you know, he was giving us the old I-walked-two-miles-in-the-snow-to-school complaint."

"But why say it was raining? If he wanted to exaggerate, he could have claimed he was farther downtown. If he wanted to make the people look bad, he could have claimed they were rude to him or someone stole his camera, any number of things. Other than rain, which would be the truth if he arrived over the weekend. And you always tell me people revert to the truth when they're caught off guard or if you wait long enough."

Matt smiled. "I love when you quote me to make your point."

We had our arms linked now and were approaching Lori's apartment. I was beginning to know this neighborhood as well as our own in Revere. I'd seen the same man leave a neighboring building with a tiny, flat-faced dog twice now, and I'd been tempted to drop in at a specialty cheese shop below street level. It seemed you couldn't walk more than ten meters anywhere in the city without seeing or smelling something interesting.

"Well, can't we at least get Buzz to think about it?"

Matt shrugged and blew a steamy breath. "Why not? But much as I'd like to pin this on someone this minute, we've got to keep our heads. Let's see, first it was some anonymous ozone violator, then Dee Dee, now Billy. For a while you even suspected Karla. It seems like you're flailing around in this case. Not like you. And it's a case that isn't yours to begin with, I might add."

Matt was right, but his words stung. He must have forgotten momentarily that the worst insult I could hear was an affront to my sense of logic. Flailing was for the uncritical thinkers of the world.

"I know I have no contract," I admitted. "Don't worry. I'm aware that this is not Revere, where I can take a few liberties."

Matt assumed an expression of mock horror. "Liberties? You take liberties in Revere?"

"One or two."

"To be serious — we have to keep looking at what we have physically. We have letters from a hotel, and you have the smell of perfume and a candy wrapper."

"And Billy's lies," I whispered. If I was going to flail, I wanted to do it right.

I felt Matt relax once Lori opened the door to us. Not that she looked in any way at ease, but she was alive and standing up — and holding a letter.

"Are Billy and Craig still here?" Matt asked.

"Nuh-uh. What's up, Uncle Matt? Am I in some kind of danger?" Lori's normally quick speech was faster yet, and higher in pitch, befitting someone holding a threatening letter. "I figured this mail was a mistake of some kind, maybe meant for Amber."

"You're probably right, honey. We want to be sure, that's all."

Matt took the letter by its corner.

"I threw it in the trash," Lori said. "I didn't think of preserving fingerprints."

"No problem. We're going to see Buzz this afternoon anyway, and I'll pass it on."

No problem, I thought. Just a letter identical to the one received by a woman who's been murdered.

"Where are Billy and Craig, Lori?" I asked. *Especially Billy.*

"Craig took Billy on the subway to South Street Seaport. It's his favorite view of the Brooklyn Bridge. Craig's playing goodwill ambassador for the city, but I don't think Billy is about to become New York City's number-one fan no matter how hard Craig tries."

"Did Billy leave his stuff here?" Matt asked.

"Yeah. He just has a duffel bag. One of

those enormous military-type pieces," Lori said. "What's up? What's this all about? He's not a suspect or anything, is he?" Lori held her arms high across her chest, each hand rubbing the opposite shoulder.

"For now, we're just taking precautions. Billy might be in some kind of trouble, so make sure he doesn't stay here, okay?"

"What shall I do with his bag?" Lori asked, understandably flustered.

"Keep it for now. We'll make sure he's not back tonight, anyway."

"Please, Uncle Matt. I'm your niece, not some interviewee. Is Billy a suspect or not?"

Matt sighed and pulled her to him. He patted her back the way I imagined he did when she was little. "I'm sorry, honey. I guess I forgot you're not ten anymore."

We took seats around a small table in the kitchen, and Matt told Lori why we thought Billy had some explaining to do before we trusted him completely to be only the grieving brother.

"It could have been a little exaggeration, about the bad weather, but we need to check it out, and you need to be careful in the meantime. Okay?"

"Okay." Lori nodded, seeming satisfied that she'd been briefed. "Do you want some tea? Or coffee?" She looked as though she needed warming up herself.

"Why don't I put some water on to heat," I said.

"Thanks, Gloria. And now that I have you alone . . ." Lori chuckled briefly, a nice sound after her nervous speech patterns. She cut it short when we didn't respond. "That's a kind of famous movie device," she said.

"We don't get out much," Matt said, and then we all laughed.

"I thought of a couple of things, but I didn't want to bring them up with the guys here. Well, first is that I have a follow-up meeting tomorrow afternoon with a company we're profiling — Curry Industries — and I'm wondering if you'd come with me, Gloria. Even though I won't be doing the CFC part right now, I don't want to take a chance that they'll still be so cooperative down the road. I could use some tech support. And since you're making a career out of educating the Revere Police Department" — Lori grinned at Matt — "I thought you might be willing to help me out."

Be still, my heart.

"She'd love to," Matt said, before I could gush.

"Great. Let me give you the first interviews, which are mostly about the ozone monitoring in the plant area, so you'll be familiar with the company. I have them on a DVD." Lori reached into her purse and came up with a thin case marked CURRY I. "I've been carrying this around with me and kept forgetting to give it to you."

"We have no way to play this in the hotel room," Matt said.

Lori and I looked at each other. We knew we were thinking the same thing — the poor guy was not privy to the ubiquity of computers in cafés.

"Not to worry," I told him.

Matt threw up his hands and laughed. "Sorry, I should have known better." I was glad he was comfortable in his low-tech skin.

Lori pulled open a desk drawer and retrieved a stack of pamphlets. "I have some of Curry's product brochures. You might as well take these, too, Gloria."

"Good. I like to be prepared."

"I'll say," Matt said, but neither Lori nor I acknowledged the remark.

"I'm hoping to get some interesting stuff, some angles that are newsworthy," Lori said.

"You mean controversial?" Matt asked.

Lori cocked her head, her face taking on a faint red hue. "I guess. We can go for coffee afterward, Gloria. Roland Hirsh opened a new place off Tenth where a string of fast foods used to be. He hired the former manager of Gilda's in Little Italy, so the food should be . . ." Evidently no word could describe the fare. Instead Lori kissed the tips of her fingers and waved them off, Italian style.

I marveled at the way Lori could spout off such details, like Rose, who knew Revere's history, businesses, and families inside and out. It was nice, too, to see Lori being enthusiastic and playful, and clearly not thinking of the danger she might be in. Being around a cop can give you a sense of security no matter what the circumstances. I knew that.

"Anything else? You said there were a couple of things?" Matt asked. Always on the job.

"The other is, you know how you asked about some of Amber's, uh, victims? Well, I did remember one, not that I even know what she had on him, but Amber talked about someone she called 'old man Fielding.' I don't have a first name or anything."

Matt had his notepad out in seconds.

I wondered what he was writing. Could he hear the noise pounding in my ears? Did he remember the names on the letter I'd stolen from Dee Dee's file?

Fielding v. Fielding.

The case that was the subject of Karla Sasso's letter to the Tina Miller Agency.

I hoped this was simply another instance of my flailing.

Matt didn't mention the Fielding connection after we left Lori, and I didn't bring it up, either. I figured he would pass the name on to Buzz and forget about it. In my mind I heard him tell me it was a very common name, and what kind of unlikely coincidence it would be that I happened to steal the very letter that connected Karla to Amber's schemes? What if all of Karla's clients were connected to Amber's scheme? I answered in my head. What better resource for blackmail than a divorce lawyer (I couldn't put Karla's face in the picture yet) who would feed clients' names and information to Amber?

This ugly mental conversation kept me busy all the way across to Sixth Avenue and up to Fifty-fourth Street. Matt was quiet, his arm around me part of the time. The light was fading, a magical time of day in New York City, which looked better to me in shades of gray than it did in color. I hoped I'd have some time before the end of this so-called vacation to enjoy more moments like this.

For now I was preoccupied by the specters of women murdered, mugged, or in danger, and a best friend who'd be devastated if she knew what I was thinking about her daughter-in-law.

Buzz had already staked out a place in the far corner of a bakery-deli between Fifth and Sixth and was leafing through a magazine I couldn't identify.

"*Spring 3100,*" he said, when he saw me looking at it. He held it up to show me the cover. "It's the NYPD magazine, named after the telephone number of the old headquarters down on Centre Street." Before he slipped the magazine into his portfolio-style briefcase, I had time to notice the announcement for the featured article: "New test robot hurls suspected bomb into container that can safely detonate the equivalent of a car bomb."

Something to tell Rose, I thought, *so she'll think I'm interested in* her *trivia.*

Matt took my coffee order, leaving me at the small, round marble table with Buzz. "Be good while I'm gone," he whispered to me, with a wink in his voice.

"That was a great lesson on ozone the other day, Gloria," Buzz said. "I went home and told my kid. He's fourteen. Turns out he already knew most of it from general science, but, hey, at least I'm caught up with the ninth grade."

"I'm glad it worked out. Let me know when you're ready for part two."

"That's where the ozone is the good guy." Buzz twirled his spoon heavenward. "Up there where it keeps sunlight out."

"Excellent." Next time I'd explain that only part of the sun's spectrum was harmful.

The midafternoon traffic at the counter was light, and Matt was back in no time with a tray of coffees. Espressos for Buzz and him, and for me a steaming cappuccino ordered mostly because I knew they were served European style in this café, in a wide ceramic cup. I was happy just to warm my hands on the bowl.

Matt retrieved the Family Suites letter and envelope from his inside pocket. He'd encased both in plastic storage bags from Lori's kitchen, a gesture toward preserving what might be left of evidence.

Buzz put on half-glasses, ruining his cool turtleneck-and-sports-jacket look, and focused on the correspondence. "You got this how?"

I wondered if he'd ask. "I, uh, found it in Lori's trash." I added quickly, "In plain sight." I was glad both cops laughed.

"Off the top of my head, without an expert, I'm going to say it's most likely the same as the pair in evidence, from Amber's things. It has the look and feel, for sure."

It occurred to me that cops and scientists had a lot more in common than people thought. Buzz had used three caveat phrases in one sentence.

"Was there anything from the hotel?" Matt asked.

Buzz shook his head. "We have a copy of the register, but that doesn't tell us much. We'd have to have someone in mind, with a photo to show them. It's the kind of place where you're not expecting real names, you know."

I thought the family-friendly name and logo spoke otherwise, but what did I know? "Can you show them Billy Keenan's photo?" I asked.

Buzz raised his eyebrows, nicely trimmed. Like Frank Galigani's, and unlike Matt's. Or mine, for that matter.

"Gloria has a theory about Billy." Matt scratched his head, a gesture I didn't appreciate.

I gave Buzz a summary of Billy's account of his visit and threw in my own ideas about a possible motive. "Can you pick him up?"

"Not on the basis of a weather mistake. What do you think, Mattie? Would the brother be on your list?"

Matt shrugged, his head shaking a slight no. "The language doesn't fit, for one thing." He fingered the plastic. "This sounds more like it's from someone who's under threat of exposure from Amber, and I don't see how that could be Billy."

"Did anyone check him out in Kansas?" I asked. "Maybe he owes a lot of bookies."

Bookies, in Kansas? What was I thinking? I looked around the bakery to be sure no other customers had been paying attention to me. I noted with relief that there were no single patrons, who were more likely to eavesdrop than ones who had companions. I knew from experience how hard it was not to listen in on conversations when dining, or snacking, alone.

"We checked Kansas, of course, just because we check out all of a victim's family. There's nothing there. Billy seems like a good guy: works on the farm, takes care of a sick mother. If he *was* in town earlier, it might have been just Sunday night, and he might be embarrassed to admit he took time out to enjoy the sights while his sister was in the morgue."

"However —" I started.

"However," Buzz interrupted, "it's Mattie's niece we're worried about here, so let's do something. We can bring him in, say there are more questions we need to ask about his sister. That gets him out of the house, and then we'll set something up outside Lori's place."

"Can't you tell him the NYPD comps all victims' relatives with a free hotel room?" I asked.

Two pairs of cop eyes stared at me.

"It was just a thought," I said.

CHAPTER TWENTY

Matt took care of refills on espresso and this time brought back a plate of cookies. It had been at least three hours since our last dessert, at Lori's. This selection was what Marco Lamerino would have called "American." No anise or pine nuts or biscotti. I wasn't fussy when it came to cookies. I chose a black-and-white from the assortment; Matt and Buzz went for the shortbread.

"So, the reason I asked you here in the first place . . . outside of the terrific company" — Buzz laughed, and I thought we were about to hear another Yogi Berra quote — "is, I know that Mattie and you have an interest in the rest of this case, too. As I told Mattie on the phone, I'm only too happy to share our progress. Not that there's much. About the only definite, and it's a negative, is the ex-boyfriend's alibi. Kevin Russell. He was in Atlantic City, losing his shirt in front of enough sober witnesses to convince us."

"Then there's Dee Dee," I said. "Is she okay?" In my anxiety over a possible attack on Lori, I'd nearly forgotten the real one on Tina's secretary.

Buzz reviewed the few details he had — or was willing to reveal. Dee Dee was at Central Hospital and on the way to recovery from broken limbs and an injured larynx. She had already implied she wouldn't be able to ID her attacker.

"She's not even sure why the guy stopped throttling her, but she thinks a biker came along and he freaked," Buzz said.

"No one hung around to be thanked?" I asked.

Buzz laughed. "Lot of times people would just as soon not get involved to that extent."

"Did Dee Dee have any candy in her purse?" I asked. My peripheral vision caught Matt rolling his eyes.

"Why? What do you have?"

What do you have? I loved that phrase. When Matt said it on our cases in Revere, I felt like a true partner, though he had a perfectly good and official one in the department.

I told Buzz about my candy and perfume theory — that I was certain I'd run into Dee

Dee in the alley next to Lori's building. If he wondered how I happened to be in Tina's office to meet her secretary the first time, or why I was snooping in the alley at night, he didn't ask. I figured that Matt had done an excellent job of prepping Buzz for this meeting — or that in New York City I wasn't the oddity I was in the smaller cities of the United States.

"So you're thinking Amber's murder and Dee Dee's attack are related."

I was about to make a grandly logical case for the connection when I caught something in Buzz's expression. "You already know that," I said, with mixed feelings about being one step behind the police.

Buzz nodded. "We're pretty convinced that Dee Dee was also getting a little kickback from Amber. We'll see if we can get a look at her bank statements. Tina, by the way, runs a squeaky clean office, from all appearances."

"Dee Dee would be in the perfect position to give Amber inside information," Matt said.

"Yup. All the files. All the lawyers that go through that office. A gold mine."

I cringed internally at "lawyers." I'd already decided not to bring Karla Sasso

Galigani or *Fielding v. Fielding* into this conversation.

Another thought came to me. "It was Dee Dee who called 911 from the loft before I got there?"

Buzz stirred his coffee, nodding in time with the movement of the spoon. "We don't figure her for the killer. Amber was probably already down when Dee Dee got there. She called 911 and split when she heard you come up. She was too sedated last night to say much, but I'm sure by now we have a better idea how she fits in. I just haven't checked back yet."

So I wasn't in the loft with a killer, just another blackmailer?

Buzz looked at his watch. "Gotta go," he said. "I'm due at the police museum. Hey, Mattie, you want to come?"

A police museum? That was one Rose never mentioned.

"What's going on down there?" Matt asked.

"I have a little meeting of the fund-raising committee. You might like to look around at the exhibits. There's a tour. Got everything from the old flintlock firearms to Harleys to uniforms. I think you'd enjoy it."

Matt looked at me. "Want to go?"

I felt part of the NYPD tradition now, and

a flintlock firearm seemed more interesting to me than a painting of hills or flowers or a dour-looking Dutchman. I'd promised Rose I'd meet her at the hotel, though. I wasn't sure what she had in mind, but I guessed she'd found a special exhibit somewhere — New York City had them even in the lobbies of high-rise office buildings, I knew — or she wanted us to choose our outfits together for dinner at the Sassos' later in the evening.

"I'd love to, except I have plans with Rose," I said. "There's plenty of time for you to go, Matt. You can tell me all about it."

As we buttoned up, Buzz said, "Hey, you have to hear this one."

"From Yogi Berra?" I asked.

"No, no. This is a cop story."

Matt grinned: He liked it already.

"A cop is interviewing a victim in a car accident, so he asks, 'What gear were you in at the moment of the impact?' " Buzz cleared his throat, getting ready for a big finish, I assumed. "The guy answers, 'Gucci sweats and Reeboks.' "

There must *be some funny science stories,* I told myself.

Buzz hailed a cab for me in less than two minutes. I turned around in my seat and saw a second one pull up for him and Matt before mine reached the corner. I wondered how he did it. He wasn't in uniform, but maybe there was a certain code, besides the lights on the roof and the finger signal Lori had told us about, that alerted the cabbies to the presence of the NYPD.

Like a true old-school gentleman, Buzz had given the cabdriver the address of our hotel as he closed the back door for me. Matt stood by, probably wondering if I was about to call his friend sexist or declare my ability to give the address myself. Instead, I humbly accepted the assistance.

I just didn't accept the destination.

"Actually, I'll be going to Central Hospital first," I told the cabdriver when we'd turned down Broadway. "Do you know where that is?"

The cabdriver gave me a look, as if I'd asked one of the old joke questions like *Is the Pope Catholic?* It used to be that *Is the Pope Italian?* worked also, but not lately.

"You're not from around here, I guess," the driver said in an accent I couldn't place. "I gotta go back the other way now, go up Central Park West and then over."

I wasn't sure if he was asking my permission or complaining. Either way, he seemed pleasant enough as he hummed carols along with a group that might have been the Mormon Tabernacle Choir coming through his speakers.

Twenty minutes later, I stepped out — curbside, not into the traffic, as the driver admonished me — in front of Central Hospital, apparently the nearest one to the jogging path where Dee Dee had been attacked.

I surveyed the area and didn't see any NYPD multitone-blue police cars. I'd gotten pretty good at recognizing an unmarked in Revere, but I was not in home territory and couldn't tell if any of the cars parked bumper to bumper outside the hospital were official.

I walked with purpose through the automatic glass doors and up to a nurse's station, easy to find in the relatively small facility.

"Ms. Sanders," I said, as if I had an appointment and was not to be questioned.

"Name?" asked a burly woman whose smock had a western theme — horseshoes, saddles, and bright pink rope — and a name badge that read POGEL.

I knew I wouldn't make any points by telling her that her name was close to the acronym POGAL, for "precision optics grinder and lathe," a special grinding machine developed at a national lab in California.

"Dr. Gloria Lamerino," I said, wishing I were wearing my old lab coat.

Ms. Pogel didn't seem impressed by my confident manner. She consulted a computer database. "Sorry. Ms. Sanders has requested only certain visitors. You're not on the list." She gave me a withering look, meant to send me far away from her desk.

"I wasn't aware that they'd forgotten to call my name in," I said, congratulating myself on quick thinking.

Nurse Pogel frowned at me. "Well, now you know."

Foiled. I slunk back from the station and took a seat in a small waiting area, outside Ms. Pogel's peripheral vision, to rethink my strategy. I glanced over at the well-staffed nurses' station and felt overwhelmed.

"Ms. Sanders."

I thought I was hearing an echo of my own voice, except it came from a tall young man with reddish-brown hair. He'd approached the desk in the same confident manner I'd tried.

"I'm her fiancé, and I should be on a list. Zachary Landram."

Zach. I remembered meeting him the

other day when he'd had simply boyfriend status.

"ID, please."

Nurse Pogel wasn't making it easy for Zach, either. I strained my ears, hoping she'd announce Dee Dee's room number.

No such luck. Apparently satisfied with Zach's ID, Nurse Pogel wrote something on a piece of paper. I could have sworn she glanced over her shoulder at me when she did it.

Zach wore a heavy army-green overcoat and a yellow and red plaid scarf. Easy to follow down a corridor. I stood and straightened my clothes. I headed in the same direction he did.

I'd taken four steps when Nurse Pogel marched out from behind the desk and blocked my path. "Is there something else I can help you with, Dr. Marino?" she asked.

She didn't seem to be in the mood to be corrected. "Not at the moment," I said, defeated.

I turned and walked toward the large glass exit doors. I'd found out one thing, at least: The police had already talked to Dee Dee. Otherwise Zach wouldn't have been admitted to see her.

I wasn't happy with my lack of progress.

On the street I began what I knew would

be the long process of getting a cab to the hotel.

I'd never felt so frustrated. Since arriving in New York, I'd been unable to help a woman dying at my feet, then incompetent at assisting in finding her killer. My ozone lessons to the NYPD had been brief, and for all I knew, useless. In fact, I'd been more trouble than I was worth to them: I'd stolen a letter, causing the police and an ADA to waste valuable time figuring out what to do with me. The small connection I'd made between Dee Dee Sanders and Amber Keenan was moot since the police had already determined it.

Now I couldn't even get into a loosely secured medical facility to talk to a potential suspect.

New York is tough, I thought.

My ride to the hotel, when I finally caught one, was fast and wild. The driver wove the bright yellow cab in and out of traffic, leaning on his horn as he spoke a steady stream of dissonant sounds into his headset. At one intersection it was a face-off between the cab and an enormous office supply delivery truck. I decided he wasn't happy with this small fare — only about nine blocks down and two over — and wanted to get the job over with in a hurry. The music blaring through the speakers was unhummable, and the name on his ID card was hard to pronounce.

It was all a nice change from my taxi experiences so far, with the drivers asking, "Where are you from?" and the sounds of "O Come, All Ye Faithful" on their radios.

Thanks to the speed-of-light transportation, I arrived at the hotel early. I thought I might have time to call around to some of the less expensive hotels in the city.

Did a young blond man from Kansas check in last week? I could ask. Then what would I say? *This is his mother?*

I had a strange feeling as I made my way through the crowded lobby, past guests or passersby sitting on the couches and easy chairs, past a Christmas tree by the stairway to the mezzanine cocktail lounge and a menorah on the registration desk. I thought I saw Billy at one point, but it was another young man with the same straw-colored hair. Tina seemed to lurk behind a luggage dolly stacked with suitcases and duffel bags. A chubby woman on a settee, surrounded by luggage, sat with the same posture as Karla. Rounding a corner, I nearly tripped over stiletto-heeled boots, and my breath caught until I realized they weren't Dee Dee's.

I needed a break and a nap. I had at least a half hour before Rose was due back from her shopping trip. I hoped she hadn't bought me anything.

I walked to the back of the hotel, past telephone banks that stood unused. I remembered the old days of conferences in hotels, and the long phone lines at break times. Now the landlines bolted to the wall were like monuments to an earlier age.

Ping.

The elevator. I checked for the white up arrow and stepped into the car, grateful not to have to pull a folding metal door closed. Unlike the one in Lori's building, this elevator moved smoothly. As the wonders of machinery carried me upward, I stuffed my gloves into my tote and fished around for the card key in an outside compartment. I couldn't shake a chill and hoped the maid had left the heat in our room on high.

Whirrr.

The elevator whined to a stop. I looked at the LED display and saw it was black. No sleek red number to indicate the floor. I waited for the doors to open. It hadn't felt like nine floors of travel, but maybe someone on a lower floor had pushed the button. It could even be Rose, back early, traveling from six to nine.

A long time passed. Probably five seconds, I told myself, smiling at the recollection of an article I'd read: People waiting for an elevator started getting impatient only seven seconds after pushing the call button.

I relaxed, thinking how short a time ago Polaroid photographs were a brand-new concept, and now they were too slow for modern life. I doubted Karla's son, William, would give a second look to any accessory that didn't plug into his computer. I patted my digital camera through the leather of my purse and resolved to take more advantage of it for the rest of the trip. Maybe catch some of those spectacular views of Central Park I heard the Sassos enjoyed from their apartment windows on the Upper West Side.

I checked my watch. I didn't have a starting point, but I'd have bet that more than seven seconds had passed. The car was still stopped. The doors remained closed.

The elevator was paneled in dark brown, with a brass rod across the back. I leaned against the pole and looked again at the display in the upper right corner of the car, shifting my head back and forth for a different reflection, to see if I could read a number.

Nothing.

I unbuttoned my coat, took off my scarf, and shoved it into my tote. My hand hurt, and I realized that I'd been digging the plastic card key into it. I put the card back into its compartment.

No need to panic yet, I told myself, looking at the knobby red alarm button. How embarrassing it would be to call out the cavalry and then start a smooth ascent to the ninth floor. I might learn that there'd been only a ten-second delay. I checked for a camera mounted on the ceiling but saw none. I saw the outline of a trap door but no way to open it. I suspected it was locked from the outside, available only to authorized rescuers.

I had a flashback to a story in the Berkeley newspaper about a fraternity prank where students figured out a way to climb onto the top of the cage of an elevator and had a beer party sitting right there. The incident resulted in a permanent termination of elevator service in the fraternity house.

I didn't need to think of spooky elevator stories, I told myself.

The only signage, lined up across the top of the elevator car, was advertising for the hotel restaurants. Looking at the backlit dinner plate, I involuntarily conjured up the smell of shrimp and felt a wave of nausea.

I pictured the figures in freshman physics books showing the force diagrams for a person in an elevator. I kept myself mentally occupied by recalling Newton's laws for the situation. If I were standing on a scale, with the elevator moving up at a uniform acceleration, the scale would read greater than my actual weight. If the cable were cut — here I gulped noisily — I'd be weightless, like an astronaut floating around in her spaceship.

The physics of the problem was unsettling, and so were the chemistry and biology. Fortunately, I didn't know off-hand how much oxygen was used up by a person per minute in a closed box.

I jiggled the STOP button, in case it was stuck somehow and that was the problem. It wasn't.

I pushed my cell phone buttons to call Matt. The only response on the green backlit screen was NO SERVICE.

I'll count to ten, I decided, *and if the car doesn't move, then I'll push the alarm button.* I took off my coat and let it drop to the floor. *One, two . . .*

Enough.

I leaned as hard as I could on the red button.

I wasn't ready for the silence. I expected loud clanging noises. I *wanted* loud clanging noises. *It's all right,* I thought. *A silent alarm, so we don't frighten all the guests.*

Just the one trapped in the elevator.

I desperately hoped there was an alarm sounding, a light blinking, a security guard's pager vibrating somewhere.

I pushed and pushed on the button, starting to hyperventilate.

Whirrr.

The car jolted into action. I let out a long, loud breath, close to a wail. I felt the car move. I stood still, sucking in my breath again. The machinery whirred, a comforting sound in ordinary conditions, but I couldn't move a muscle in anticipation of another malfunction, if that's what I'd experienced. I longed for the bumps and clanging noises of the old elevator on West Forty-eighth Street to tell me I'd reached some upward milestones.

Ping.

The elevator stopped again. This time the doors opened, and I was at the ninth floor. I rushed out of the car, leaving my coat behind. I glanced back while the doors were still open. My comfortable, old black coat, lying in a heap in the middle of the floor, beckoned, but the wide, gaping hole left by the opened doors was frightening, and I didn't dare enter the car again.

I rushed down the corridor to our room, digging the card key out. It took me three tries to get a green light.

Once inside I leaned against the door and tried to get my breathing to a normal rate. I tried to determine what had upset me so much and decided that if I'd been sharing the car with anyone at all, it would have been more bearable.

How many elevator cars were there in New York City? I asked myself. Thousands? Maybe tens of thousands. This afternoon one of them happened to malfunction, and I happened to be on it. That was all.

Still, my nerves were on edge.

Ring ring ring.

Three short, loud rings in quick succession. I jumped and dropped my key card. The elevator alarm, finally?

No. It was the hotel landline. We'd all been using our cell phones, and I'd never heard what the ring sounded like.

Ring ring ring.

I was startled again.

Ring ring ring.

I picked up.

"I'm back, Gloria. How was your day?" Rose's merry voice.

It took me a moment to adjust to the cheery sound. "I nearly suffocated in the elevator," I said, before I thought about it.

"I know. Those cars are so overheated, aren't they?"

"Right," I said, and collapsed on the bed.

CHAPTER
TWENTY-ONE

The dark young man at the desk, with RAN-JIT on his narrow name badge, was only too happy to check at Lost and Found for my coat.

"I still don't understand how you could have left it in the elevator," Rose said as we waited at the counter for his return. "It's not as if you had a lot of bundles." She frowned and squinted at me. "Did you go shopping without me?"

"No, Rose. I would never do that." I crossed my heart. "The coat just fell, and the doors closed before I could grab it."

It wasn't easy lying to my best friend, but the truth was too scary to relive and too embarrassing, given my overreaction.

I'd called down to the lobby and asked if there had been any reports of elevator problems in the last hour or so. None, I was told.

The thought of reentering the elevator to

go down to the lobby had been too much for me. I convinced Rose to come to my room first so she could help me choose which shoes to wear and we could ride down together. She took it as a chummy gesture and loved it.

"Well, I hope they don't find that coat," she said to me now.

"Rose!" I feigned shock, though I knew exactly what she had in mind — a little shopping trip to help me find a new, chic wrap like the one she'd bought that very day while cruising Madison Avenue with Grace.

"Here it is," the young man said with the smile of success.

Rose looked disappointed.

I snatched the coat and shook it out. Getting rid of the bad memories.

A doorman was on hand at the hotel entrance to hail a cab for us. We were to meet Matt at the Sassos' residence for dinner.

The ride to the Upper West Side was uneventful, compared to my earlier trip to the hotel. Compared to much of the last couple of days.

In between comments from Rose, acting like a tour guide as we passed the new Time Warner Center and various statuary at

Columbus Circle, I tried to rehearse bits of conversation that might lead to a discussion of Tina Miller, Amber Keenan, and a Fielding or two.

"I hope Karla can relax and not say a word about business," Rose said as we pulled up in front of the building. "Don't you?"

"My turn to pay," I said, unzipping my wallet.

The Sassos had a magnificent view of Central Park, leading me to think that all the photos I'd seen of the Wollman Rink through the years, some of them on holiday greeting cards, had been taken from their living room windows.

"Not many ice skaters out there tonight," Roland Sasso said. He poured sparkling water into lovely stemware for Matt and me as we all crowded around the window. "Too cold. The winters are getting worse. So many of our friends have moved to Florida, but could you give up this view?"

"I'd never get anything useful done," I said. I thought I saw a horse-drawn carriage circling one of the ponds but figured it was an imaginative addition to the scene on my part. Even without the magic of snow, the bare winter trees seemed strategically placed for maximum beauty and dramatic effect.

I'd had a decent view from the windows of my Berkeley condo, looking out over the University of California campus, its impressive campanile, and the San Francisco Bay. On a good day I could get a glimpse of Alcatraz and the Golden Gate Bridge. Here, the combination of Central Park's Great Lawn, the lakes, the gardens, and the monuments laid out against the layers of skyscrapers beat it all.

"Gloria's trying to see the Ice Cream Café," Rose said. "That's the way I used to get her to go from the Frick to the Met. I'd promise her a hot fudge sundae in between."

I wasn't sure I wanted to broadcast my lack of culture to the Sassos, but it wouldn't be breaking news to them, anyway, I decided. I'd met Roland, a manager of some of New York City's housing projects, a few times on his trips to Revere, and Grace on her more frequent visits to spend time with her grandson, William.

The couple were almost a duplicate pair to Rose and Frank. All four were trim in physique, elegant in dress and style. Grace and Rose had the same red highlights in their hair and shared a love of the finer things in home décor. As in the Galiganis' residence, everything in the Sassos' West

Seventy-fifth Street dining room matched. Wine glasses were all the same size, the silver a consistent pattern, and the china plates supported by larger pewter plates underneath them.

Karla's own kitchen in Revere, on the other hand, was homey. You could tell a teenaged boy lived there, and she'd be likely to hand you a bottle of mineral water without a glass. She wasn't what you'd call trim but fell somewhere between Rose and me on the BMI charts. Although her home wasn't as perfect and orderly as that of her parents or parents-in-law, Karla herself always looked ready to appear as an officer of the court, as she did tonight in a navy blue three-piece suit.

"It's terrific having you here, Gloria and Matt," Karla said, giving us each a spontaneous warm hug. "This is a great time of year to be in the city, isn't it? And I always wanted you to come to Mom and Dad's."

The tender, welcoming gesture caused me to wish I'd never heard of *Fielding v. Fielding.*

Rose's first order of business at dinner was to invite Karla and her parents to our wedding reception.

"Can't you just call it a party?" I whispered, not wanting to spoil the chicken with the sweet-smelling feta cheese and basil stuffing that Grace had served.

Rose glared at me. Not a hard glare, but a glare nonetheless.

"Gloria and Matt were married in September. Tell us about the ceremony, Gloria," Rose said.

My turn to glare.

Matt took the floor, so to speak. "It was nice and simple, at a B and B in Vermont at the height of foliage season. We had a minister from a local church who came right to one of the parlors. They have weddings there all the time."

"You mean *planned* weddings?" Rose asked.

Matt gave her a silent smile, then turned to me. "Gloria looked lovely."

How could I argue?

"What did you wear, Gloria?" Grace asked.

My first thought was *Nothing as wonderful as you're wearing tonight.* Grace had on silk pants and a tunic top in many shades of burgundy and gold, complementing her short brown-red hair. I knew her garnet pendant was not from an unjuried crafts fair at the local church. Roland's delicately knit beige sweater vest, worn under a brown sports coat, looked like silk also.

"Good question, Grace. I have no idea what you wore, Gloria," Rose said, clearly not uncomfortable sharing her distress with the Sassos.

"A dress and jacket."

"Matching?" Karla asked, suppressing a laugh.

"Yes, matching." I didn't mention that the sleeves of the jacket were too long and I'd pinned them up. I'd bought the outfit in a hurry at an outlet store on our drive north to Vermont.

"And Matt?" Roland asked. The Sassos were into this joke.

Matt looked down at his Wednesday suit.

Rose lowered her head and put her hand over her eyes.

"This," he said, trying to look sheepish but ending with a broad grin that made even Rose laugh.

Grace and Roland offered their guests the best east-facing view as we sat in the living room after dinner. Dessert was poached pear with ice cream and a delicious caramel biscotti sauce. Rose and I had brought truffles from a shop in Rockefeller Center, which nicely filled the chocolate gap.

Our storytelling tradition, reminiscent of kindergarten sharing time, extended to the

Sassos. I could hardly wait to hear Karla's story, but Matt, excited from his police museum visit, started off.

"Well worth the trip downtown, if you ever have the mind to. They've got photography exhibits and cases full of old uniforms and guns." Matt looked around the circle, gauging, I knew, whether this was the right audience for a discussion of revolvers, double-breasted jackets, and batons. He switched to department history, giving us an account of the first law enforcement officer in New York City. "His name was Johann Lampo, and he patrolled the streets, well, the trails and paths, in 1625, settling disputes, warning the citizens if a fire broke out at night, and so on."

"We would still have been called New Amsterdam back then, right?" Roland said.

"Yeah, and they called the residents 'the colonists.'" Matt paused and took a deep breath. "There's a 9/11 exhibit, too," he said. Everyone's head seemed to go down at the memory. "You really ought to see it."

"Kathleen Gustafson, the DMORT woman Frank and I met on Sunday, talked about 9/11 a lot," Rose said, her voice somber. "Dr. Gustafson's team was part of the emergency response in the days and weeks following. She said all told they processed more than fifteen thousand human specimens. Even after all this time, she remembers every detail of that day. I'm sure it will always be with her."

"It will always be with all of us," Roland said.

As if no other story could follow immediately after a reminder of the 9/11 attack, we all got up and refilled cups, visited the restroom, checked the view again, and came back to different seats in the living room.

Grace chose not to follow the how-was-your-day format we usually used. She took us back in time to her mother, an Austrian immigrant, who was milliner to the stars.

"Karla is named after my mother. She might have told you how her grandmother worked for Saks in the old days and did custom millinery for very famous and wealthy people," Grace said.

"I knew," Rose said, "but I don't think I've ever told Gloria."

Once I heard Grace's tales — that Sophie Tucker ordered one of her mother's designs in three colors; that Eleanor Roosevelt wore a special creation to one of FDR's inaugurations; that she had a contract with nearly every first lady for twenty years — I was surprised Rose hadn't told me.

Much as I enjoyed hearing about celebrity hats, I was itching to hear Karla. When she finally took a turn, she began with her "jerk of the year, who shall go nameless here." I had a feeling she adapted the title to substitute "jerk" for what was probably a stronger, more contemporary epithet, for the benefit of the elders in the room.

"This guy, we'll call him Joe, it's his mother's ninetieth birthday. So he plans a big party. Nice, huh? But he plans a *ski trip.* Now, the woman can barely walk."

"Tell them what he said, about how his mother could spend the time," Grace prompted.

"He said she could sit in the lodge and drink hot chocolate. So this poor old woman would be up in the mountains of New Hampshire, away from all her support system, all her doctors, sitting in a ski lodge while everyone else is having a good time. I ask you, who is this ski trip for?"

"People can be thoughtless sometimes," Rose said. This was about as harsh as Rose could be about another human being.

"No wonder my client wants to be rid of him. She cares more about her mother-in-law than the woman's own son does," Karla said.

Is your client's name Fielding? I wanted to ask. In the back of my mind all evening had been the question of how — or whether — to bring up Amber Keenan or Tina Miller. I wanted desperately to clear Karla in my mind of any wrongdoing, victimless or otherwise.

I saw my opportunity when Matt and Roland left the living room to look through Roland's collection of jazz.

Rose was the only one left who might mind my bringing up something work related to Karla, but Karla had already opened that door, as they say in the courtroom, by talking about "Joe."

I couldn't think of a smooth segue, so I decided to go with a rough one. "By the way, did you hear about the young woman murdered in a loft downtown?" I asked Karla and Grace. "Amber Keenan. She was Matt's niece Lori's camerawoman."

Rose frowned, as if the mention of the crime had turned her French vanilla sour.

I searched Karla's face for a telltale response on hearing Amber's name. I caught a nervous twitch but knew that I might have placed it there myself, like a Photoshop embellishment to a snapshot.

"Mom told me," Karla answered. "What an awful thing."

Now what? I hadn't planned very far ahead, I realized. Might as well spell it out. "Amber also worked for a private investigator, Tina Miller, and some lawyers in town." An exaggeration, but not my first. "So I thought you might have run into her."

"It's a big city, Gloria," Rose said. "And there must be a million lawyers."

"Almost," Grace said. "Didn't you tell me there were nearly thirty thousand attorneys in Manhattan alone, dear?" she asked Karla.

"Something like that." Karla's tone said she'd rather talk about anything else.

"Karla could make ten times more money in New York, but she can't talk Robert into moving back here," Grace said.

Rose's eyebrows went up higher than I'd ever seen them. "Of course, for Robert it wouldn't be moving *back*," Rose said, with a thin smile.

Congratulations, Gloria, I told myself, *you've managed to create tension in an otherwise ideal family gathering.*

I knew that the subject of long-distance families had come up before, with the Sassos often complaining how hard it was to be part of their grandson's life when he lived so far away. By California standards, the distance between Boston and New York, about a four-hour drive, was trivial: If you could leave your home in the morning and be at your destination by lunchtime, you were almost neighbors.

"I don't know what I was thinking," I said. "Of course there are tens of thousands of lawyers in New York City. Sorry." Looking at Karla's face, though, I was glad I'd raised the issue.

My bumbling remarks were rewarded a half hour later in the kitchen. Matt and Roland were still back in the den. I could hear strains of a Cab Calloway album that I recognized from Matt's collection at home.

Rose and Grace were talking about fabric Grace had bought. I realized with astonishment that it was for a dress Grace would wear to my upcoming wedding party. I remembered Rose's telling me that Grace was an accomplished seamstress and still did freelance dressmaking for many celebrities, whose names had all escaped me.

Karla pulled me aside, leading me toward a corner of the kitchen where the noisy dishwasher provided cover for her voice.

"What's up, Gloria?" she whispered. "Are you trying to set me up in my own parents' home?" Karla seemed to be struggling to walk a line between anger and the respect she'd always shown for me.

"You tell me, Karla. Why did you deny knowing Tina Miller?"

"I don't see why it matters."

"It matters. Did you have dealings with Amber Keenan?"

Karla took a deep breath and leaned on the marble counter, no longer facing me directly. "Not exactly."

"Does that mean *approximately?*"

I saw part of a smile in her profile, in spite of the tension that had arisen between us.

Karla picked up a colander and pretended to dry it when Rose's and Grace's voices seemed to grow louder.

"False alarm," I said, as the two women retreated again to Grace's workroom. "Please tell me, Karla, or . . ." *I'll think the worst* came to my mind, but I trailed off instead of admitting it.

"I talked to her, okay? We met through Tina. You may not be aware of this, but Amber was a . . . not a nice person. She had access to every dirty deed filed away in Tina's office. A lot of times a client or a client's spouse will have a shady past, and it would be very bad for them if it came to light."

"Like Mr. Fielding?"

Karla turned to face me, her eyes wide. She might have been looking at a witch with

314

superpowers instead of just a nosy pseudo-aunt. "Gloria, do you know my client list now?"

"Karla, I know about Amber's schemes. Did she want something from you?"

Karla nodded. "She needed a lawyer in her pocket, for referrals. Someone to tell her who was financially a good candidate. We never talked about a specific client, though now that I think of it, Fielding would have been a good candidate. I guess you could say she wanted to expand her business."

Maybe Amber should have been among New York's most successful businesswomen of the year. Except it might have been her business that killed her, with one of the Fieldings, or any number of other so-called clients, involved. My head reeled as I considered the possibilities and how lacking I was in the information necessary to rout them out.

I was also upset that I'd put my best friend's daughter-in-law through an ordeal that served only to bring her distress and shed no light on the murder investigation.

"I'm sorry, Karla. I —"

"Gloria, believe me, I feel better talking to you. I swear to you, I never, ever helped Amber. I'm embarrassed to think I considered it for a split second. I have no doubt that she got to some of my clients another way. She had this way of making things sound so innocent and appealing."

"So I've heard."

"Every time I bumped into her in the office after that, I felt guilty, even though I didn't do anything wrong."

"Do you think Tina was involved in Amber's business?"

"Off the top of my head, I'd say no, though we never discussed it. It's just that Tina's a no-nonsense person, and I think she would have fired Amber on the spot if she knew. Many's the time I thought of telling her, but then I decided, no, just keep out of it. It's not that I could have proven anything. Just my word against hers. Now, of course, I wonder, if I had spoken up . . ."

Lori and I weren't the only ones wondering if we could have prevented Amber's death, it seemed.

"How about Dee Dee?"

"Geesh, Gloria. Is there anyone you don't know? I can see how you'd have connections in Revere, but I'm amazed that you were able to put all this together in Manhattan."

Karla's smile told me she'd dropped her defenses, and I consoled myself with the thought that my nosiness might at least have relieved her of pent-up guilt or stress.

"I'll take that as a compliment." I smiled, thinking of how Matt would have responded. That kind of question always drew his *It's what I do.*

"I'm not so sure about Dee Dee," Karla said. "In a way she was a better link, with not so much to lose as Tina. She had all the files at her fingertips, but I can't say for sure. Like I said, I just tried to keep my distance. When I heard Amber was murdered, I thought about how close I'd come. I mean, *I* could have been killed, Gloria."

"Did you think of going to the police then?" I asked.

Karla shivered. When the dishwasher made a loud noise switching to its next cycle, she jumped. "Of course I did, but I had nothing. We never talked specifics. It was all this general *Hypothetically, suppose a person had a past he was ashamed of . . .*"

Karla was struggling to keep her makeup intact, dabbing here and there at her face with a tissue. I looked at her straight on and knew I should believe her.

As sorry as I was that I'd put her through a grilling, I was thrilled to be able to scratch Karla Sasso off my list.

In the taxi on the way back to the hotel, I mulled over the events of the day and my next steps. An update on Karla Sasso and the Fielding nonconnection would have to wait until Matt and I were alone in our room.

I'd decided not to tell Matt or Rose my elevator story. By now the event had faded, and I saw it for what it was: a brief glitch in a machine. Still, I couldn't imagine ever stepping into an empty elevator again. Fortunately the number of elevators in Revere was limited; most of them were in the new high-rise apartment houses that had replaced the amusements on Revere Beach Boulevard.

"You're going off to work with Lori tomorrow, right?" Rose asked, as the cab ducked in and out of lines of traffic heading south.

"Yes, we're going to Curry Industries in the afternoon."

Oops. I shouldn't have put limits on my time not available for shopping.

"So we could do something in the morning," Rose said.

Too late. "What did you have in mind?"

"Aren't you all shopped out, Rose?" asked

318

Matt, who should have known better.

"I have everything but your present, Matt."

"Good one," he said.

I wondered if I could commission Rose to pick out Matt's present from me. I'd come to New York thinking all the city's energy and resources would give me an idea of what to get him for Christmas. So far the only thing that emerged as a possibility was a book of Yogi Berra quotes.

Matt was half asleep as I finished up my Karla briefing, but I wanted to be rid of the issue once and for all, so I pushed forward on it from my side of the bed.

"So Fielding was Karla's client and Amber's victim, but I really believe Karla had nothing to do with blackmailing him. Amber fished around in the files — with or without Dee Dee's help — and approached all the lawyers Tina worked with, for fodder. I'm convinced Karla resisted the temptation."

Our usual pillow talk.

"That's a relief," Matt said, wiping his brow. Not easy to do from his prone position, he had to hoist himself on his elbow to accomplish it.

"I know you think I see nonexistent connections everywhere, whereas you never were worried about this."

"I'm just amazed that while I was listening to music with Roland, smoking a cigar, you were on the job."

I raised my eyebrows. "Smoking?"

"Gotcha. Now that I have your attention — have you given any thought to going home?"

"Home? To Revere?"

"Apparently not."

"Goodnight, honey," I said.

CHAPTER
TWENTY-TWO

Lori had cabin fever. She'd stayed cooped up in her apartment since Uncle Matt and Gloria left, missing a gorgeous afternoon. She picked at leftovers from lunch and paced the long wooden floor. She walked to the large window on the West Forty-eighth side, separated two adjacent slats on her old metal blinds, and checked the street. This time the unmarked was for her protection, at least, and not to drag her away.

The breeze that wafted through a window facing east was cold and crisp, with a dryness that made the air crackle — her favorite walking weather. If it weren't for her fears, she'd be out walking right now, soaking up the energy, getting inspired, meditating.

That was exactly what she was going to do.

It was just getting dark. She'd go for a walk and later grab the subway to SoHo and cruise some of the shops, take in a movie at the Angelika, maybe get an idea for her next video. Lori wasn't one to work on only one program at a time, especially now that she felt she had a real handle on this ozone project.

Always be on the lookout for the next subject, she reminded herself, remembering the day she wrote that in class and underlined it.

Lori got dressed — short skirt, boots, and the only jungle print she owned, a short, faux-fur-lined jacket, just for moods like this.

She left her building and headed west toward Eighth, waving to the cops in the sedan as she passed them, on the other side of the street. She wondered if they had a photo of Billy taped to the dashboard — well, that was how they did stakeouts in the movies, anyway. She hoped by now they'd cleared up the little problem with Billy's story.

She turned south on Eighth and stopped to look at fuzzy scarves hanging from a makeshift post. The street vendor was packing up. Sometimes you got deals if the guy wanted to push some goods quickly before he left for the day. She tried to figure how long the feathery scarf fad would last and whether she should bother buying some yarn and knitting a few for Christmas presents. She'd done a pathetic job so far on her list, but maybe she could get back on track now.

Behind the vendor, at the curb, was a mounted policeman, his pale blue helmet catching light from a streetlamp just coming on. Lori wondered if it was the same redheaded cop who'd blocked her out of her apartment the other day. The cop had pulled his horse between two parked cars. Two young women in tight jeans and jungle prints not unlike her own were cozying up to the horse and rider.

"So, you have any advice on where to have a good time around here?" one young woman asked the cop. She ran her hand along the yellow band across the animal's forehead.

The horse had reflector lights strapped to its ankles. Lori wouldn't have been surprised if there was some kind of mechanism in the lights to keep the animals docile while cars whizzed by and single women flirted with their riders.

"You asking about a good time in New York?" The cop snorted, the way Lori imagined his horse would while clearing his nostrils. "All over the place. There's all kindsa things goin' on."

"How about you? Where do you go for a good time?" the other woman asked, twirling her scarf, a pink and turquoise boa.

Lori dropped the nubby peach and cream scarf she'd been thinking of buying. She contemplated giving up all the scarves she now owned, trading them in for a good, smooth-textured, woolen one. As of this moment, the fashion had run its course as far as she was concerned.

The cop laughed, tilting his head back. "Me? Hey, I'm married, you know. But tell me what kinda guys you're lookin' for. I know a lot of single cops, believe me."

Lori moved on, smiling. It was the little things in New York City, she mused — things like these one-minute vignettes — that made a filmmaker's life easy.

An image of the letter with the vague threats flashed through Lori's mind, ruining her good mood. She'd been so worried about it since she learned it wasn't junk mail. *Enough people have been hurt. Do not expose this.*

Uncle Matt told her about the similar note the cops had found in Amber's apartment. That letter had talked about footage. Maybe if she'd seen the word "footage" in her own mail she would have responded more like a professional investigator. She might have tried to determine the origin from the partial logo.

Funny how she lost her journalistic edge when it came to her personal life.

Lori tried to rid her mind of the whole affair, but the cartoonish family logo stuck in her mind. It seemed downright twisted, the contents of the letter being so *not* family-friendly.

Closer to Times Square, Lori cut over to Broadway, where the crowds were elbow to elbow from the store and restaurant windows all the way out to the curb. There was nothing like teeming masses to give you anonymity and the freedom to let your mind wander. Lori loved it. She did her best thinking while she was walking on a street bustling with activity or sitting alone in the middle of a busy coffee shop. Now that most cafés had Internet access, her home-away-from-home offices were even better.

Just before the next intersection Lori stopped in her tracks, an idea taking hold. This maneuver nearly caused the couple behind her holding hands to trip over her. *Even pedestrians tailgate in New York City,* she thought.

She crossed the street to the semicircular driveway of a big hotel and got in line for the cab dispatcher, ignoring the sign about the service being for hotel residents only. *As if!*

She was about sixth in line. Definitely a better shot than trying to wave down a cab on her own. After a few cold minutes, she was on her way.

"Family Suites Hotel," she told the cabbie.

Lori had asked to be let out a block away from Family Suites so she could get her bearings and a feel for the area. She'd never been on this street, but she was pretty familiar with the Lower East Side from the days when she volunteered at the Tenement Museum. She knew she was close to the leather district and other trendy shopping. Every other parking meter had a bike attached to it with a simple chain, so the residents must have some feeling of security, Lori thought.

Here and there she saw a new high-rise apartment house with still-unweathered light red brick, but the deep red hues of the older tenements reminded her of an Edward Hopper painting. Like many New York neighborhoods, this one would look better on the inside than the outside, Lori was sure. She remembered tracking down an address in a district that was new to her and being put off by graffiti on all the roll-up metal security doors; once inside the building, she'd found fresh paint, polished fixtures, and newly sanded floors. Not that much different from her own building, now that she thought of it, which was no treat to look at on the outside.

Family Suites was in the middle of a block. She hoped it had undergone a similar interior renovation, because it was about as run-down a place as she'd seen. Not one you'd be likely to take your kids to without a solid recommendation.

Also, she'd happened to choose the evening before rubbish pickup for this zone. She passed mounds of black garbage bags at the edge of the sidewalk, toppling into the gutter and often in her path. From the smell Lori figured more than one of them had sprung a leak.

She smiled at the sign warning about a penalty for honking your horn. In fact, the traffic was relatively quiet, she noticed, now that she was paying attention. Now *there* was a tough job for a cop — find the honking horn and slap a fine on it.

Lori realized she had no plan for what she would do once inside the hotel. It wasn't as if she had a photo of Billy Keenan to show the clerk. She recalled the familiar scene replayed on so many TV crime dramas: The cop shows a photograph to someone behind a counter. *Have you seen this man around here?* She should have thought to look among Amber's things to see if there was a snapshot of her brother, although the police still had most of what Amber had left behind in her corner of the loft.

She should at least be able to finagle a copy of the letterhead to compare with the partial logo on the letter she'd received, to be sure the note originated here.

A card shop across the street gave Lori an idea. Sure enough, they had a small office supply section. Lori bought an inexpensive leather-like portfolio. She wished she hadn't worn her jungle print jacket, but she couldn't afford to buy a new coat just for a prop. She tucked her hair demurely under her black chenille hat and pulled at her skirt. She'd have to wing it.

She climbed the half flight to the front entrance of Family Suites and opened the door. She was in luck. Not a scary dump. The lobby was small but well maintained, decorated with tall plants — she couldn't tell if they were real or not — and a single grouping of a wicker sofa, three easy chairs, and a small table with a lamp.

Lori approached the registration desk, waiting her turn after a man in a dark overcoat. The clerk was young and pimply, as she'd hoped. She wasn't ready to deal with a veteran of the hotel wars. The lobby was otherwise empty, not a family in sight.

The dark overcoat slipped away toward the elevator. Time for Lori's performance. She cleared her throat and silently rehearsed a more professional-sounding name than Lori Pizzano.

"Good afternoon, Ms. Margaret Burnside, of Cutting Edge Stationery," Lori said. She placed her new portfolio on the counter, hoping there was no other price tag than the one she'd peeled off moments before. She extended her hand. "Eddie, is it?" she asked, reading his cab-yellow name badge. "I'm here about the new stationery designs you wanted to talk about. I know I'm a little late, but my plane was delayed."

Eddie, who reminded her of the pudgy boy everyone laughed at in seventh grade, scratched his head. "Gee, nobody told me about this. And there's nobody else here right now," he said. Lori wondered if he heard her sigh of relief.

Lori clicked her tongue, an I'm-slightly-annoyed sound. "Well, that's disappointing," she said.

"I'm really sorry. You probably made the

appointment with Mr. Braguine, the manager."

Lori nodded. "Yes, that was the name."

"He won't be in until the morning, about ten o'clock. I have his emergency number."

A stationery emergency? Lori waved her hand. "No, no, I suppose my secretary could have gotten the message wrong. Well, how about this, can you at least get me a copy of your current letterhead?"

"You mean, like the paper and envelopes?"

"Yes, the paper and envelopes," Lori said. *Geesh.*

Eddie reached down and fumbled for a few seconds and came up with an information folder like the kind in hotel rooms everywhere. "It's all in here," he said, poking at the package with a chubby finger.

Though she'd known what to expect, Lori's stomach did a small flip when she saw the logo on the outside of the folder. Multicolor stick figures. Mommy in red with a triangle skirt, Daddy in blue, and a gender-neutral green and yellow child between them. "Thank you," she said. "I'll start with this."

"Okay, and I'm sorry about the appointment and all."

"Well, you've been very helpful. Oh, one other thing. Would you mind terribly if I just sit here in the lobby for a few minutes and catch up on my paperwork? I've been traveling all day." Lori hoped all this lying counted as a research technique and was not a sin. Or, even more important to her earthly life, a crime.

Three young women entered the lobby, probably for legitimate reasons, distracting Eddie for a moment. He turned back to Lori. "Uh, sure. I guess it would be okay," he said to Lori, scratching his head again and making Lori wonder about when the exterminator was next due to visit the building.

"Thanks so much," Lori said. She pretended to fish around in her empty portfolio. "I guess I'm out of business cards, but I'll write down my contact information before I leave."

By now Eddie's attention had shifted entirely to the new customers, who'd produced a printout of a reservation form.

Lori sat on one of the dark wicker easy chairs where she was partly hidden but could see both the front entrance and the bank of elevators. What had made her think this was a good idea? she asked herself. Even if she did see Billy, it wouldn't mean he'd been here longer than since Monday. Nor would it mean he wrote the notes.

Well, it was warm inside and she had nothing better to do. She settled back and surveyed the lobby, making a note of the location of the exit signs. She wouldn't want to miss someone coming in a side door.

She wished she'd thought to bring a Thermos of coffee, to make the picture complete.

Forty or so minutes later, Lori was about to call it quits. If Billy ever did have a room here, he'd probably checked out anyway. There was very little traffic in the lobby, and she couldn't stay much longer without appearing suspicious. It was hard to fake paperwork when all she had was her small steno notebook and the folder Eddie had given her. Besides, the thin pad on the wicker chair was getting uncomfortable. Eddie glanced over at her every now and then, causing Lori's heart to skip as she imagined his finally seeing through her act and calling the police about a fraud and a loiterer.

Lori made a show of zipping up her portfolio after a fruitful work session.

Ping.

The elevator doors opened, as they had about every ten minutes since Lori arrived. She barely gave them a glance this time. Then she stopped halfway off the chair and sat back down.

One of two women exiting the elevator looked familiar. Lori squinted to favor her long-distance eye. Rachel Hartman? Well, well, it *was* the PR woman from Blake Manufacturing. She was with a woman of approximately the same height, a little younger, and much frumpier.

Her sister from L.A. Lori remembered Rachel's comment about her sister and downtown lodging.

Lori used her elbow to push her purse to the floor behind the small table next to her, between her chair and the sofa. She twisted around to retrieve the bag, turning her back on the women, fumbling until she was sure they'd passed her.

Rachel Hartman was writing threatening letters to her and Amber? Or, even more incomprehensible, Rachel's sister, if that's who the other woman was, authored the letters?

Lori had no idea what to do. They were still at the exit, wrapping scarves around their necks and pulling on gloves. Lori could hear part of their conversation — bits of weather talk mostly, plus the mention of a martini. Rachel's distinctive voice, with its slight lisp, ended whatever uncertainty Lori had about who the woman was.

She thought of confronting the women. She might ask them, *Have you written any letters lately?*

Not a good idea. She considered waiting until they left, then going to the desk again, to see if she could find out Rachel's sister's name, room number — something that might give her a clue as to whether the letters were generated by either of them. No, she'd shot her wad with Eddie; she couldn't make up another story for him.

When the two women left the building, Lori gathered her things quickly and followed them out the door. The good news was that Eddie must have been on a break in back and didn't see this part of her act.

Her ad hoc plan was to follow Rachel and her companion at a discreet distance — but just as Lori got to the street, she saw her marks get into a cab, probably the quickest pickup she'd ever seen. Why wasn't taxi service slow when you needed it to be?

Lori let out a long sigh, watching her breath float after the cab, disappointed in her own investigative skills.

For now she'd have to be content with a folder of Family Suites stationery and information as the fruit of her labor. She'd lost her desire to cut over a couple of streets to the major shopping area and decided to go home instead. She had homework to do for tomorrow's meeting at Curry Industries, and maybe a glass of wine would help her figure out how and if Rachel was connected to the threatening letters.

Lori walked to the nearest subway stop and headed down the stairs. No way would two fares be lucky in the same place on the same night, she thought — it would be impossible to catch a cab before she froze to death.

On the train rattling through a tunnel somewhere between West Fourth Street and Twenty-third Street, Lori's subconscious kicked in and made some connections. She needed to cue up the Blake video and look more closely at the ankle Craig had been so fascinated by.

CHAPTER
TWENTY-THREE

Lori got to work as soon as she shed the several pounds of outer clothing it took to keep her warm in these temperatures. She was glad she'd left the heat up in the apartment while she was gone. Wasteful, but she figured it was an okay trade-off for having no A/C in the summer.

She loaded the Blake video into her second VCR, next to her computer, plugged her video capture card into a USB port, and hooked the patch cable to her Mac. She clicked on the editing suite and brought up the footage. Not footage anymore, she thought, just a bunch of pixels.

On the subway Lori had remembered the strange scene on the Blake video at the end of the series of welding interviews. When Lori had first seen the image she'd had the same thought as Craig — someone was doing the deed on the floor of an office in the Blake Manufacturing building. But the woman who belonged to the foot could have been crawling around the floor to find something she'd dropped.

Or maybe she'd fainted. Lori gulped. Or was dead.

Back to the adulterer theory, she thought, pushing a vision of Amber away. Maybe it would have been better if she'd seen Amber's body, instead of having her mind conjure up one horrible scene after another as it had been doing the last few days.

Now she'd try to determine if that was Rachel on the video. Rachel's calf and foot, anyway. It was a long shot, but worth a try. Maybe she'd be able to tell whose office the person was in or see a snatch of clothing of the alleged sex partner.

She pulled her chair closer to the monitor and found the frames she needed: most likely an office floor, showing the edge of a desk, the bottom of a file cabinet, and a woman's leg, from midcalf to shoe. With her box tool she drew dashed lines around the file cabinet, capturing the top of the lower drawer. She zoomed in. Maybe the printed label would tell her something. She clicked in as far as she could, but all she could make out were letters of the alphabet, *N* — or *M?* — to *T*. Nothing useful.

Lori stepped along, frame by frame, moving across the floor to the woman's leg, down to her ankle, until she came to a bracelet. *Aha.* She remembered that Rachel wore an ankle bracelet on the day of their interview — *and so did fifty percent of the women in Manhattan,* Lori thought. Her memory of the design of Rachel's bracelet wasn't that good, either, just that it was gold and shiny and had a flat plate where a name might have been engraved. Another dead end.

She scanned forward and backward among the frames a few times and finally gave up. Lori knew that even with all her zooming and enhancement capabilities she wouldn't be able to find what wasn't on the tape in the first place, and that was determined by the camera settings. She and Amber shook their heads all the time over television crime shows where a technician would enhance a videotape of a license plate that was shot at a great distance, or a blurry reflection from a mirror, and the images would end up clearer than if you'd been standing there.

Right now she wished she could zoom up and see if there was a name and title on that office door. Preferably PRESIDENT, or better yet, MARRIED PRESIDENT WITH A LOT TO LOSE. Speaking of a lot to lose, Rachel might be in deep trouble if whoever was subsidizing her lifestyle found out. It took a minute for Lori to admit to herself the extent to which she was building a case out of pure imagination. She had no direct evidence that Rachel even *had* a sugar daddy, let alone one who would object to extracurricular activities. For all she knew, Rachel's ankle was in the sugar daddy's office.

Nevertheless, she told herself, she did some of her best work this way. There was nothing wrong with a little wild theorizing as long as no one was listening just yet.

If that shapely calf was Rachel's, then it was likely that Rachel was another potential victim for Amber. Lori figured Rachel approached Amber and tried to talk her out of blackmailing her. When that didn't work, she wrote threatening letters, including one to Lori just in case. She'd obviously gotten smarter the second time, with Lori's letter, and had torn off the letterhead.

The big question was, Did Rachel stop at letters, or did she end up suffocating Amber with one of Lori's pillows? The police had taken the offending pillow, but Lori still glanced over at her couch, where similar ones were stacked, and shivered.

The second big question was what she

should do next. She could go to the NYPD directly, or to Uncle Matt, but with what? The tape certainly didn't show anything incriminating, not even that it was definitively Rachel on the floor.

She thought back to their interview. What if she had Rachel's fingerprints on something? The police could compare them to the prints on the two letters they had in custody. If Rachel was dumb enough to leave the hotel letterhead intact the first time, she probably didn't use gloves to handle the paper.

Too bad Lori hadn't stuck one of those expensive china teacups in her purse. Rachel had offered to take her jacket, but Lori had kept it. Well, probably fingerprints didn't stick to fabric anyway. It would have to be wood or ceramic or paper or —

Paper. That was it. She jumped up and went to her desk. Luckily she hadn't tossed the PR package Rachel had foisted on her.

Lori rushed back to the kitchen, found her rubber gloves under the sink, and looked for a plastic storage bag big enough to hold the nine-by-twelve envelope. She settled for a freezer bag from the bagel shop and carefully inserted the package. *Too little, too late,* she thought, but she might as well do what she could to preserve any evidence.

An image flashed through Lori's mind. Rachel's ankle bracelet again. *What if . . .*

She removed the envelope from the bag and emptied the contents onto her kitchen counter. Rachel had mentioned a recruiting brochure in the packet.

There it was, and sure enough the team photo on the cover featured Rachel standing at the front tip of a small triangle of people. *Rachel Hartman, PR, and her team,* the caption said.

Rachel Hartman had a wide smile across her face and a thin bracelet around her ankle.

Lori switched from her thick kitchen gloves to the thin white cotton gloves she kept handy in the darkroom and took the brochure to her scanner. What she needed was a dual image on the screen so she could compare bracelets. The triangle of people had been shot from an angle, from above, but Amber had shot from above also. Not the same angle, since in the brochure photo Rachel was upright on the lawn in front of Blake's, but it might work.

Lori scanned in the front page of the brochure and worked at the two pictures on her monitor — the frame from the office video and the photo from the brochure — so the dual images were the same size and magnification. No doubt in Lori's mind. It was the same ankle and the same bracelet. She figured the NYPD had a better system and could make some meaningful measurements, but this was a good start.

She printed out the two photos and looked up at the clock over the sink. Eight ten. Not a good time to reach Uncle Matt. She remembered they were all going to visit someone in Rose's family in the West Seventies. She'd be seeing Gloria tomorrow afternoon at Curry's. That would be soon enough to lay out her theory and her evidence.

Lori went to the window and peeked through the blinds. The unmarked was there. Nothing to worry about. It wasn't as if Rachel was going to come after her tonight. Funny how Uncle Matt thought it was Billy Keenan she should be wary of.

"Make up an excuse for him to not come here," he'd said.

She drew a nervous breath and stretched out on her couch. After a minute she got up, took the remaining pillows that matched the one used to smother Amber to the kitchen, and stuffed them all into a large garbage bag. She dragged the bag across the loft to the fire escape window and threw the pillows four stories down to the Dumpster. She should have done that right away.

She checked the chain on her door and went back to her pillowless couch.

Lori woke up with a stiff neck, disoriented, and hungry. Midevening naps were not her norm. Neither was skipping dinner. It was almost ten o'clock, and as good as lunch had been, it was way too long ago. If she was going to work for another couple of hours she needed sustenance.

She was glad her fridge was full of leftovers from Raoul's. Lori piled a plate with helpings of roast chicken and olive salad and two slices of dill bread. She grabbed a sesame cookie from the jar on the counter on her way to the living room.

This session called for her TV setup only. She planned just to review the latest Curry DVD so it would be fresh in her mind for tomorrow. She shifted a couple of pillows from her chairs to the couch and placed her dinner and a glass of white wine on the coffee table. She'd spend a few minutes reviewing the video and then take a break and watch the news or a Lifetime movie.

Lori looked through the DVDs on her Currently Active shelf. She plucked CURRY II, the second of the Curry DVDs Amber had burned. The police still hadn't returned all her videos. She pictured some rookie bleary-eyed going through boring outtakes.

She opened the neon green jewel case and stared at the round label on the disk inside.

Julia Roberts, her hair blond and in an upsweep, carrying a child, looked off to the side of the cover art.

What?

A DVD of the movie *Erin Brockovich* was in the case marked CURRY II: CFCS. Strange. How had this happened? Where was the CURRY II disk?

A *duh* moment. She must have put the Curry DVD in the *Erin Brockovich* case she'd returned to the video store.

She'd recently rented *Erin.* It was the kind of movie she wished she'd written — a little person bringing a big corporation to its knees. Like the old Paul Newman favorite *The Verdict,* but with even wider social consequences. She'd studied *Erin* and then returned it when she got her third late notice from Red Carpet Video. She hadn't gotten around yet to buying her own copy.

Now she wondered what was in the CURRY I case she'd given Gloria.

You'd think the video store would have called her. Probably some kid, like chunky Eddie at Family Suites, logged it in without opening the case, just marking time at a minimum wage job.

She picked up her landline and her address book and punched in the number for the video store.

"Red Carpet." After about ten rings, a voice as young as Eddie's. At least they were still open and had an actual human answering.

Lori told the clerk about leaving a personal DVD in the *Erin Brockovich* case.

"Oh, yeah. We were just going to call you."

Right. "Can I come down now and switch them?"

"Uh, no. We're almost closing. We open at nine tomorrow."

"I'm just a couple of blocks away, and I really need to see that other DVD."

"Sorry. I'm all packed up here, and I got a date. And you know you're gonna have to pay for the extra days."

"Yeah, yeah," Lori said, and hung up. Fat chance that guy had a date.

Not that she did, either. It had been a while, in fact. Too busy. She sighed loudly, puffing out her cheeks. More likely just too lazy to try again. She'd been with Sean for so long she didn't even know the dating protocol, as evidenced by her pitiful attempt with Craig.

Lori thought of the box full of photos she had of Sean and of the two of them together. She couldn't bring herself to toss them, but she didn't display them, either. They were in the basement with other relics of her past. She pictured Sean in a Back Bay apartment now with — who knew? — some hotshot lawyer. At least Sean had never lived in this loft, so it was easier to move on.

Well, no Curry footage, and certainly no date. The perfect excuse to watch a Lifetime movie. She had several in the bank on her DVR. She scrolled down the list. Kelli Martin and Tori Spelling in that cheerleader movie. Susan Lucci seducing her hunk of a contractor, with the sexy stubble on his cheeks. Nancy McKeon as a Mafia wife. Gail O'Grady leading three lives.

Lori clicked on the Mafia movie. She cleaned her plate of the last shreds of chicken and pasta, then leaned back. She was ready for Julia's brother, Eric Roberts, who always made a convincing bad guy.

Thump! Creak!

Lori snapped upright. The elevator. Passing the third floor. She pushed the mute button and tipped the glass of wine over putting the remote back on the table.

Click. Click. The noise sounded louder than a welding torch.

She sat still, listening.

She remembered the unmarked and took a breath. They must know not to let Billy up — but would they be suspicious of an attractive, nicely dressed woman?

Bzzzz. Bzzzz.

She tightened her sweater around her and went to the peephole.

CHAPTER
TWENTY-FOUR

"A hat shop? I don't think so," I told Rose at breakfast in the café attached to our hotel.

Matt and Rose had brought their outer clothing downstairs so they could leave after breakfast without going back to their rooms. It was the same at every table in the café — one chair per group was used exclusively to hold all the coats, scarves, hats, and gloves that were needed in the increasingly low temperatures outside. Although I'd planned to stay put for a while and use one of the computers at the back tables, I'd brought my outerwear, too. I tried to convince myself that it was *not* because I didn't want to take a chance on being in the elevator alone again.

Rose picked at a low-fat bran muffin. "Grace wants to show us the shop her mother opened up on her own years ago. It's over on East Sixty-fourth, off Lexington. The place has been sold many times over since then, and they've added some pre-made things, but they still do custom millinery for special clients."

"That's very interesting, Rose. I wish I could join you, but I have to do a little prep work for my trip to Curry Industries with Lori this afternoon."

Matt pretended to choke on a crumb. He and I should have been eating low-fat muffins, too. Instead Matt had a frosted lemon scone, and I was enjoying a thick slice of pumpkin bread with cream cheese frosting. A seasonal treat. Might as well have it while it was available, I told myself.

Rose looked at Matt, smiled, and pointed at me. "You'd think I'd be used to the idea that she'd rather be in a welding shop than a hat shop."

"They both take a lot of creativity," I said. A weak argument, one that made them both smirk.

"You don't see this kind of craft much anymore," Rose said. I assumed she meant hatmaking and not joining two metals together at high temperatures. "Young people don't even know what a milliner is."

"Are you planning to have a hat made for yourself?" Matt asked her.

"I'm thinking of ordering one for MC for Christmas, to go with the scarves I bought.

And maybe for Karla, too, as a surprise. They'd really be good for just about any-one."

I had a sudden insight into what Rose was getting at. "Not for me, Rose, okay?"

"Of course not." She cleared her throat. "I'd never buy you a hat, Gloria. Matt, maybe, but not you." Chuckles rippled through the air between the two of them. "Where are you going this morning? Want to meet us for lunch in Little Italy?"

"I have another cop date," Matt said.

Lori and I were due at Curry's at two o'clock. I could have an early lunch with my friend to make up for rejecting her hat shop — and her hat.

"I could meet you at, say, eleven thirty?"

"Grace likes the more upscale places down there," Rose said.

"I can do upscale."

Another choking sound from Matt.

"Good," Rose said. "I'll call you on your cell and tell you the address once we pick a spot."

Rose wrapped herself in her fashionable winter outerwear and went off to meet Grace. Matt stood and got ready to head in the opposite direction to a precinct on the West Side where he'd been invited to see the latest in gun technology.

"They call it a shot spotter," he said. "It does this computer calculation, and it can tell you almost exactly where the gun was located when the shot was fired. Some kind of automated triangulation, like figuring out where a telephone call came from."

It sounded a lot better than a hat shop.

"I'm glad you met so many nice people at the conference. I'll bet you could spend a week just taking them up on invitations to visit their squads."

"You mean you're glad I have enough to keep me busy."

I stirred my foam. "Well, that, too."

Rose had her felt and ribbons. Matt had his shot spotter. I had my DVD on chloro-fluorocarbons.

New York had something for everyone.

I took a seat at a new table at the back of the shop and slipped the Curry disk into the DVD drive on one of the PCs available for a small hourly fee.

I'd read through the Curry brochures Lori gave me and learned that the company made refrigeration products for large restaurants and supermarkets and for other commercial and industrial uses. Their literature contained detailed descriptions and photographs of enormous coolers and freezers and entire refrigerated buildings and vehicles. In case I'd ever need such information, a separate illustrated booklet gave me tips on icing problems in walk-in freezers.

The DVD was disappointing. Most of the content comprised headshots of administrators answering standard questions with stock answers. What did I expect from a company that made refrigerators? Nothing fascinating like cyclotrons or atomic force microscopes or grating spectrometers.

A young man at the computer station next to me in the bakery was watching an animated movie featuring creatures wearing headpieces that reminded me of welding helmets. Even his video looked more interesting than my upright freezer displays.

I turned back to my screen. Off camera, Amber asked questions of a group of men in suits and ties. It was unnerving to hear her soft, intelligent voice. I couldn't help picturing her in the only position I'd ever seen her in — dying at my feet. I had a hard time imagining her gentle intonations extorting money from devastated clients. Here, her tones were quiet and smooth, meant to evoke confidence and trust from her subjects. Not that it worked. The Curry subjects gave her the party line anyway.

"Do you believe that additional UV exposure due to ozone depletion will eventually be significantly harmful to humans?" Amber asked. She sounded as though she were reading from a script. I guessed that Lori had written it. The answers were equally scripted. (*No, the data showing the connection is weak, and such claims are premature* was the bottom line after three men spoke.)

Hmmm. I thought I'd read that the FDA found evidence linking sun exposure to skin cancer, with twice as many melanoma-caused deaths in lower latitudes, closer to the equator.

"Do you think the ozone depletion we've already measured is significant enough to warrant government regulations prohibiting CFCs?" (*No, the changes are too small to be concerned about,* said one executive after another.)

Hmmm. I knew that an infinitesimal amount of CFCs could deplete an enormous amount of ozone. Besides that, there were countless examples in science and mathematics to indicate that even a small change made to an apparently stable system could alter the system radically.

Would the bureaucratic answers have anything to do with the estimated 130 billion dollars it would take to refit industrial equipment across the country?

I was getting ready for my Curry meeting, all right, but not in a way that put me in a good mood.

I scanned past the boardroom scene to see if there was anything more riveting in later chapters on the disk. I played the DVD at regular speed now and then to hear bits from employees in work clothes on the plant floor.

A refrigeration and air-conditioning mechanic declared, "This is a cool career."

Cute.

A graduate of the New England Institute of Technology in Rhode Island explained his duties as "complex." "We have to read blueprints and do all the cutting and welding," he said.

I paused to learn the difference between *reach-ins* (refrigerators with pull-out trays, more like pizza ovens I'd seen) and *roll-ins* (refrigerators with space to wheel in an entire rack of many shelves).

"Five years ago I used to repair ice machines," another worker said. "Now I have my degree and I design them."

Curry seemed to have many happy workers.

I thought I'd inadvertently clicked on another program when a mortuary prep room appeared on the screen, but evidently mortuary coolers were among Curry's products. I had a flashback to my former residence above the Galigani funeral home and the noises and smells of its basement prep room.

"Our designs store up to six bodies," a worker said. He stood in front of a large box set on casters. "The unit is ready for the funeral home to put into use immediately. A team of funeral directors assisted us in the development of this product line."

In all my years as friend and then tenant of the Galiganis, I'd never thought to wonder where they bought their refrigeration units. I made a mental note to ask Rose if she or Frank had ever been approached for their input into mortuary cooler design.

I thought I'd seen enough until a tall young man with reddish-brown hair walked across the screen behind a worker who was demonstrating a small refrigerated vehicle that reminded me of an ice cream wagon. I wondered who had the contract for such wagons for New York City. I'd run into them everywhere.

One scene I'd never noticed on a New York postcard had been the appearance of a giant flatbed truck on Fifth Avenue around six o'clock on our first evening. The trailer section was loaded with six or eight hot dog and ice cream wagons, their umbrellas deflated, stuffed together so tightly their wheels intertwined. Not only had the vision shattered my image of the little old vendor in business for himself, but it also made me wonder where all that wonderful ice cream was going to spend the night.

I promised myself a chocolate Drumstick after I completed my homework: finishing the Curry DVD.

The young man in the background in the last section tweaked my memory. I scanned back and took a closer look at his broad shoulders and the trendy stubble on his chin and cheeks. Before he walked out of the frame, he turned his head and glanced briefly at the camera.

The final glimpse sealed it for me: The man was Zach Landram, Dee Dee's fiancé.

And a Curry employee?

I had no tools to zoom in or enhance the frame, but I was sure enough who the man was without any special editing capability. He had on a pale blue dress shirt and tie and carried a clipboard. I pictured him in profile standing in front of Nurse Pogel. Lacking a split screen and dual imaging, I still had to say the noses matched.

I scanned ahead to the end of the DVD, but Zach didn't appear again. I reached into my bag and took out the Curry brochures. A man in a dress shirt walking among employees in stained jumpsuits might be a manager, I thought, and managers often had their names and faces in company literature.

By the time I'd leafed through the brochures this second time, I was warming up (so to speak) to refrigeration technology. Not that I'd trade my scientific supply catalogs for details of cooling systems, but I had to admit there was something fascinating about structural steel frames, observation windows, pressure relief ports, and diaphragmatic speed locks.

My diligence was rewarded by the fourth pamphlet: "The Curry Industries Team Working for You." The first pages featured an organization chart with photographs of all the managers. A broadly smiling Zach Landram was regional purchasing manager.

I looked at the details of the photo of Zach at a desk, surrounded by what looked like cubicle furniture — L-shaped surfaces with cabinets hanging on the wall. I looked for a snapshot of Dee Dee in the cluttered area, but the resolution was poor. I could make out only generic stacks of papers, books, and files. I winced at the sight of a tall metal organizer that reminded me of my clumsy pilfering at Dee Dee's desk.

I ran all the coincidences through my mind, drawing imaginary lines. From Amber to Curry Industries, working for Lori. From Curry to Zach, one of their managers. From Zach to Dee Dee, his girlfriend. From Dee Dee to Tina Miller, Amber's other boss. I factored in Dee Dee in the alley and Dee Dee being attacked in Central Park.

Too many *D*'s, I decided. I needed a face-to-face with her.

I retrieved the disk from the drive and went to the counter to pay my fee. While I was there I ordered another cappuccino.

I needed to be alert for my upcoming interaction.

I was on hold for several minutes before someone in Dee Dee's ward picked up the phone.

"Ms. Sanders is back in her room now and will be on the line shortly," I heard. I was glad she didn't sound like Nurse Pogel.

I waited about five minutes, sipping cappuccino and checking my battery power icon every now and then. It wasn't even ten o'clock, but lunch smells were already taking over the café. I breathed in the aromas of pastrami, panini sandwiches, vinegary salads, and garlic bread. Too early. The huge slab of pumpkin bread I'd eaten felt heavy in my stomach, and I resolved to try to be more like Rose and not feel obliged to eat every crumb I was served.

Finally, "Hi, this is Dee Dee."

"Dee Dee, this is Dr. Lamerino. You may remember I met you at your office earlier this week."

"Oh, yes. Dr. Marino."

Close enough. I wouldn't expect a secretary to remember the name of every non-client who passed through her office, even ones who absconded with correspondence. I still didn't know exactly what had become of Karla's letter, or whether Tina Miller or Dee Dee had been made aware of its absence, temporary or permanent. Every time I asked Matt where the letter was and what, if any, explanation had been given to the women in the agency, he'd answer, "I'll tell you when we're safely back in Revere."

". . . nice of you to call," I heard Dee Dee say.

I realized my mind had wandered to my recent brush with felony status.

"I hope you're making a good recovery," I said.

"Oh, yes. I should be out of here tomorrow."

If Dee Dee was surprised that a relative stranger would be calling her hospital bed, she didn't let on. I'd seen the same ability to interact with hundreds of background people in most of the secretaries I'd known in my lab career. I, on the other hand, had a hard time keeping track of the few foreground people in my life.

Time to own up to the reason for my call.

"Dee Dee, I've been looking into Curry Industries for a project I'm working on. Imagine my surprise when I saw Zach Landram on a video of the facility."

I heard a big sigh, and something like a whispered "Uh-oh."

"Will you talk to me about it?"

"I've already talked to the police. They keep coming back." She sighed, as if the cops were a persistent virus.

"Did you tell them your boyfriend is a manager at Curry Industries, where Amber Keenan shot some video for a documentary?" The *murdered* Amber Keenan, I meant.

"I told them what they needed to know. I went to the loft on some business for Tina. Amber gave me that address, and I found Amber . . . dead. I got scared and left, but I called 911 first. There wasn't anything else I could do for her. I didn't do anything wrong."

Nothing wrong?

I'd given a lot of thought to my own failure to act to help Amber. Matt had told me once about the scarcity of what were called duty-to-rescue statutes in most states: "If you stand around and watch someone die, you may be a moral coward, but you're not a criminal," he'd said. He'd told me this long before either of us knew I'd be the coward.

I decided not to tell Dee Dee that Amber was alive when she left. Why have anyone else feeling guilty as I did that we might have saved her life?

I focused instead on the puzzle that was Amber's murder. "That's not the whole truth, is it?" I said. "About why you were in the loft. I think it's in your best interest to talk to me, Dee Dee." I paused for effect and lowered my voice. "Or I could just go directly to the police."

Another big sigh from Dee Dee. Another whispered phrase. "I'll put your name on the list."

I was glad Dee Dee didn't ask why I hadn't gone to the police already. My first thought on seeing Zach on the Curry video had been to approach her and not Buzz — because I was anxious to be of maximum assistance, I'd reasoned. I'd have to give that some thought when this vacation was over.

I needed to move quickly. I wasn't sure how long I could trust Dee Dee not to split from the hospital or to put a special DO NOT ADMIT note next to my name.

I checked my watch. Getting a cab to the hospital would be easy since I was still essentially inside the hotel lobby and the doorman on duty could just whistle for one. That would put me on the Upper West Side by about ten thirty. I'd have to allow at least forty minutes to get a cab from there unassisted and travel all the way down to Little Italy by eleven thirty. Even in the middle of the day traffic was dense everywhere on the main streets and avenues of Manhattan, no matter what the direction. That would leave me twenty minutes max with Dee Dee.

It would be close, but I could do it.

I called Rose's cell phone, trying to maneuver into my coat at the same time.

"Are you enjoying the hat shop?" I asked her. I stuck my right arm into the sleeve of my coat and flung the rest of it across my shoulders.

"It's wonderful, Gloria. They'll make up our designs and ship them in time for Christmas." She paused. "Not for you, of course. Though I was thinking that a lovely little white hat for your wedding reception might be perfect."

I switched my cell phone to my right ear and shoulder. "I'm not going to wear white."

"Well, you're not going to wear black, are you?"

"Rose, I have to run. I might be a little late for lunch." I wrapped my scarf around my neck. "Do you have the name of the restaurant yet?"

"Yes, the New Vineyard. It's on Spring Street. You can't miss it. It has a brand-new green awning hanging over the sidewalk, with ferns everywhere." Rose interpreted my pause correctly. "I told you it would be upscale," she said.

"Not a problem. I'll see you there, but don't worry if I'm a little late."

"Just tell me the color," Rose said.

I thought of pretending I didn't know what she meant, but I decided to give my long-suffering friend a break.

I looked down at the dregs of my cappuccino. "Maybe a coffee color," I said.

CHAPTER
TWENTY-FIVE

Bzzzz. Bzzzz. Bzzzz. Bzzzz.

The insistent doorbell was nearly shattering Lori's eardrums. She pressed her eye against the peephole.

Rachel Hartman was at her door.

"Lori, please, open up." Rachel sounded frantic and out of control. Her hair was disheveled, her eyes puffy, even allowing for the peephole distortion. "I know you're in there."

Lori stepped back, her breathing loud and raspy, like after the breast cancer run she did every year in the park. She paced the small area in front of her door. The mayo from the pasta salad was making an unpleasant comeback. She thought of the cop in the unmarked downstairs. A lot of good it did to have him four flights down. She should have set up some kind of signal to get him up here in case someone sneaked by. The way Rachel did.

Too late now.

"There's a cop right downstairs," Lori said. She couldn't believe how weak her voice sounded even though she was telling the truth. If she were Rachel she wouldn't believe it.

She had an idea. She walked to the switch that controlled the living room lights and flicked it on and off, on and off, eight or ten times. Maybe that would get the cop's attention, since a crazy woman walking into the building didn't catch his eye.

Lori checked the peephole again. Rachel was pacing also. Gone was the PR woman's trim, confident demeanor, her luxury environment. Lori tried not to be swayed by the pitiful, scruffy woman outside her door. A woman who might have killed Amber. Who might be here to kill her.

"Listen to me," Rachel said, turning back toward the peephole. "I've been a wreck all night, since I saw you in the lobby at Family Suites."

Lori started. *I need to work on my spy skills,* she thought.

"I know you have the pictures Amber took of me and Ricky Blake."

Ricky Blake? The son and heir of Blake Industries? Clearly Rachel didn't know what a tiny portion of her body Amber had caught on video. Amber must have convinced Rachel she had up-close-and-personal views of an office tryst.

"Did you write those letters?" Lori asked. Start with the minor offenses.

"Lori, just let me in to talk. This is ridiculous." Three sibilants in a row emphasized Rachel's lisp. "I can barely hear you through this door. I promise I won't stay long. I just need to explain."

"It's this way or with the cops," Lori said, hoping she sounded tough.

She flicked the switch again. She wondered if Rachel could see the lights go on and off through the crack under the door.

"Yes. I wrote the letters," Rachel whispered, as if she couldn't bear to admit it out loud. "I sent a note to Amber first. Then when she was murdered, I worried about where the video would end up. I figured you must have it."

Now that she'd started her outpouring, Rachel couldn't be stopped. "I had to do something," she said. "If it ever got out, everything would be up in flames. Ricky's married, for one thing, and it's his wife's money that keeps the business going. And then there's Max . . ."

Rachel trailed off. Lori heard the sounds of sniffling and nose-blowing.

"The guy who's paying your rent and buying you Tiffany vases," Lori said.

She took Rachel's pause as an admission that her wild guess was correct.

"I talked it over with Amy, my sister from L.A., and she convinced me to come here. She said you weren't necessarily like Amber, that you might be reasonable." Rachel paused. "I need to have that video. It's nothing to you, and there's no reason the police or anyone else has to see it. I didn't kill Amber."

"Why should I believe you?" Lori asked. Then she asked herself, *Why am I challenging a potential killer? And where is the cop?*

She flicked the lights on and off again. This time she counted — twelve times.

"Why would I kill Amber before I got the video from her? I need that video."

"So you've said."

Click! Creak! Thump!

The elevator going back down.

Lori didn't know whether to be relieved or more anxious. It was either help on the way or more trouble.

Thump! Creak!

It seemed to take much longer than usual for the cage to descend and start back up. Rachel sobbed even louder. Lori checked the peephole, half expecting Rachel to have

367

a gun drawn. But she was standing like a defeated doll, her arms loose in front of her, her shoulders shaking.

The elevator doors opened, and an NYPD uniform walked out.

"Everything okay here? I thought I saw the lights flicker."

No kidding. Lori felt her shoulders collapse and almost laughed out loud.

Rachel gave her a miserable look, and Lori lost the sense that she was negotiating with a killer.

"We're fine," Lori said. *Okay, don't be completely stupid.* "My friend would like someone to wait with her while she hails a cab."

"No problem." The young officer held out his arm to Rachel, as if to lead her to a dance floor.

Rachel turned back to the peephole and mouthed a thank-you.

Lori went to the window and stayed there until she saw Rachel get into a cab. She was 90 percent sure Rachel hadn't killed Amber. She was ambitious and annoying (so was Amber), but she didn't seem the type, whatever that might be.

If she were really a good person, she'd ease Rachel's mind about what was on the video, or even give it to her. The more she thought about it, the flimsier her bracelet photos seemed, and finding usable fingerprints on the letter was always a long shot.

For a minute Lori considered bargaining with Rachel. Maybe she could get something juicy about Blake's ozone practices, some undercutting of OSHA regulations they might have engaged in.

Then a little voice reminded her — that's exactly what Amber had done.

CHAPTER TWENTY-SIX

This time I was able to give the cab driver the hospital address. I was beginning to feel like a native New Yorker — keeping a busy schedule, visiting a friend who was recuperating, meeting another group for lunch, my husband off to work. My gasp was hardly audible when the cab nearly plowed into a double-decker tour bus.

Not that Billy Keenan was off the hook in my mind, but I'd worked out a scenario in which Amber meets Zach while working on the Curry video material. They become too friendly to suit Dee Dee, so Dee Dee kills Amber. I had no room in the theory for who attacks Dee Dee, unless it's a random mugging. Or that Zach, angry with Dee Dee over his new girlfriend's murder, teaches Dee Dee a lesson.

Weak, but not completely out of line.

A tiny flaw appeared in my reasoning when I realized that Dee Dee would probably know Amber's home address from the office files and wouldn't have to stake out the loft. Counterargument: Amber had lots of roommates, and it would be more efficient to track her down alone at Lori's apartment.

Another hole was that Dee Dee did not fit my profile of a killer (my profiling skills having been acquired while reading FBI articles over Matt's shoulder). There were a lot of reasons for that, starting with her sweet name, her lovely perfume, her upbeat disposition, and (very high on the profile list) her love of candy and willingness to share it.

As the cabdriver headed up Eighth Avenue, honking all the way, I heard the *blip blip blip* of my cell phone and checked the caller ID.

Matt. My husband had uncanny timing.

"What's new in guns?" I asked him.

"I learned more about RUVIS, that ultraviolet fingerprinting technique I told you about. It can also pick up shoe impressions on tile and other surfaces, smooth or porous, plus explosive residues."

"Fascinating," I said, my mind still on the Zach-Amber connection.

"For those who care."

"I've been meaning to ask you — what's happening with Billy Keenan? Has he been told not to go back to Lori's?"

"I haven't talked to Buzz yet today. I'm sure he came up with something. So where are you?"

It had been foolish to hope he wouldn't ask. I cleared my throat. "In a cab."

"On the way to lunch already?"

"Not exactly."

"Gloria, do I have to come and get you?"

I needed voice training — lessons in how not to sound guilty when I'm not telling my husband the exact truth (*lying* seemed a harsh way to put it). Now I had to decide whether to conceal my destination. Until I had those classes, I figured, I might as well be honest.

"Dee Dee's boyfriend Zach Landram is a purchaser for Curry Industries," I said.

Silence while Matt processed this information. I pictured a crooked expression, his left cheek scrunched up.

"Go on."

"Well, it means Zach knew Amber." I realized this was a stretch since Zach was merely in the background on the Curry video, but it did put them in the same place at the same time. "What if Zach was cheating on Dee Dee with Amber? It gives Dee Dee a motive for murder. She went to the loft to confront Amber, and things got out of hand."

"It's worth mentioning to Buzz," Matt said.

Was it my imagination or was this the first of my theories this week that Matt thought respectable? Maybe the air was changing.

I bolstered my idea with more information. "Dee Dee never mentioned to the police that her boyfriend worked for Curry. She told them she went to the loft with some business question connected to the Tina Miller Agency."

"You know this how?"

"Uh . . . well, first, I'm glad you're interested in pursuing this motive."

"I'm surprised you're not trying to connect this to ozone."

A light went on in the cab.

Or was it my brain finally putting things together? I was embarrassed that Matt had thought of it first. Wasn't I getting paid (in Revere, anyway) to study potential links between science and crime?

Here it had fallen into my lap and I hadn't thought of it. We were all thinking that Amber's blackmail enterprise was limited to the personal secrets of Tina's clients — infidelity or a past that included lap-dancing, perhaps — but a true businesswoman like Amber would see opportunities everywhere. It occurred to me again that if Amber had applied her business skills to something legal and worthwhile, she might have been pictured next to Tina on the cover of *New York City Today.*

If Curry had ozone problems, Amber might very well approach the management — Zach? — with the same kind of proposition she used with her other clients. She was the cameraperson and could easily have kept evidence from Lori.

There was no end to the problems Curry or any other industry could have with ozone. Faulty monitors and poor ventilation were the key issues for Blake, Lori had told me, whereas she was looking into Curry for potential CFC violations. In any case, all provided excellent material for blackmail.

"Where are you going now?" Matt asked.

"You're a genius, Matt. Your investigative skills are unmatched."

We both knew I was setting him up, and he humored me with his reply. "It's what I do," he said. Then, "And now you're on your way to . . . ?"

"To see Dee Dee." I hoped the traffic noise, not to say my own driver's incessant honking, would drown me out. I made a note to investigate the routes of the water taxis I'd heard Lori talk about.

"Gloria, let me speak to your cabbie."

I nearly bought it, but ultimately heard the tease in his voice.

"I thought I might get more out of Dee Dee than . . ."

"Than the NYPD?"

"Well, woman to woman, you know."

"I'm going to have to call Buzz, you know that. He needs to know that Zach works for Curry. What he does with it is up to him."

I nodded, as if he could see me. "I'll call you in a while — and don't worry. I'll be in a public place," I said.

And what better place to be attacked than in a hospital? I thought.

In the moments between hanging up with Matt and paying the cabbie, I almost talked myself out of visiting Dee Dee. I knew Buzz would send detectives back to the hospital as soon as Matt gave him the new information. I should bow out now. Even so, I couldn't shake the idea that, number one, Dee Dee would feel less threatened and maybe inadvertently confess to me (although that had never happened in all my cases with the Revere Police Department), and number two, I might relieve a little of the guilt I still felt at letting

Amber die (expert opinion notwithstanding) if I could be of any help now.

Number three was a little worrisome: There was a tiny but nonzero possibility that I wanted to get a little ahead of the NYPD. Finally, since I was already here, I might as well follow through.

From the hospital entrance I could see the outlines of the American Museum of Natural History and the planetarium. If I lived near here, I'd volunteer as a docent, I thought. I made a mental note to check into such opportunities at Boston's Museum of Science. I told myself it was a good sign that I was beginning to picture myself at home.

I'd looked forward to having Nurse Pogel see that my name was on Dee Dee's welcome roster, but a different woman, wearing a different pastel smock, was behind the desk.

"Twelve-thirteen," the new nurse told me.

I made a stop at the small gift shop, then walked toward the elevator. The doors opened, letting out an elderly man and two children. There was no one standing with me to get on.

I stood still, waves of tension flooding my body.

This is not good, I thought. *Middle age is*

no time to develop new phobias, and New York City is no place to have elevator issues.

"Are you coming?" A woman's voice.

I shook myself alert. While I'd been frozen in place, a middle-aged woman had walked around me and entered the elevator car. She was pushing the button to hold the door open for me.

Saved. For now I could put off the phobia discussion with myself. I was beyond happy when I saw that she'd selected the eighteenth floor. She'd be alone for six floors, but I doubted she'd mind.

On the way up, the elevator made only one stop, for a wheelchair-bound man in the custody of a candy striper. Good. The more company the better.

I reached Dee Dee's wing (already hoping for elevator company when it was time to return to street level), rounded the corner, and followed yellow dots on the floor and arrows on the walls to Room 1213. Though I couldn't see a kitchen, I smelled boiled peas and baked potatoes — odors much less enticing than those of the many delis we'd been in lately.

Men and women in hospital uniforms moved about with clipboards and trays. I saw few civilians, but one of them was familiar.

Tina Miller was walking toward me.

We closed the gap between us a few doors from Dee Dee's room, if the numbering system meant anything.

We both stopped.

"We meet again, Gloria. Visiting a relative? A close friend?"

"You might say that. We're all neighbors in a way, aren't we?"

Tina bit her bottom lip, the most visibly annoyed I'd seen her (though no one could say I hadn't been trying). "Nice of you to think that way."

"How is Dee Dee?" I asked. "I'm sure she's anxious to get to the bottom of what put her in the hospital."

"Not that I doubt that you're a Good Samaritan, Gloria, but if you're still on a mission to connect everything to Amber Keenan's murder, you're on a wild goose chase. Just because a person comes in contact with a shady character or two doesn't mean that everything that happens to them is related."

"I guess you're right." I leaned in a bit. "By shady character I assume you mean Amber, the murder victim herself. Her blackmail schemes were unconscionable."

"No, I did not mean poor Amber. She was a part-time consultant for us, and her work for me, at least, was above reproach. I'm talking in general about all the dirty little secrets that you learn in my business. But it's the stuff of movies and bad novels that PIs or their employees are in constant danger of being attacked. We're just doing a job, is all, like anyone else."

"I guess I'm just a novice," I said, surprised at how close Tina had come to losing her self-control.

"In fact, I thought I addressed this very point in that *New York City Today* article — the one you were so fond of. The PI business is a profession to be taken seriously, and not full of slimy characters pulling dirty tricks."

I recognized the sentence from Tina's acceptance speech and pictured her giving the same talk at power breakfasts all over town.

"I guess time will tell whether it's the center of this particular case."

Tina glowered and looked at her watch. No telephone call or crowded room to save her from me this time. "Well, I have a meeting."

As much as I wanted to think of ways to detain Tina and pursue the current dirty-trick count, I wanted more to get to Dee Dee before the NYPD showed up.

"Nice to see you again," I said, without

trying for sincerity.

"Enjoy your visit."

As I walked on toward Dee Dee's room I felt a chill.

Someone had brought Dee Dee a bed jacket in the peachy quilted fabric that I hadn't seen in years. Maybe they were making a comeback, like ponchos and capri pants (née pedal pushers). Dee Dee had makeup on, also. I knew I looked more under the weather than she did. I recognized an iPod on her lap and figured she was on her way back to normal.

I added a small plant and a package of chocolate-covered apricots to the array of flowers, cards, and gift bags, many in Christmas designs, that filled the top of the nightstand beside her bed.

"This is so sweet. Thanks, Dr. Larino."

Another interesting variation. "Call me Gloria," I said. "I hope you feel as good as you look."

"Oh, the makeup helps. I'm still bruised everywhere, but not bad, considering."

I didn't want to be insensitive to a woman who'd been attacked, maybe by her own boyfriend, but I was conscious of my time restrictions. I needed to be in Little Italy close enough to eleven thirty that Rose wouldn't take it as a slight against Grace Sasso and her gentrified taste, and I needed to be out of the hospital before the police arrived. Tina's comment had brought home to me the fact that she'd been working with the NYPD on a routine basis for several years. I knew I'd aggravated her this morning, and she'd had other firsthand experience of my meddling ways. She might be on the phone with them at this moment, tattling on me.

"Dee Dee, you need to tell me about Zach and Amber."

Dee Dee frowned and winced, as if she'd just eaten green gelatin with rancid marshmallows. "Zach and Amber? As in —" Dee Dee crossed her middle finger over her index finger. "I don't think so. She was definitely not his type, and we're practically engaged."

Dee Dee wouldn't be the first woman to be loyal to a philandering almost-fiancé, but I had to move on. "What were you doing in that loft, Dee Dee? Other than fighting with Amber?"

Make it sound like an accident, so she'll make a deal for manslaughter, no intent to cause death, I thought, forgetting I wasn't an ADA.

"I had to get something for Zach. A DVD."

"Is this about Curry Industries and some ozone problem?"

Dee Dee winced again. "I don't know what that is."

Though it pained me to leave her uninformed, I had no time for a complete lesson on O_3. "Amber shot some footage at Curry for a documentary. The production company she worked for was investigating environmental issues involving a form of oxygen called ozone. Have you heard of ozone depletion, CFCs, the hole in the ozone layer, anything like that?"

Dee Dee brightened. "Oh, like global warming?"

"A similar problem." Always one to give partial credit. "Dee Dee, was Zach involved in something illegal at Curry? Something that would be against the government's environmental regulations?"

Dee Dee picked at the threads of her bed jacket. "Zach said Amber had a video of Curry that wouldn't be very good for the company image."

The image, I noticed, not the environment or the workers. "But Zach isn't the president or —"

"I guess he was" — Dee Dee took a breath

— "involved in whatever it was."

"So you went to the loft to get a DVD and . . . ?"

"Two DVDs," Dee Dee said, correcting me. "Zach said it would be better for me to go in case someone saw me. It would be better than anyone seeing a man hanging around, he said."

Nice going, Zach, I thought. "And . . . ," I prodded. I wanted to hurry Dee Dee along without losing any bits of information. Every time a shadow crossed the doorway I started, expecting the NYPD to come for both of us. Dee Dee, on Buzz's orders; and me, on Tina's orders.

"I went on Saturday the first time, and I saw Amber on the sidewalk in front of the building. She was fighting with someone — a young guy. I didn't know if she was coming or going, so I just left."

"A young guy? Can you describe him?"

"Tall. Big, but not fat, just broad shoulders. Very blond. Some kind of sports jacket. Nothing special about him."

"Could it have been Amber's ex-boyfriend?"

"Kevin? No, I would have recognized him. He used to hang around the office all the time."

The young blond man could have been

Billy Keenan — or any one of a million and a half other young blond men, I mused.

"Okay, so you went back on Sunday morning."

Dee Dee nodded. "Zach found out somehow that Lori went ice-skating every Sunday morning, so the loft was supposed to be empty. It wasn't that hard to climb up the fire escape and get in through the window. See, that's where it was better for me to go than Zach. If anyone saw a guy climbing up, they might have —"

"I need you to concentrate, Dee Dee."

She shifted in her bed, and I knew this wince was from pain. "When I got there, Amber was on the floor and there was all this blood."

Dee Dee broke down in tears. I had to ease off. The last thing I wanted was for a nurse to hear her and usher me out.

"I'm sorry to bring it all back, Dee Dee. I'm just trying to find out what happened so everyone will be safe."

Or in jail.

Dee Dee nodded and gave me a brave look. "I wanted to forget the DVDs and just get help and make up a story about why I was there, but I knew Zach would kill me." Dee Dee waved her hands wildly. "No, no, not kill me, but, you know . . . be mad. He'd

384

told me to switch DVDs. I was supposed to find two movies in Lori's loft and put them in the cases marked CURRY — he knew there were two Curry DVDs because Amber told him. I mean, this would take a long time, and all the while, Amber was over there. She was facedown . . ."

I realized Dee Dee didn't know that I'd seen Amber also. "Try not to picture it," I said. To both of us.

"Anyway, I couldn't do it. I totally had to get out of there, so I called 911 and left."

Dee Dee drew a long breath and took a sip of water from a plastic cup.

I felt sorry for her, but there were still gaps to fill. "Then did you go back to the building later? Did you nearly knock me over in the alley?"

She nodded. "Zach made me go back. I told him one more time and that was it."

You tell him, Dee Dee, I thought.

"At least the next time there was no body. I was still freaked out, though. I made the switch between a movie and one of the Curry DVDs, but I couldn't find a second one after all that."

That missing DVD would be CURRY I, and Lori had had it in her purse to give to me.

"Why didn't you just take the Curry DVD? Why the complication of putting a movie in its case?"

Dee Dee sat up straight and gave me a proud smile. "Zach had it all figured out. If Lori opened the Curry cases and found them empty, she'd be suspicious that someone stole them, but if she found movies, she'd think she just made a mistake and put the wrong DVDs in the cases."

"But the movie cases would be empty. When she opened them —"

Dee Dee interrupted, clearly way ahead of me. "Who checks the cases before they bring them back to the store?"

I couldn't answer that, primarily because Matt and I hardly ever rented movies. I went back to the more important question. "You're saying that you don't know what was on those DVDs that Zach had to have so badly?"

"I honestly don't."

Dee Dee might be the best liar I'd met lately or the most innocent, uncurious person. I took in the sight of the patient in her pastel wrap, her thin legs barely making lumps in the hospital-issue bedspread. I chose to believe Dee Dee had no idea of the content of the DVDs — however hard it was to accept the notion that a bright young professional woman would put herself in harm's way acting blindly on the orders of her boyfriend.

When would there be a magazine article on that? I wondered.

"You told the police that you have no idea who attacked you in the park. Is that the truth?"

"It's the truth."

I'd reached my limit on the Dee Dee interrogation. I realized that if any of the hospital staff had been paying attention, I'd have been blamed for a great setback in her recovery process. Dee Dee's hair looked disheveled from the many times she'd run her fingers through it while I grilled her. She'd drained her pitcher of water, and now her lips looked parched.

I thought of one more question. "Did Tina know about your little escapade to the loft?"

Dee Dee's blue eyes widened. "Oh, no. She'd have been furious. She was raging mad at Amber when she found out what she was doing to our clients. In fact, I'm not supposed to talk about that at all. It's bad for the agency image to even acknowl- edge it, Tina says. We're just lucky there won't be any more of it."

Another image problem solved. Lucky indeed.

I was relieved not to see anyone I recognized on my walk back to the elevator. I had no time to stop to make notes, but I reviewed what I'd learned mentally so I wouldn't forget.

CURRY I was the DVD I'd just looked at, and other than the appearance of Zach in the background I'd seen nothing worth his feverish attempts to retrieve it. From Dee Dee's story, I gathered Zach was now in possession of CURRY II, and Lori had a movie in its case.

The scales of my suspicions had tipped away from Dee Dee (it was hard to think of a woman in a peach bed jacket as a cold-blooded killer) and toward Billy (who may have fought with his sister while he was supposed to have been home in Kansas) and — a newcomer to my list — Tina (who'd lied to me early on about knowing Amber well, and lately about her knowledge of Amber's schemes). Granted, Tina's lies might be construed as professionally acceptable, in the interests of not broadcasting her agency's business, and might be nothing to dwell on.

I wondered what the NYPD list of suspects looked like. Orders of magnitude longer than mine, I figured. What betrayed lover or unhappy victim had they discovered whom I didn't know a thing about? What would they uncover from an exhaustive search of Amber's work records, any of Tina's files that involved her, and Amber's friends and neighbors? I felt my efforts were like those of a scientist who'd been given only hydrogen, a single-proton element, to work on, when there were more than one hundred other elements in the periodic table.

I followed the yellow dots around the corner and suffered a slight panic attack when I saw no one waiting by the elevator.

So many people were passing by in the hallway. Was no one ready to go down?

Off to the side I saw a door marked STAIRS. USE IN CASE OF EMERGENCY.

Did my newly developed fear of being alone in an elevator car constitute an emergency? More important, could I walk down eleven flights of stairs and still be upright at the bottom?

I waited a few more minutes, reading the literature on a little table by a grouping of chairs. I learned tips for treating severe burns, acid reflux disease, bee stings (in New York City?) and knife wounds (I chose to think of these as resulting from kitchen accidents).

Finally I gave in to my fear and turned away from the elevator. I headed for the door to the stairway and went through it.

The heavy door closed behind me with a loud thud that echoed in the bare stairwell. Ahead of me were gray metal railings with matching steps and walls. Even the sound of my rubber soles hitting the treads made an echo.

The stairwell was creepier than an empty elevator.

CHAPTER
TWENTY-SEVEN

This was a first for Lori. Up early on Thursday morning to go to a video store. She figured if she ran down and picked up the CURRY II DVD that ended up in the *Erin Brockovich* case, she could come back and review it before lunch.

She stuck the CURRY II case with the movie into her tote and headed out her door.

The weatherwoman said it wouldn't be as cold today, but Lori still put on her thermal gloves before she left the building.

It was an easy walk to Red Carpet Video on West Fifty-first Street near Ninth Avenue. Lori enjoyed the overcast sky, the bare trees, the occasional puddle left by an overnight shower. New York was a Stieglitz photograph. A Hopper painting. A Woody Allen movie. She was into this now. A Frank Sinatra song. A Marge and Gower Champion musical. A Lori Pizzano documentary. Lori smiled and mentally bowed to adoring fans of the future.

She stopped for coffee and a muffin, sat at the café counter, and looked out at the street, already busy with people on their way to work or early shopping. Lori felt lucky to be here — and not in jail. She knew with a certainty that didn't come often that she'd never succumb to anyone again the way she'd given in to what Amber Keenan offered. No amount of money was worth giving up her freedom to enjoy mornings like this.

Red Carpet Video was at street level, below tony apartments in one of the clay-brown town houses that lined the street. Lori pulled open the heavy glass door and entered a small buffer zone of a foyer. She knocked on the inner door and got the attention of the clerk, who had to buzz her in. Lori had been in art galleries with less security. She figured the procedure was left over from when videos were new, hot merchandise and worth seventy or eighty dollars each. Uncle Matt had told her that back then you had to leave a large deposit, like fifty dollars, before you could take a videotape out of a rental store. Now — well, now you could get them for ten bucks in a store or two for five on the street.

Bzzzz. Bzzzz.

The buzzer sounded like her doorbell at home. Annoying. She pushed the door quickly so it wouldn't sound again.

"Hey," said a young guy with silver studs on his chin and the side of his nose, and hoops on his lower lip and eyebrow. He wore a brown Black Eyed Peas hoodie that looked new. Lori thought there might have been a concert recently.

"Hey," Lori said. "I called last night about a DVD mix-up. I'm not sure who I talked to."

"Uh, that'd be the night guy. Garrett."

"Okay, well, the problem is I thought I was returning *Erin Brockovich,* but it turns out" — Lori pulled the CURRY II DVD case out of her tote — "I put the movie in this case by mistake, and you have a personal DVD of mine in the *Erin Brockovich* case that I brought back."

The guy scratched his head and squinted. *He's really trying to concentrate,* Lori thought, *but he has all those holes in his face.*

"I could look on the racks out here, but it's not a new release. Whoever it was got it for me in the back. So can you just show me all the *Erin Brockovich*es you have, and we can look through and find my DVD and

I'll give you this one? I'll pay for the extra two days, of course."

That seemed to get him thinking in the right direction. He held up an index finger and then disappeared into the stacks.

He came back with eight DVD cases. Lori and the brown hoodie each took four from the pile and started opening them.

Julia Roberts came up on all four of Lori's and the first one (he was slow) of the clerk's. Lori slid a case from his pile and opened it. The sixth case was empty.

Uh-oh. Lori opened the two remaining cases. Julia again. And again.

"I don't understand this," Lori said. "Where's my DVD?"

The clerk scratched his head, causing his oily black hair to fall close to the eyebrow hoop. "Dunno." He took the *Erin Brockovich* DVD from where Lori had placed it on the counter and plopped it into the empty case.

"Well, can you look around? Maybe someone went through and checked and realized it wasn't the movie in the case so they put my DVD somewhere else." Not in the trash, Lori fervently hoped. She realized her voice was getting higher and louder. She knew she wouldn't get anywhere if she showed anger. She took a breath. "Wouldn't someone call me if they found the wrong disk in my case?"

"Uh, yeah. We're supposed to call if anything like this happens, like if we get an empty case. I always do."

Lori had a hard time believing he cared enough. She inhaled deeply. "I'm sure *you* would never let something like this get by you. Do you think you could check in the back, or under the counter here? Where would *you* put something like that if you found it?" She hoped she sounded utterly confident in this guy's ability to handle unusual situations.

The clerk's eyes brightened. "We have a lost and found. I'll check there." He disappeared behind a wrinkled fabric divider.

Lori waited, leaning against the counter, scanning the rows of movies. She remembered only a couple of years ago when videotapes predominated in this store and only about ten movies were available on DVD. Now Red Carpet displayed DVDs almost exclusively. She fiddled with a bag of M&M's from a pile of candy for sale. One corner of the store was devoted to snacks and drinks. Popcorn, candy bars, chips, and giant soda bottles were stacked three deep. One-stop shopping.

Lori was tempted to buy some corn to pop

while it was handy, but she knew it would be more expensive than in a regular market. She tapped her fingers on the counter. Where was Jewelry Man?

When he finally emerged from behind the deep blue curtain, he was empty-handed. Lori's heart sank.

"No luck," he said. "I left a note on the bulletin board back there. Maybe someone else knows where it is."

Lori thanked him and left the store. Halfway down the block she realized the guy hadn't charged her a late fee. She'd have to think about where that fell on the roster of crimes. For now, she walked on.

Lori stopped at the same café on her way back and got a coffee to go, more to steam her face than anything else. She considered her next steps. She'd look on her computer and see if Amber had left a file. She didn't hold out too much hope of that, however, and the police still had Amber's camera, she was sure. She'd check the other DVD cases that had been in use lately. Maybe Craig or Billy had been looking through her collection and misfiled some of them. Craig should know better.

Speaking of Billy — where was Billy Keenan? Lori wondered how the police talked him out of returning to her loft without telling him why. Had they found something else suspicious so they could charge him?

Her own feeble attempts to investigate had turned up nothing on Billy, but a big surprise in Rachel Hartman's confession. She knew she had to tell the police what she'd learned, but she felt sorry for Rachel. She'd tell Uncle Matt first, and then he could filter it to Detective Arnold. Maybe they'd be more inclined to give Rachel a break that way.

Lori walked down Eighth and took a left on West Forty-eighth Street. Almost home.

Murder suspects, threatening letters, flimsy alibis — these weren't her usual topics of meditation on her walks around town. She preferred thinking about how to list her videos on independent documentary sites, being sure she had all the deadlines straight for the film festivals, identifying concepts and themes that could be included in a curriculum study guide — something that would work especially well for her ozone project.

She looked forward to being able to get back to working on . . .

Lori stopped short. Fortunately no one was directly behind her. She was having too many of these moments lately. This time it wasn't a bright idea that stopped her.

Billy Keenan was sitting on the front steps of her building.

Lori stepped partway into the doorway of Lou's Pizza. She squinted and strained her neck to locate the unmarked. The car that had been there at eight thirty this morning was gone, and she didn't see anything else that seemed likely.

This is silly, she told herself. How could a cute farm boy be dangerous unless he'd had one too many and a pitchfork in his hand?

She stepped out of the doorway and looked toward her building again.

Her stoop was empty.

CHAPTER TWENTY-EIGHT

The hospital stairway to the street, empty and hollow, painted in shades of gray, stretched above and below me.

Once again, I was alone in Manhattan. How did I orchestrate so many moments of stark solitary confinement in New York City? The next time I heard about the throngs of visitors, the thirty-seven hundred buses (this from Rose), or the urban jungle, I'd have an experience or two to share.

I moved as quickly as I could down the long multilevel flights, ran out of breath, then stopped at the next landing. I was grateful for the large, dark gray numbers painted on the wall to tell me what floor I'd reached, but disappointed to see the *8*. I wasn't even halfway down. I sat on a step and listened for footsteps.

Nothing. I didn't know whether to be glad or upset that the stairwell was quiet and vacant.

No hospital sounds got through the thick stairwell doors. No noisy gurneys or food racks or beeping monitors. Not even the heavy smells of medicines and boiled food that had permeated the hospital corridors made it through to my perch.

I was trapped in a solid insulated chamber. Larger than a single elevator car, but no less frightening. *At least this one isn't sealed shut,* I reminded myself.

I stood up, my knees shaking, but more from the eerie environment, I thought, than the physical exertion. At least so far.

Four more flights, and I barely had feeling in my calves. I was on the fourth floor. *Almost there,* I told myself, struggling to ignore the pain in my chest and the dryness of my mouth. So this was why people joined health clubs, I mused. To be in shape for this kind of emergency.

Thud.

The sound of a stairwell door closing on a floor above me echoed down the shaft; it was unclear from how high up. I pressed my back against the wall and heard muffled voices. A picture of two goons, the size a private investigator might hire, on their way to kill me came to my mind.

I closed my eyes, unable to move. *This is it,* I thought. It could be weeks before a power outage sent people scurrying to the stairwells where my bloody body would be found.

"Come on, Sheila, no one's gonna see us." A deep, urgent voice.

Then a giggle and "I don't know, Stevie . . ."

"Just relax, baby. You're on your break, right?"

Lovebirds. *Don't do it, Sheila. Hold out for a nice hotel.* Or were these two hit men trying to throw me off? I couldn't risk waiting to find out. I zipped down the last three flights, convincing myself there really were knees and legs under me though I felt neither.

I reached the bottom of the stairs and pushed the door marked STREET.

I expected the comfort of daylight and a busy city sidewalk but found myself instead in a narrow alley, dark even at this hour of the day, because the buildings were so close together. The sky was overcast, as gray as the stairwell, leaving the alley bereft of warmth or sunlight.

I was breathing hard and thought of researching an elevator support group.

I made my way to the street where a most wonderful vision awaited, better than sunshine: a line of yellow taxis.

■ ■ ■ ■

As my cab pulled away, I looked around for signs of the NYPD. Would Dee Dee be arrested once they knew she'd lied to them? Or Zach for whatever was on CURRY II? Or me, if Tina alerted the police that I might be hindering their investigation?

I looked at my watch. Oddly enough, I'd be at Zach's company in a couple of hours. If they'd already posted a job opening for regional purchasing manager, I'd have my answer and I'd be able to go home soon.

This time I called Matt.

"Where are you now?" he asked immediately.

"On my way to a nice, relaxing lunch with Rose and Grace."

I heard a combination grunt-sigh. All he really needed to know was that I was safe; he didn't have to believe I was relaxed.

"What have you got?"

Back on the job. I briefed him on what I'd learned from Dee Dee about her three trips to Lori's building, starting with the possible Billy sighting on Saturday.

"The day before Amber was murdered, and two days before he says he arrived in town," Matt said. "I'll see if anything like that is in the police report from canvassing the neighbors."

"Do you know where Billy is now?" I asked, hoping they'd convinced him not to go back to Lori's.

"Buzz says they told him that Lori's apartment might be a dangerous place to be, possibly the killer is coming back, Lori is moving out also, and so on. I think they offered to get him a room in a Y and take his duffel bag to him. As far as I know, that ploy worked."

"I'll bet Billy is all too willing to believe New York is a bad place and no one is safe," I said.

"It's not great to have to play on someone's fears, but whatever works. Back to that Curry video. If Dee Dee's report is correct, Zach now has a disk that Lori thinks she has but doesn't?"

"Right. Unless she's tried to view it. My question is, Why bother doing that? Eventually Lori would see that it was missing." I wondered if Matt's explanation would make any more sense than Dee Dee's.

"They're just buying time, figuring that by the time Lori discovers it's gone, she won't be able to trace back to when she saw it last. It's amateur, but most criminals are amateurs. I'll give Lori a call and see if she's figured it out."

I started to say good-bye, but Matt interrupted. "I almost forgot. Buzz made me promise I'd tell you this one."

I groaned.

"Listen," Matt said, "Buzz doesn't usually take to laypeople horning in on a case, so count it as a compliment that he wants to send you a message. It's his way of saying he likes you."

"In that case, give it to me."

" 'I always thought that record would stand until it was broken.' "

"Okay, mildly funny. Aren't you getting carried away with these baseball quotes? You don't even like baseball."

"The Yankees are different. They're not just a team, they're an institution. Also, when in Rome . . ."

"Wait. I thought of one," I said. "Here's an Einstein quote. Just to show Buzz I like him."

"Give it to me." Matt tried to mimic my churlishness.

"From Einstein. 'The only reason for time is so that everything doesn't happen at once.' "

"Whoa. I like it. Worthy of Yogi himself," Matt said.

I thought Einstein would have been pleased to hear it.

I made it to the New Vineyard for lunch by eleven forty-two. The restaurant comprised one sprawling new-looking dining room with sparkling glasses hanging from the ceiling over the bar and plants fanning out from the rafters everywhere else. Small Christmas trees twinkled here and there throughout. I breathed in deeply to enhance the smell of zeppole, the fried dough that had been a staple of my youth.

I made my way through the busy area, partially knocking over a top-heavy coat chair in the process, to join Rose and Grace at a back table.

Fortunately Rose's watch was always fifteen minutes slow, so I knew she'd consider me right on time. When I approached, she and Grace were deep into a conversation about the many specialty shopping areas Manhattan offered.

"I never knew there were so many districts, Gloria," Rose said, helping me get settled and placing a small zeppoli on my bread plate. "Silver district, diamond district — well, I knew about that one, of course." Rose wiggled her earlobe with her finger to call attention to the diamond studs Frank had given her when their first child, Karla's husband, was born. "There's even a shoe district, down on Eighth Street. That's one I need to get to on my next trip."

"The hat district is still my favorite," Grace said. She dipped into a green-and-red-striped shopping bag by her seat and pulled out packages of thick felt, colorful ribbon, and several decorative buckles and pins. "It's *the* place to buy materials for custom millinery."

Grace had told us at dinner that the hat district was in the West Thirties between Fifth and Sixth avenues, east of the garment district, but still on the West Side. "I thought you were going to shop on the East Side," I said.

"We covered a lot of ground," Rose said. "Including a glassmaking store on Madison Avenue."

Rose and I had visited with the Sassos on previous trips, but usually only for dinner and a performance of one kind or another. Staying in town longer this time gave Rose a chance to indulge her shopping fantasies with a native New Yorker. I wanted to hug Grace for making my friend so happy and not involving me in the process.

I made appropriate excited sounds over Grace's purchases. Then I noticed that one of the packets of ribbon was coffee-colored. *Uh-oh.*

I could see that Rose had been waiting for my reaction: Clearly Grace had been commissioned to make a hat for me for my wedding party, which Rose kept referring to as a reception.

"It's going to be a tiny, tiny hat, Gloria. No one will even know you have it on."

"Then why should I wear it?"

"Just for the appearance."

For some reason this exchange sent Grace into a fit of laughter. For Rose and me it was business as usual.

Rose's purchases had come from the shops on Mulberry Street, the heart of Little Italy. She had found a gold mine of Italian souvenirs: the long, skinny red pepper that brought good luck, on key rings, pot holders, and T-shirts; and the mal'occhio fingers that kept away bad luck, also on key rings, pot holders, and T-shirts. Something for everyone back home.

I envied Rose and Grace and other people who could get so excited about shops that had nothing that plugged in or required calibration.

I needed to buy something soon, I thought, just to prove I'd been to New York

City during Christmas season.

Aware that I had a meeting with Lori at two o'clock, Rose had ordered for me. I accepted a steaming plate of clam linguini from a young blond server wearing a Santa hat, as did the other restaurant staff. He set identical plates in front of Rose and Grace.

I knew Rose preferred the smaller restaurants with middle-aged waiters who lived in the apartments above the establishments and hardly spoke English. After one taste of the delicious clam sauce, though, we all agreed it didn't matter that the floors were new and shiny instead of old linoleum with wax buildup.

Blip blip blip. Blip blip blip.

My cell phone. I checked the caller ID and clicked it on.

Rose frowned.

"My husband," I said to her. "Maybe it's about our wedding."

Her frown disappeared.

"Is Lori with you?" Matt asked.

The lack of preamble worried me. "No, we'd planned to meet at Curry's. What's the matter?"

"Maybe nothing."

"But?"

"Buzz says Billy is out."

My stomach clutched. "How?"

"I guess he's not as much of a country bumpkin as he seems. Apparently he just asked a uniform who brought him a soda if he was under arrest. The cop says no and Billy says 'bye. The good news is that the canvass did turn up a neighbor who saw Amber fighting with a young man on Saturday morning. Between Dee Dee's claim and this one, they can bring him in as soon as they find him."

"That's something." I swallowed hard. "When they find him."

"I'm going to hang up now and try her cell again," Matt said. "I'll let you know."

CHAPTER
TWENTY-NINE

I left Rose and Grace in the New Vineyard and, after a nearly fifteen-minute wait, caught a cab to Curry Industries on the West Side. Looking around the neighborhood, with no sea of yellow four-doors as in midtown, I knew it would be even harder to get a cab back uptown.

First things first. I tried to concoct a Plan B — what I'd do if Lori didn't show up. Other than worry.

Curry Industries, just south of the Holland Tunnel to New Jersey, was a large concrete and glass building. So was MOMA, I realized. Different architects, obviously. Where MOMA gave the impression of blending seamlessly into its environment through its enormous windows, walkways, and connecting hallways, the Curry building was a solid block, with no graceful lines to break up the austerity. It looked like most lab buildings I'd worked in, so why was I disappointed in it?

Was New York City turning me arty, as well as mushy?

The wide glass doors parted as I approached the entrance, up one flight of concrete steps. Inside, a reasonably pleasant carpeted area held a reception desk and giant posters of refrigerators and freezers. I recognized the designs as the same ones used in their literature. Here, too, I was reminded of labs I'd known and loved, where technical illustrations provided the décor. I was happy to note that I still enjoyed close-ups of technology and science in action and hadn't completely lost my appreciation of gears and switches.

Hallways ran off in three directions from the front desk. I wondered in which wing the regional purchasing manager sat.

The young woman at the desk was wearing elaborate dental appurtenances and a school ring on a thin gold chain around her neck. Right out of high school, her first job, I thought. Not much of a challenge.

"I have an appointment at two with Zach Landram," I told her.

She consulted a large calendar-ledger combo. "Your name, please?" Her voice was sweet and high-pitched. I imagined her last job being at an establishment where the next question would be *Do you want fries with that?*

"Dr. Gloria Lamerino. I'd be listed with Ms. Lori Pizzano, who isn't here yet. Is it all right if I wait in this area?"

She ran her finger down a page of the book. "Oh, okay, I see it. Mr. Landram is running a little late anyway. Can I get you some coffee?"

Curry Industries was decidedly more hospitable than the hospital, despite the etymology of the word. That didn't mean I'd break my no-office-coffee rule.

"No, thank you," I said.

I took a seat in the reception area facing two of the hallways. I glanced at the array of booklets and saw that they were duplicates of what I already had. Lori had been thorough.

Although I carried my own reading material in my tote — copies of *Scientific American, New Scientist,* and *Physics Today* — I flipped through one of Curry Industries' magazines of choice for its visitors: *Popular Mechanics.* It was nice to branch out once in a while, I told myself, and skimmed an article that was a retrospective on the icebox.

By two thirty, Lori still hadn't shown up. I called Matt. "She's a half hour late."

"That's not like her."

"What about calling Buzz?" I asked.

"Technically, she's been missing for only thirty minutes."

"Technically isn't all there is to it." As if he didn't know.

"Dr. Lamerino?" Zach Landram had come up behind me. His office was evidently in the wing to the far right of the reception desk, out of my range of view.

"I'm going to check on whether they've located Billy," Matt was saying. "I'll call you back when I have anything."

I hung up with Matt and extended my hand to Zach, who was jacketless but wearing a crisp blue-and-white-striped shirt and a wide blue tie.

"You might remember me from Dee Dee's office at the Tina Miller Agency," I said, my mind still half on the missing Lori.

"Of course, I remember you," he said. *Barely* was what he didn't say. "Let's go back to my office." He snapped his fingers as he passed the receptionist. "Kelly, have Lynn bring us some coffee."

This was the Zach who'd sent Dee Dee to do his dirty work three times. It seemed he commanded an entourage of willing females. Just annoying enough for me to forget my manners.

"Did Dee Dee tell you I'd be paying you a visit?" I asked him, hardly waiting for him to close his office door. I'd been wrong about the cubicle. Zach had his own office, just one with inexpensive, cubicle-like furniture.

Zach hesitated, then said, "She called me, yes."

"Let's not waste time, Zach. What's on the DVD that you risked Dee Dee's life to retrieve?"

Zach had gone from cool manager to flustered suspect in less than a minute. I was conscious that I'd counted on my looks to throw him off track — not a new trick, but one employed usually by the young and beautiful. People often have low expectations of someone who's middle-aged with a matronly figure and frizzy hair (especially on damp days like those this week). *She looks frumpy; she must also be mentally dull* might be their reasoning. The perfect image for an investigator, when you thought about it. Maybe that was why Matt had chosen the rumpled look, I mused, allowing myself a tiny diversion. In any case, it had worked on Zach.

"Okay, I know you're helping the police," he said, running his fingers through formerly well coifed hair. "I don't want any

414

trouble. It's not as if Dee Dee or I killed Amber. It was just a little violation, that's all."

"A CFC violation." I spoke as if I already knew.

"We had to finish this one project, for a major customer. The regs came into effect at a bad time. One more shipment of CFCs and we'd be done."

I sat comfortably on a padded chair while Zach paced. "Amber was there when the shipment arrived." By now I could write the story without him.

"Amber happened to be around with her camera on the loading dock just when the stuff came in. She got suspicious because of the way the guys were behaving, not wanting her to see the labels. If they'd played it cool, she'd never have known. Then all she had to do was come on to one of the idiots."

The rest was obvious. "She approached you for money."

"Yeah. No way was I going to pay."

I raised my eyebrows. "So you killed her." Even as I said it, I had a feeling — based on the dubious judgment of a police consultant — that I was not in an office with a killer, nor the fiancé of a killer.

Zach threw up his hands. "I didn't kill her. I figured I'd just get the DVDs somehow.

Look, the regulations are a laugh in the first place. You're a scientist, you should know that. It's just busywork for some bureaucrat."

It was hard to disagree completely. Like every consumer, I'd been annoyed by laws that had their origin in a single isolated incident: One person trips over a step and the next thing you know all steps have to be painted a bright yellow.

"I've never viewed the law that way," I said simply.

"Let me tell you a story. A certain group in the city government that shall go nameless called here about six months ago. Turns out they moved their offices and in the process lost all the files relating to our safety procedures in the fab shops. All the paperwork on ventilation, helmets, safety glasses and shoes, signage, you name it. Not to mention applications, permits, inspection reports, correspondence to and from us and them."

I moved to the edge of my seat. Zach's report was mind-boggling. "They, uh, actually told you they lost all your files?"

Zach had his hands on his hips. He nodded rapidly, his eyebrows up. "They wanted us to make photocopies of everything, starting from January 1980, and send them to their office."

I was aghast. "That means you could send whatever you pleased."

"You got it. Now you tell me, can you have respect for an outfit like that? What makes you think they know what they're talking about?"

I certainly saw his point, but —

A knock on the door startled me. I'd been lost in a sea of logical fallacies that gave Zach his rationale for ignoring federal regulations and committing a crime in the process. Not to mention endangering his fiancée.

Zach's secretary, Lynn, appeared in the doorway. "Ms. Pizzano is here," she said.

Lori was right behind her. I restricted myself to a smile and a deep breath, when I really wanted to jump up and hug her.

"So, *so* sorry I'm late." She extended her hand to Zach and took the seat he indicated. She gave me a smile. "I'm sure Dr. Lamerino has done very well on her own."

"Very well indeed," Zach said, clicking his tongue.

"We missed you," I said.

Zach loosened the collar of his shirt and gave me a pleading look that shouted, *Don't tell her, please.*

I had what I wanted and didn't see the

point of embarrassing the man further at that moment.

I looked at my watch. "You know, Lori, I think I've learned enough to help you fill in your narrative. Maybe we should let Mr. Landram go to his next meeting."

"Right, right," Lori said, her tone telling me she'd picked up my cue. "Well, it was at least nice to meet you, Mr. Landram."

As much as I felt sorry for Zach and his plight, I looked forward to turning him in. To the appropriate agency and to Lori.

For now I was happy to leave the building with Lori by my side.

"My phone went dead," Lori said as soon as the wide glass doors shut behind us. "I can't believe I forgot to charge it. Anyway, I knew you'd be worried, and as soon as I got here I gave that teenaged Curry receptionist Uncle Matt's number and asked her to tell him I arrived, so he should be okay now."

Lori hadn't taken a breath. I responded with a long one, trying to keep up with her outpouring and her quick pace as we walked toward a more cab-friendly neighborhood.

Lori had a lot of news. She'd headed home from the video store, where she thought she'd find the CURRY II DVD, and seen Billy Keenan on her doorstep.

"I panicked. I didn't see a cop on the street, so I hid. Then he was gone, but I didn't feel like taking a chance. I went back to the café where I'd had my coffee. I hated to be all wimpy and call the cops, but I was still all freaked out about Rachel Hartman confessing to me —"

I gasped. "Rachel Hartman confessed? That Blake PR woman who was at the awards breakfast?"

"Yeah. Well, no, not to Amber's murder."

As Lori explained, I was fascinated by a thread of the case that I hadn't been aware of — Rachel's connection to Family Suites and the threat of her ankle (intertwined with Blake's, so to speak) being exposed to the world. Another reminder of the narrow vision I'd had trying to solve this puzzle.

Lori went back to her timeline for the morning. It made my schedule of visiting Dee Dee and enjoying lunch with Rose and Grace seem leisurely.

"I decided to call Craig and see if he'd come and get me and walk me to my apartment, but like I said, my phone was dead. By the time I found a working pay phone, I don't know what time it was, but Craig came through." She paused and blew out a breath. "We might hook up some time."

"Hook up?"

Lori shrugged her shoulders and blushed. I got the idea. "Anyway, he showed up with this big bruiser of a buddy, and they walked me to my place and waited while I changed and then caught a cab here."

"And Billy?"

"Not there or anywhere in sight. I have no idea where he is." She lowered her voice, and I could barely hear her. "I guess I'm a coward."

"I'd say you were smart, Lori, especially after all that's happened."

"Thanks, Gloria."

"I hope you don't equate meeting me for the first time with all the misfortune of this week."

Lori stopped, came around to face me, and threw her arms around me. We had a long, teary hug, right in the middle of the sidewalk. Pedestrian traffic flowed around us on both sides, like water around an obstacle in a pipe.

No one paid attention otherwise.

All was well. Except that Billy Keenan was on the loose.

CHAPTER THIRTY

"It's definite that Billy was in New York earlier than he claimed," Matt said. "Buzz is on it. He put a car back in front of Lori's building, just in case, though I doubt Billy would go back there. He's probably on his way to Kansas by now." Matt paused for a sip of mineral water from a six-pack of bottles Rose had brought to our hotel room. "But we can be happy that a few pieces of the puzzle are crossed off the list." Matt started to tick off the successes. "We know who was in the loft with Gloria and why; we tracked the letters, explained the missing DVD —"

"If Billy was in New York already, how did the police get ahold of him to notify him of Amber's death?" Rose asked.

"I guess it took a while," Lori said. "That's why they didn't release the information about Amber until later on Monday."

"With cell phones and remote access to

answering machines, no one has to know where you really are anymore," Matt said.

"That's spooky," Rose said.

She had a point.

The biggest piece of the puzzle, Amber's murderer, had eluded us, but we'd done our best. Something nagged at me, however. Something a little off-center. I had the feeling that eventually it would come to me and all would be clear. Like the last turn of a potentiometer, finally reaching the right frequency and clicking in to give a sharp signal.

"Who's up for a trip to the Met?" Rose said, always ready for action. Nothing was nagging at her.

I'd promised Rose one evening at a museum that was open, and she was collecting on my pledge.

"I think I'll pass," Matt said. "Frank called with a little RPD story." He emphasized the *R*. "They caught that guy who's been a fugitive for almost ten years — the one who killed his own grandfather when he found out the old man was an FBI informant."

"Silvio Di Gregorio," Rose said. "I remember the case."

I was grateful she didn't give us the genealogy of the family. "Are you sure he wasn't from Everett?" I asked, needling

Matt about the town he grew up in, a few miles from Revere.

He hummed a few bars of the Everett High fight song, then reminded us, "You know, at some point I need to go back to work. It might as well be tonight. I'm expecting some faxes from Berger. You remember George, my partner from long ago when we were in Revere?"

I gave him a big grin. "We'll be home Saturday morning."

Matt said he'd be happy grabbing a fruit-and-cheese dinner at the all-night market on Eighth Avenue.

Rose promised me an excellent cappuccino and pastry at one of the cafés in the Metropolitan Museum of Art on Fifth Avenue.

A museum with coffees and pastries was okay with me.

Rose was smart enough to start me off with a meditative visit to the Met's Christmas tree, set up in the medieval art gallery. We stood in front of an enormous tree decorated only with a magnificent array of silk-robed angels. The largest Nativity scene I'd ever encountered surrounded its base, and the strains of heavenly Gregorian chant filled the darkened area. A moving experience. If Rose had more information about the crèche, she wisely kept it to herself.

We made a plan to separate and meet in an hour and a half for coffee (me) and wine (her) at the café-bar by the main restaurant. Rose headed downstairs to the Costume Institute. I went to seek out the American Wing, where I knew there was a replica of a room designed by Frank Lloyd Wright. In the end, it was geometry that pleased me most.

I wandered through the galleries, deciding not to use the site map in the booklet I'd picked up but to enjoy whatever was on the way. An hour passed quickly, and I realized I was on a completely wrong path if I wanted to visit the American Wing. I checked the floor plan and saw that I should have walked north from the tree but had strayed to the northeast. I'd gotten lured into the arms and armor gallery by the sheer enormity of the pieces. There was something about the seven-foot-tall suits of armor sitting on giant horses that was irresistible.

I wished the museum designers had used a system of numbered streets with orthogonal, numbered avenues, like the efficient midtown layout. Then a docent could say that a certain painting was at Fifty-ninth and Fifth, for example.

According to the legend on the map, it was nearly a quarter mile from the Temple of Dendur, which was just to my left, to the café and bar at the far southern end of the museum. I thought I'd better skip American this time and head for my date with Rose.

I made my way back, arriving again at the entrance to the building. Crowds of people were sitting on the benches, milling around the information desk, standing in long, snaking lines to deposit or retrieve coats and bundles. The chatter echoed in the Great Hall.

Once I cleared the hall and headed down the long rectangular gallery of Greek and Roman art, the crowd thinned out. I'd always had the idea that this gallery served more as a passageway to the restaurant. I stopped at the restroom off in a corner by the elevator. When I came out, looking down to be sure my clothes were reasonably well adjusted, I bumped into someone.

Not an unusual occurrence. This was New York City, after all. Except that I knew this person.

I heard a whispered "Not a word, *Doctor.*"

Tina Miller.

I felt a gun in my ribs, my arm in a vise that was Tina's fist.

Before I knew it I was inside the elevator

next to the restroom. Tina pressed her gun into me. Even with my extra pounds as a cushion, I felt the muzzle. With great ease Tina used her other hand to push first the CLOSE DOOR button and then the P button. Screaming was out of the question since my vocal capability had shut down. My entire respiratory system was in shock. I felt smothered.

"Do you know how long it's taken me to pull this off?" Tina said. "To get just the right time and place?"

Keep them talking, I remembered from police lore. "How long?" I squeaked.

"Remember that elevator in the hotel? I came close, but some tour bus emptied out into the lobby and I couldn't follow through."

"How?" A peep from my strangled throat.

"It's not that hard, really. Frat boys pull that trick all the time to scare their pledges. And it's even easier now with remotes. Not to mention a greased palm here and there. You forget my training, Gloria."

The elevator had jerked into motion, propelling us downward. I remembered from the map that the ground floor had only the Costume Institute on the northern end and some classrooms and parking on the southern end. Tina must be taking me to her car.

"Why?" More inarticulate muttering. I felt my knees go weak, as if I'd made another trip down eleven flights of stairs.

"Why did I kill Amber?"

I'd meant *Why are you doing this to me?* But I'd take any discussion that put off what seemed the inevitable. Me in Tina's car headed who knew where. It was dark out, and she could dump me in any of the dozen districts Rose had mentioned.

"Millions of reasons," Tina said, on her own track. "Have you ever heard of Toyland? They're the biggest conglomerate of kids' stuff in the country. I had that account in the palm of my hand. I'd have been vetting employees, including up to one hundred new hires a month all over the country. I could have moved in across the street from Trump Tower with that kind of income." Tina slammed her hand against the elevator door. "I have worked hard. I have earned success."

Even in my weak state, I could figure out that Amber's schemes would eventually bring down all that Tina had worked for. She didn't have to spell it out, but she did.

"Amber screwed it up. She actually tried to blackmail Mr. Toyland himself over a little fling in the Caribbean last summer. It was to his advantage to tell me but not to press charges against the little twit. That was the last straw. I knew that firing her would do no good." Tina smirked. "She'd end up blackmailing me. Either way, I'd be in the middle of a scandal."

The elevator was slow. I didn't know if that was good or bad. I didn't know much other than fear. I was conscious of the pain in my ribs, the closeness of Tina. I could smell her perspiration and a hint of alcohol.

"Dee Dee?" I asked. A frightened chirp.

"I like Dee Dee, but she had troubles of her own with that foolish boyfriend. I just needed to scare her. But you —" Tina pushed harder into my ribs. I wouldn't have thought it possible. "I knew it would be only a matter of time before you figured it out. My first clue that you were trouble came when Dee Dee told me the Sasso file had been messed up. There had been no one else in the office but you. Then the next day the cops brought that letter back to my office."

At least I'd die knowing how Buzz had resolved the issue of Karla's *Fielding v. Fielding* letter that I'd lifted from Dee Dee's file organizer.

"Those dumb uniforms claimed they'd

found it in the street and thought they'd return it. Right. Now cops pick up street crap and spend time on special delivery. How stupid do they think I am?"

I wondered what strange body chemistry gave us clear thoughts at moments like these: I finally realized what gave away Tina as the killer. In her office that Monday noon, she'd already known Amber was dead, claiming she heard it on the news — but the police didn't release the information until much later because they couldn't locate Billy. I'd had the one important link nagging at me to pay attention.

The perverse thing was that Tina thought I'd made the connection, and that's why we were here.

If I'd realized that day in Tina's office that Amber's murder was known only to the killer and a very small circle outside of NYPD . . .

If we'd returned to Revere as scheduled . . .

If I'd left Tina alone in the meantime . . .

If, if, if . . .

I caught a whiff of Tina's body odor as she switched gun hands and prepared to exit the elevator with me. I wondered if she'd worked up the sweat digging my grave.

I didn't have much time. I needed to think

about a possible weapon. The sharpest thing I had on me was the one-inch-diameter clip-on button we'd received when we bought our tickets. Not very useful. I mentally surveyed the contents of my purse. No keys, since we'd taken Matt's car to Logan. Not even the flashlight I usually carried. I'd last used it in the hotel bathroom to locate the tiny soap I'd dropped behind the sink, and I'd forgotten to put it back in my purse.

What was left? My bag was heavy enough to weigh me down. Now was its chance to come through for me.

"She not only sold real evidence," Tina said. "She'd started doctoring photos. Putting in different backgrounds and all the tricks you can do with software these days."

You don't need me here, I wanted to tell Tina. *You're talking to yourself anyway.* Tina had been yammering incessantly. She continued to berate Amber Keenan, young people in general, and idiot clients who did foolish things and thought they wouldn't get caught or have to suffer the consequences in the end. I wanted to suggest she explore a different line of work, but it wasn't the opportune moment.

"I'm married to a cop," I said. A whine this time. I had no control of my voice. The padded green walls of the elevator oscillated, closing in on me at one instant, fading away to infinity the next.

"I know who your husband is." Tina seemed angry that I would question her ability to learn everything about me.

Where *was* my husband? Learning a new technique for catching bad guys while his wife was in the hands of one?

Back to the contents of my purse. A multicompartment wallet. Nail clippers that I'd had to stick in check-in luggage before going through airport security. Pens. A notebook. Neatly packaged tissues and hand wipes. A fold-up travel hairbrush. A *New Scientist* magazine. A laser pointer.

A laser pointer? I felt my cheeks flush. I had a laser in my purse! So what if it was only a Class IIIa, less than five milliwatts. This meant that the risk of a permanent eye injury was very small, but even a transient exposure would bring on a bright flash, if I aimed straight for Tina's eye. It would be enough to dazzle and distract her.

I'd have to time the shot right. When we stepped out of the elevator would be best. I could then swing the pointer around and get the attention of anyone else in the garage. With the luck I'd had this week, however, I couldn't guarantee that the garage wouldn't be completely empty of cars or people.

It was my one shot. I had to take it.

First I had to get the laser out of my purse. I kept it in a small compartment near the top with my business cards. I made a plan.

During the ride, Tina had held me to her right, against the wall farthest from the control panel. Though she was not as heavy as I was, she was a lot stronger, to say nothing of the weapon she wielded. My right side was pressed against the wall, my purse hanging slightly to the front.

The elevator bounced to a stop on the ground floor.

Tina held my left arm with her right hand and the gun to my ribs with her left. While she adjusted her hands to usher me out of the cage, I dug into my purse and found the laser. To her it would have looked like I was rubbing my sore hip.

The doors opened. Tina stepped out and I followed.

One step, two steps.

Then, hoping to catch her off guard with a quick motion, I flung my purse on the ground, open end up so the contents would spill out. I pushed the button at the end of the four-inch laser pointer. The 630-

nanometer red beam blasted out of the narrow tube. Tina turned to me with a startled look, giving me a clear shot at her left eye. I trained the laser on her eye, tracking as best I could her jerky motions as she dropped the gun and tried to protect her eye. I kicked the gun as hard as I could, sending it scuttling across the cement floor of the garage.

Tina tried to wrestle the pointer from me, at the same time dragging me back toward the elevator.

New York City, crossroads of millions of private lives, came through with a busy parking garage. I waved the laser wildly while I ducked away from Tina. I heard shouts of "Sniper!" from an adult and "Laserman!" from a little boy.

Ping.

The elevator doors closed behind me, with Tina inside. She was on the run, but not for long.

I found my cell phone and called my husband, the cop.

CHAPTER
THIRTY-ONE

On Friday afternoon, Matt, Lori, and I had our debriefing with Buzz at the precinct, comparing notes and tying up loose ends of the case.

Traffic on Lori's elevator and fire escape had been high that Sunday morning as Dee Dee interrupted Tina's attack on Amber, and then I interrupted Dee Dee's B and E.

I learned that Dee Dee and Rachel had hired lawyers to take care of their respective misconduct, a B and E charge for the first and misuse of the U.S. Postal Service for the second.

I sincerely hoped Dee Dee would consider unhooking herself from Zach.

I was satisfied that Blake Manufacturing and Curry Industries would be accurately represented in Lori's documentary and duly fined for their real-life violations — Blake for poor ventilation in the welding area and Curry for illegal CFC purchases.

"Thanks for all your help, Gloria," Buzz said, giving me a surprise hug.

"Probably as much nuisance as assistance, I know," I said, conscious of all the little false leads I'd gotten excited about.

He shook his head. "Don't think about it. In the end, you know, cops just want a case solved, and it doesn't matter where we get the help to solve it."

I was happy to get away without another Yogi Berra quote.

The second debriefing took place in Rose's room. She wanted to combine a case update with showing us her purchases for the week and giving us each a present.

"Presents? Now? But we'll all be together in Revere for Christmas," I said. I was embarrassed that I hadn't done any December twenty-fifth shopping, let alone end-of-vacation shopping.

"Lori's coming, too," Matt said, clearly pleased that his niece would be joining us for the holiday.

"And maybe Craig," Lori said. We clapped at the news.

"These aren't really Christmas presents," Rose said. "They're just . . . souvenirs."

She lined up three small red and green foil gift bags on top of her luggage. The rest of the room, including what most likely used to be Frank's side of the bed, was piled high with shopping bags. A couple of the logos were familiar — the lowercase *b* for Bloomingdale's and the rose for Lord & Taylor. Other names I recognized from previous trips with Rose, though I'd never been in Bergdorf's, Dolce & Gabbana, Barney's, or Harry Winston's.

"First, a little clarification," Rose said. "What was the story with Billy Keenan? I never met him, but I thought you suspected him for a while."

"She suspected everybody for a while," Matt said, meaning me. He'd given his solemn word, however, never to bring up the matter of Karla Sasso and the *Fielding v. Fielding* letter.

"I never suspected Rachel Hartman," I corrected.

"And you, Gloria, I can't believe what you went through with Tina. I didn't think they let people use those elevators without an operator."

"They don't. Buzz said Tina evidently drugged him. She has a lot of resources, remember."

"Maybe I don't want to hear all this," Rose said. "As long as you're safe."

Lori raised her hand, as if asking permission to speak. "Billy called me last night, from his home in Kansas. He wanted to explain why he'd come to New York in the first place. He thought he could talk Amber into going back home or at least giving him some money to help out the family. I don't think he has any idea where Amber's money came from, and I didn't tell him. He just knew she had a lot of it, from her general lifestyle, and he was ticked off since he and his mom were just making it on the farm. That's why they fought."

Another breathless report from Lori, who was hard to stop once she got going. Like Rose. I felt so lucky to have such energetic, engaged people in my life.

"So once his sister was found murdered, Billy lied because he knew we might suspect him," Matt said.

"Yeah, you bet," Lori said. "Especially when he was told not even to pick up his stuff from my apartment. He wanted to talk to me yesterday, but he saw me run away from him and figured, why bother? I'm really sorry I wasn't nicer to him. I think he has a very bad opinion of New York."

"We'll just have to invite him back," Rose said.

I waited for her to offer to take him shopping.

Though we'd been there often through the years, Rose talked us all into an excursion to the Empire State Building for our final evening in New York.

"Only if you promise not to give us too much history," I said.

She agreed — but found a way to slip in her data on our walk, four abreast, toward the Fifth Avenue skyscraper, probably the most famous in the world.

"It's so familiar, I don't have to tell you it's been in more than ninety movies."

"And a number of documentaries," Lori reminded us.

"It has 1,172 miles of elevator cables," Rose said. "Oops. Sorry, Gloria. Well, you'll be safe in these elevators, I'm sure."

Rose dropped her last stack of postcards in a mailbox in Times Square. She'd written at least a dozen postcards a day since we arrived, sometimes scribbling quickly or applying postage before our meals arrived.

"Who's getting all these cards?" I'd asked her after the first three mail drops.

"Let's see, there's MC, John, Robert, and William — he likes to get one addressed especially to him — and Martha at the office. There are fifteen people in my Rotary Club group, and ten on the committee for the historical society's auction. Also, all my cousins who go to Florida for the winter. They're always sending me cards. So that's Paul and Lu, and Don and Liz, and —"

I held up my hand. "I get it."

"And since Frank left on Tuesday, I've sent him a couple every day."

"Of course."

I had three possible candidates for post-cards: my cousin Mary Ann, who insisted on calling me Gloria Gennaro no matter how many times I explained that I hadn't changed my name and neither had Matt; Andrea Cabrini, a technician friend at the Charger Street Lab in Revere; and my best California friend, Elaine Cody, a technical editor at the Berkeley lab where I'd worked. I told myself I went for quality, not quantity.

We entered the art deco lobby and *oohed* and *aahed* over the metal relief sculpture of a glowing Empire State Building. We were all sporting the "souvenirs" Rose had given us, from one or another museum shop she'd been in during the week. For me, a beautiful green enamel Christmas tree pin, with tiny white beads strung around the branches. For Lori, a lovely ceramic pin in the shape of an old-fashioned Santa bent over with presents. For Matt, a tie tack with a pattern of a tiny sprig of holly.

Once upstairs (the elevator and escalator rides were smooth and without incident, but the source of much teasing), we headed first for the view to the south, walking above clusters of skyscrapers on all sides. What struck me most about the absent Twin Towers was how much I missed them on this trip even though we hadn't visited Ground Zero. They'd been your anchor walking around midtown, a compass pointing south to the tip of Manhattan at any hour of the day, in any weather.

"I never did get to tell you all the memorabilia that was in the police museum," Matt said. "They've got interviews, photographs, plus Ground Zero artifacts." Matt shook his head. You might have thought he'd been there himself, instead of men and women he considered part of his professional family. "It's heartbreaking. You see pieces of glass and chunks of building, and burned-up respirator masks and police radio caps, flashlights, yellow harnesses . . ."

His voice trailed off, as did our minds, back to the terrible day.

Rose and I had begun our New York reunion trips when I first moved to California, long before the Twin Towers were built. The World Trade Center was an exciting new place to visit in the early seventies. We'd gone up in the sleek elevators and looked down to Staten Island on one side and up to the Bronx on the other.

Now they were gone. I felt like we'd lived through their birth and their death.

It made me feel very old — and very sad.

On Saturday morning, Lori and Craig came to see us off. Our bags were on a luggage dolly in the hotel lobby where we were saying our good-byes.

Lori was wound up about a sponsor who'd contacted her about including her documentary, *Oxygen — Like Any Good Thing, Too Much or Too Little Can Ruin Your Health,* in the Green Scene Festival next spring.

"They told me they've been wanting someone to take on the ozone issue," she said. "Can you believe it?"

Craig beamed as she talked, adding his own excitement about the "totally cool invitation." I sensed an excellent hookup was in the works.

Rose felt obliged to include some last-minute trivia — that New York is now known as the second home to the world, for example. Her facts overlapped Lori's exclamations, causing a happy confusion of words to float up to the high ceiling of the lobby. "This reminds me of a Yogi Berra quote," Matt said.

"Oh, no," we women cried.

"Go, dude," Craig said.

Matt smiled and prepared his throat for a performance. " 'It was impossible to get a conversation going; everybody was talking too much.' "

Everyone within earshot obliged him with a laugh.

I was ready with a random fact of my own.

"Did you know that all of New York City's drinking water is treated with a fluoride compound, at a concentration of one-point-zero parts per million?"

I tuned out the groans and thought how much I would miss New York.

ABOUT THE AUTHOR

Camille Minichino has been a regional president and board member of the Mystery Writers of America, the California Writers Club, and Sisters in Crime. Like Gloria Lamerino, the author has a Ph.D. in physics and a long career in research and student instruction. She currently teaches physics at Golden Gate University in San Francisco. She also instructs on writing fiction and works as a scientific editor in the engineering department of Lawrence Livermore National Laboratory. Ms. Minichino lives with her husband and satellite dishes in Castro Valley, California.